THE NIGHTWALKER

Diane Guest lives in Connecticut with her husband and children. She is also the author of *Lullaby, Forbidden Garden* and *Cristobel*.

DIANE GUEST

The Nightwalker

A BERNARD GEIS ASSOCIATES BOOK

HarperCollins*Publishers*

HarperCollins*Publishers*
77–85 Fulham Palace Road,
Hammersmith, London W6 8JB

This paperback edition 1994
1 3 5 7 9 8 6 4 2

Previously published in paperback by Fontana
(Special overseas edition) 1993

ISBN 0 00 637781 5

Set in Palatino

Printed in Great Britain by
HarperCollinsManufacturing Glasgow

Prologue

The last small eddy of air drifted across the foothills and whispered through the century-old maples that lined the drive leading to Clairemont. Then all was still. The moon rose high over the deserted gardens and cast long, shadowy patterns where two tall Tuscan statues guarded the entrance like sentinels, secretive and silent.

The front of the manor house was already closed up for the night, lights off, doors and windows shut tight against the cool, damp air. And yet, precisely at 10.30, just as William Blackmarsh and his son Robin were finishing the last of their brandy, from outside in the walled garden there came a mysterious, soft, rustling sound, as if someone in a long skirt had just swept up the wide stone steps, and then the heavy panelled door leading into the entrance hall slowly swung open. An odd circumstance. Without explanation. And yet it happened all the same, and so quietly that no one noticed.

Moments later, in the library, the sweet scent of Persian lilac filled the air, though that too was impossible to explain. The perfume could not have come from the gardens. There were no more Persian lilacs growing there. Still, it was as if Claire herself had just walked in.

A deep, eerie stillness descended upon the house, a stillness so pervasive that, in the kitchen, the housekeeper, in the process of scolding one of the maids, stopped in mid-sentence, struck dumb by the sudden silence. Upstairs, William Blackmarsh's valet looked across the master bedroom towards the door, startled, as if for some reason he thought it was going to open by itself.

For an instant there was an absolute lack of sound. And then came the crash. An ear-piercing, splintering crash, and all of the priceless pieces of Rose Mandarin that Claire had collected so painstakingly for so many years were swept from the mantel in the library and smashed to bits on the marble hearth.

Later, some of the servants claimed that the damage had been caused by some kind of earth tremor. Others insisted that one of the great beams in the cellar had shifted. But if anyone had cared to ask old John Weeks the gardener – no one did since they all considered him well past his prime – he would have said with a shudder that it was Miss Claire. Miss Claire, coming home.

Only minutes before it happened, William Blackmarsh and his son had been sitting in the drawing-room, enjoying their brandy. Discounting the difference in their ages, the two men might have been taken for twins, so alike were they in looks and mannerisms. Not only did they share the same handsome, patrician features and tall, fine-boned physique, but even the younger man's voice was an echo of his father's.

'I don't suppose anyone has heard from Lenore,' Robin was saying. There was obvious displeasure in his tone.

William Blackmarsh leaned against the back of the chair and wearily rubbed his temples. He had an unbearable headache. 'I forgot to tell you. She phoned today. She said to let you know she'll be home on Friday.'

Robin frowned. 'My wife ought to learn to say no to people. Lenore spends her life saying yes. Her latest involvement with these vagabond children is ridiculous. Thank heaven it's at an end.'

His father's only response was a thin smile. 'What is it, Robin?' he said. 'Obviously you have something you want to discuss, and it isn't Lenore. So let's get on with it. What is so ungodly important that it couldn't wait until morning?'

His son hesitated, but only for a minute. 'I think it's time, Father,' he said quietly, leaning back in the soft leather chair, relighting his pipe. 'Time to talk about your daughter.'

His father groaned. 'What has Amanda done now?'

To the casual observer Robin seemed the picture of calm. Only the most perceptive would have noticed that his hand was shaking. 'Not Amanda, Father. I'm talking about Gillian. In this instance Lenore and I see eye to eye. We think Gillian has suffered enough.'

Across from him William Blackmarsh didn't move, his pale blue eyes expressionless.

Robin kept his voice level. If there was one person in the world he did not care to offend, it was his father. Still he pressed. 'What about Gillian's children?'

'What about them?'

'Don't you ever want to see them? After all, they're your grandchildren.'

No response.

'You wonder about them. I know you do.' Robin

paused. 'Gillian's children have never harmed you. Why do you punish them for something that was none of their doing?'

For a moment William Blackmarsh looked blank, as if he did not understand what his son had just asked. Then his face went hard, the way it did when he had reached the limits of his patience. 'You overstep your bounds, Robin. Let me remind you that what I do is none of your business.'

The younger man's face tightened, his next words edged with anger. 'This was Claire's estate and her mother's before her.' He made a sweeping gesture with his hand. 'And when you are gone, we both know what will happen to it. In her will Claire made it perfectly clear. No matter how you feel about it, there is nothing you can do to change that. It's time you prepared for it. For all our sakes.' His tone softened, grew pensive. 'Don't you ever wonder how Claire would feel if she were still here? She wasn't my mother but I knew her well enough to know how much she loved Gillian and Amanda. How precious her two daughters were to her.' A sharp breath. 'I think she'd hate you for what you've done to Gillian. And for what you keep doing.'

In a spasmodic movement William Blackmarsh half rose in his chair, and suddenly the mask of cool control that he had worn for eighteen years fell away, leaving the true wreckage of his life exposed.

In the face of his father's pain Robin looked away, but he did not let up. 'End this, Father. At least let Gillian see what life at Clairemont is like. Let me bring her home before it's too late.'

Slowly, deliberately, William Blackmarsh sat back in his chair, his handsome features arranged in an icy mask once more. 'Unlike you, Robin,' he said quietly, 'I'm not sure how Claire would have felt about anything I've done.' His eyes narrowed. 'Nor am I sure of your motives. But since this seems to mean so much to you, so be it. Bring your half-sister home.'

Once spoken, his words seemed to hang suspended in the air, and at the same time, the two men heard a swift, rushing sound outside the door, as if someone were pacing back and forth at a frantic rate, wanting to stop what was happening, not certain how to do it.

There followed the most unearthly silence that either man had ever experienced.

Stunned, Robin looked over at his father. 'What the hell . . . ?'

A moment later, as both men sat immobile, staring at the door, they heard the splintering crash, and Claire's antique Rose Mandarin shattered into dust.

Thus begins the nightmare.

Chapter One

Max Norlund woke up in a sweat to find the room still dark, and instinctively he knew that his wife was gone. Dear Jesus, he thought wildly, she's doing it again. Before the idea had even registered, he was out of bed like a shot. The sleepwalking thing hadn't happened in over two years, and he had begun to hope that maybe it never would. Clearly he was wrong.

Their bedroom door stood ajar, and in his bare feet he hurried out into the hall. From the far end, his daughter's night-light cast an eerie shadow on the wall, and he shivered, wondering not for the first time how such a dismal glow could possibly be a help to anyone in the dark of night. It certainly wasn't doing him any good.

Trying to keep calm, pushing back the memories of other sleepwalking episodes, other nights best forgotten, he made his way down the hall, opening each door as he went, as quietly as he could, not wanting to wake Daisy or Will. Or worse, Gillian, wherever she was.

As usual, the door to Daisy's room was open a crack. She hated to sleep behind a closed door. He peeked in, quickly, just long enough to assure himself that his daughter was fast asleep, his wife not in the room.

The door to his son's room was shut tight. Silent

13

testimony to the boy's fearlessness or, more likely, Max suspected, his fierce determination to set himself apart from his twin. Max opened the door. In the bed along the far wall he could see the lump that was ten-year-old Will. But no Gillian.

The guest rooms too were empty.

Max felt his heart give a sickening lurch. Could Gillian somehow have got past the locked door at the end of the hall?

The answer was waiting at the top of the stairs. The door that was locked every night to keep his wife safe stood open. Beyond, the narrow stair-well curved down. Harmless enough to someone fully awake. Dark, steep, dangerous to a sleepwalker.

He didn't call to her. Experience had taught him the futility of such a thing. He had lived with her for twelve years, and he knew without question what he had to do. Find Gillian quickly, wherever she had wandered. Find her before she could come to any harm and, without waking her, lead her gently back to the house, back to the safety of their bed.

And in the morning he would not mention a word about it. That, too, he had learned he must never do.

During the first years of their marriage, when he was still in law school at Georgetown and she was designing jewellery for a Pakistani who had a shop in Dupont Circle, they had lived on the third floor of an apartment building on Columbia Road. Gillian had never told him about her night walks – in fact she had never told him anything at all about her past except to say that she was estranged from her family – so the first time she walked in her sleep he had been frantic. He had wakened in the early hours of the morning to find her gone. He had searched the apartment, the hallways, the roof, finally locating her

14

blocks away, his sweet, his darling bride, sitting on the steps in front of the Perpetual Bank, eyes wide open, full of tears. But inside, she was still fast asleep.

The next morning she remembered nothing, and he, laughing, had made one of the worst mistakes of his life. He told her what she had done. He never forgot her reaction. He doubted he ever would.

For a full minute she stood staring, not at him but past him, with such a desperate look in her lovely blue eyes that he was stunned. Her pain was unmistakable and yet so private that he felt like a stranger, seeing something he wasn't entitled to see. When she spoke it was as if he were not even in the room. 'Oh, God,' she whispered. 'I thought it was over. I thought I was forgiven.' Then the tears came. Deep tears, coming from wherever tears begin, sliding silently down her cheeks. And no matter what he said, she was beyond consolation. Nor would she explain why she was so devastated. But he knew one thing: the horror she felt had something to do with her estrangement from her family.

That morning he hadn't gone to the university. He stayed with her until she was calm, keeping himself busy, not daring to ask why she was so shattered, grateful when she brushed the last tears from her cheek and told him in a trembling voice that she was okay. He could go to class. She would be all right.

He remembered that when he got home that night she was waiting for him, pacing. Said she wanted to show him something she had made. It was a braided harness, made from strips of cloth.

She slipped it over her head, fastened it tight across her chest, and when she got into bed she tied the loose end to the bed-post. 'I'll never do it again,' she

15

whispered, and her voice was like a child's, promising. 'I won't.' And without waiting for him to respond, she began to talk about her childhood. Before that she had told him very little. He knew that her father was *the* William Blackmarsh of publishing fame, that her mother had died when she was young, and she had spent most of her life in one school or another. He knew she had a half-brother, Robin. And a younger sister, Amanda. Beyond that she had never spoken about her life except to say that she had lived at Clairemont, a house in Connecticut that had been built for her grandmother. 'Her name was Claire too,' she had said. 'Just like my mother's.' Pause. 'They are both dead.' And with that, she had gone silent. She never spoke about her past again.

Not that he found her silence easy to accept. He didn't. But each time he questioned her, she withdrew, as if she had a disease she was trying to forget and he kept reminding her of it. 'I have no one but you,' she told him once. 'I've lost all the others. Must I risk losing you too?' And after that he never pressed her again. Because he sensed that what little she had been able to share with him had come at immeasurable cost to herself. He loved her too much to inflict such pain in an effort to satisfy his own curiosity.

Now, attached to the bed-post with her makeshift harness, her face chalky white, she told him that when she was thirteen years old, her father had sent her away to boarding school. Because, she said in a faltering voice, she had been a wicked, wicked child. Max never forgot the way she spoke those words. Wicked, wicked child. So full of self-loathing. So full of guilt. 'Don't ask me what I did to deserve it because I can't tell you,' she choked. 'Just know that my father was justified. I deserved the worst. I never

16

went home to Clairemont again. He couldn't bear the sight of me and I don't blame him. And it's all because I was so wicked. So very, very wicked.' Her next words were almost inaudible, her lips barely moving. 'I had hoped the sleepwalking was over. But it's not. It's not.'

'I love you, Gillian,' he said. 'And whatever you did, I don't care. It's over.' Gently he unfastened the harness. 'This is not the fourteenth century. You don't need this contraption.' He held her then, and smoothed her dark hair, wanting to ask a hundred questions, asking none. At first it was because he didn't want to cause her any more torment; later he didn't want her to think her past mattered to him at all. She seemed so relieved that her guarded confession hadn't changed his feelings for her.

And it hadn't. Knowing her, loving her was enough. He hoped that one day she would tell him. When the pain was behind her. Until then he just wouldn't think about it. Nor would he remind her of it. He never brought the subject up again. The past was past. When she was ready, if ever, she would tell him. In the meantime he was happy. And so, he told himself, was she.

Although he never asked her what had happened all those years ago at Clairemont, he did insist that they go to one of the professors at Georgetown, an expert in the field of sleep disorders. During those sessions he gathered a lot of information, none of it very useful. He could still rattle it off in textbook fashion: sleepwalking in children is not uncommon and they usually outgrow it; in adults it is rare, sometimes caused by emotional trauma; it occurs primarily during something called Stage Four of the sleep process, a period when it is most difficult to

17

wake the subject. But in the end, it all came down to a single bit of advice: Be patient. And in the meantime, take precautions.

And he had. He learned all the rules. In the course of twelve years of marriage, each time they moved to a different place, he followed the same rituals. Special locks on the doors to keep Gillian from falling down the stairs; bolts on the shutters so that in her sleep she couldn't mistake a window for a door and jump to her death; and most important he learned how to sleep with one eye open.

But after the twins were born, Gillian changed. A serenity came over her, a peacefulness that hadn't been there before, and it almost made him forget her secret pain. He was quite sure *she* hadn't forgotten it, but at least he couldn't see it any more in her eyes.

And gradually the sleepwalking episodes became less and less frequent until finally they stopped altogether.

Nevertheless, when they moved to Arlington two years ago, Max had a special door installed at the top of the stairs and had all the windows on the second floor fitted with double locks. Just in case. But even as he went around Gillian-proofing the house, he couldn't help but think that it really wasn't necessary any more.

Max was happy. Gillian was a wonderful, loving mother. And more than that, she was his best friend, his lover, his life. Her past no longer mattered to him. The here and now, he told himself, was all that counted.

Sometimes, in fact, he felt that his life with Gillian had grown too perfect, too idyllic. That no one could go on forever without some adversity.

Later, looking back, he wondered if he shouldn't

have simply accepted their happiness without question. As if somehow, by questioning, he had brought a terrible evil into all their lives.

Now, heart pounding, Max made his way down the stairs and across the hallway to the living-room. At the door he stopped to listen.

Silence.

'God damn it, Gillian,' he whispered, 'where are you?' He moved into the room but the blinds were drawn and he could see nothing. Turn on the lights, he thought. Before you trip over something and wake the kids.

He made his way back to the door, but before he could find the light-switch he heard her voice.

'Max. I'm all right.'

He turned round. She was standing very close. 'I'm here,' she said. 'And I haven't been sleep-walking.'

He reached out to turn on the lights but her next words stopped him. 'Can we just sit here in the dark for a minute? Please?' There was fear in her voice.

He took her by the arm and together they made their way to the couch.

She didn't wait for him to speak. 'Robin called today.'

Max was struck by the intensity of her tone. It wasn't unusual for her half-brother to call. Gillian heard from him periodically. So this time why did she seem so frightened?

She reached over and in the dark she found his hand, squeezing it hard. 'He wants me to come home.' The words came out like a pronouncement of death.

'Home?' He thought for a minute how stupid he

sounded, but it was all he could think to say.

'Home. To Clairemont.'

He could feel the storm gathering. He knew he had to be careful. 'What exactly does that mean?'

'It means that my father has given me permission to come home.' Then she buried her face against his shoulder, but she didn't cry, and somehow the lack of tears unnerved him more than all the tears she had ever shed before.

Gillian lay alone. Max was sleeping quietly beside her, but all the same she felt isolated. She tried to lie still so he wouldn't wake up, wouldn't feel her trembling. What am I to do? she wondered. What am I to do? The thing that she had known would never happen had happened. Her father wanted her to come home.

No, Gillian, said a quiet voice in the back of her head. He doesn't want you to come home. He is simply allowing it because Robin wants it. When you asked him, Robin told you the truth.

Robin. Her half-brother. Her only family contact. How odd that the person she had been the most distant from all those years ago would be the only one that she ever spoke to now. Five years older than she, but light-years away in terms of open affection. Robin. Always remote, cool, an onlooker. But he had kept in touch. And he always told her the truth. Even when it hurt.

I'm thirty-one years old, she thought suddenly. Father, do you know it? I'm thirty-one years old. For eighteen years I have waited, hoping. Too much hoping. And now here it is. A chance to go home.

But could she? Could she ever, ever go back?

With a painful effort she made herself think about

her father. What he looked like, the sound of his voice. She hadn't allowed herself to do that consciously in eighteen years. True, sometimes in her dreams he would be there, the god figure, the supreme being, judging her, always finding her guilty, but when she woke she would force herself to forget about him, knowing that he would never forgive her, certain that she would never see him again.

She tried never to think of her mother either. Claire. That memory was more than she could bear. But sometimes, when she looked at her own face in the mirror, she would be caught off guard, startled by a momentary flash of recognition. As if someone else's face were there in place of her own, someone impossible to forget.

Did she really look so much like her mother? And, realizing that the answer was yes, she would cry. But always they were silent, hidden tears so Max wouldn't see.

She turned to him in the dark. Poor Max. He never pressed her to tell him. His understanding of her pain was that complete. Some day . . .

Damn you, Gillian, she thought, rolling over to bury her face in the pillow. First things first. Father is allowing you to come home. What more can you expect? Isn't this more than you ever dared hope for? To go home? To have your children know their grandfather? To see Clairemont again?

Please, please God, then why am I so frightened?

And deep inside, she knew. Going back to Clairemont meant more than facing her father. It meant facing herself, and those terrible memories of what had happened there. Was she strong enough to do that? Did she have the courage?

21

The same distant voice whispered a warning. You're weak, Gillian. You'll never be able to face him.

Panic-stricken, she sat up with a jerk, tiny beads of perspiration standing out on her forehead. 'I can't do it,' she whispered. 'I can't.'

Half asleep, Max stirred beside her. He reached over and pulled her close. 'It's all right, sweetheart,' he mumbled. 'Everything's all right. Sleep.'

So she lay inside the curve of his body, forcing herself to be calm, and as the first light of dawn sifted into the room, Gillian finally fell asleep.

Gillian dreamed of her mother. Claire was in her rose garden. She was reciting her favourite verse.

> *Footfalls echo in the memory*
> *Down the passage which we did not take*
> *Towards the door we never opened*
> *Into the rose garden.*

Gillian smiled in her sleep.

And then Claire reached out her hands. Her skilful, caring hands that could make anything grow. And she began to cry. It all seemed so real. Until Gillian realized with horror that, instead of falling from her eyes, the tears were dripping from the tips of her mother's broken fingers.

Chapter Two

When Will was little, he thought his mother was the Queen of England because she named their first dog Buckingham. And that meant, of course, that his grandfather had been the king. And the reason they never saw him was because everyone knew that the King of England was dead.

He had given up that notion long ago when he got to first grade, because when he told the class, even though his teacher had tried to look serious, he had seen the smirk on her face. He knew then that it wasn't true. Still, their grandfather might just as well have been king *or* dead for all they ever saw of him.

They didn't see their other grandfather either, but that was because he really *was* dead.

'Do you think Parch is going to be all right?' Daisy asked. She was sitting beside Will in the back seat of the car they had rented at the airport.

'Of course,' their mother said without turning round. 'Parch loves the kennel.' She said it but Will knew she didn't believe it.

'Parch hates the kennel,' he said. 'He was shaking like a leaf when we left him, right, Dad?'

'Well, I've seen him happier,' his father admitted. 'But it's only for two weeks.' Will noticed how he kept looking at their mother strangely out of the corner of his eye, as if he was expecting her to get sick or something.

'I wish I was a vet,' Daisy said. 'When I get to be one, we'll never leave our pets behind.'

'I have to go to the bathroom,' Will said.

'Again?' Daisy said, looking disgusted. 'How come you always have to go?'

'I don't.'

'Do so. Every time we get in the car you have to go.'

'So?' He made a face. Sometimes he got along with his sister. Like when she was in a good mood and like when they played Monopoly or Jungle Animals. Other times he wanted to pinch her head off. 'How much farther do we have to go till we're there?' he asked his father.

'About an hour.'

'I'm excited,' Daisy said, jumping up and down on the seat.

'It's going to be weird seeing our grandfather,' Will said. He had been thinking about that for almost a month, ever since their mother had told them that for their vacation they would be going to Connecticut. To Clairemont. To visit their Uncle Robin and their grandfather. He still wasn't exactly sure how he felt. Some of his friends had grandfathers. Dave Winters had two and they were both nice. But still Will couldn't help but wonder about his. And about why their grandfather had never wanted to see them before, but now he did.

He and Daisy had talked about it and Daisy said she thought maybe it was because their grandfather was sick and tired of being so rotten and mean. Mom said it was because he was getting old and wanted to see them before he died. But she looked funny when she said it. Sort of nervous. Dad said: Who cares? We'll all have a great time, no matter what.

24

Will pressed his face against the window and looked out at the passing scenery. It was so different from home. Home was wide streets and sidewalks and deep, shaded lawns. Here the trees on both sides of the road grew almost touching, and there were stone walls that were falling down or covered with poison ivy. At least that's what the vines looked like. A great place for snakes, he decided.

He glanced over at his sister and smiled. If there was one thing Daisy hated it was snakes. And thunder. And ghosts. And spiders. And the dark. In fact, when he thought about it, Daisy was afraid of just about everything. As for himself, there wasn't much that he was scared of. Except (and he admitted this only to himself, never to his mother or father, and especially never to Daisy, even though somehow she seemed to know) sometimes he was scared of the dark. As for snakes, he really liked them.

'Do you think there are any snakes at Clairemont?' Daisy asked, reading his mind the way she did a lot.

'I love snakes,' Will said, looking over at his twin, flaring his nostrils. 'I bet there's a million of them. Big ones. Vipers with holes in their heads where their noses should be.'

Their mother, who was still being awfully quiet, didn't say anything, but their father said, 'I don't think you have to worry, Daisy.'

'I have to go to the bathroom,' Will said, remembering. 'I really mean it.'

'We're almost into town,' Max said. 'Can you wait five minutes?'

'I guess.' Will sighed, sat back, and began to pick small pieces of rubber from the side of his sneaker.

Out loud, Daisy began to count telephone poles.

* * *

A few minutes later, Max pulled into a gas station just outside Norfolk and told the attendant to fill the tank. With a last glance at his wife, who still sat in stony silence, he went off with Will to the rest-room.

Right up until this morning, when they had boarded the plane at Washington National, Max hadn't been sure she was going to have the courage to take this trip. He could feel her uncertainty, and underneath, even though she thought she was hiding it from him, her fear.

As for himself, he had his own reservations. Not that he minded going to Clairemont. If anything, he was eager to meet her family. To judge for himself what kind of people they were. But the big question remained: Had Gillian come far enough to face what she still wasn't able to talk about? Her father? Her brother? Clairemont?

After Robin's phone call, she had put up a good front. She was cheerful, and when she told the children about their impending visit to Connecticut, she actually seemed eager. Until yesterday morning.

After breakfast, just as he had been gearing up to drag Parch off to the kennel, she had turned to him. 'Max, do you think I'm strong?' She had asked the question thoughtfully, as if she had been wondering about it for a long, long time.

'Strong like what? An ox?'

She shook her head, holding both hands out in a gesture of helplessness.

He remembered his sudden uneasy feeling as he sat down again at the kitchen table. Outside on the swing-seat he could hear the twins yelling at each other. He could hear Parch in his favourite spot beside the sink, licking his paw. He could hear his wife breathing. 'Sit down,' he said.

She did.

He reached across the table and took her hands in his. 'Gillian, we don't have to go to Clairemont. You know that, don't you?'

She looked at him sympathetically, as if he were a child who didn't understand. 'Don't you see?' she said sadly. 'If I don't have enough courage to go back, then what's to become of me? I can't hide forever. Can I?' The last two words were spoken as if for one wild moment she was hoping he would say yes.

'You do whatever you need to do,' he said. 'You lead. I'll follow. You know why?'

She shook her head.

'Because you are the best thing that ever happened to me.'

She smiled. 'As always, you sing in praise of simple comforts.'

He nodded. 'In praise of simple comforts.'

She stood up and came round the table and kissed him. 'So it's settled. I'm off to face my father,' she said. 'Maybe then I'll be able to tell you what I did before someone else does.'

The way she said it made Max wonder if he really wanted to know.

They headed west, passing through small Connecticut towns with white churches and village greens and miles of woodland in between.

In one town Gillian finally spoke up. 'That's where I bought my first two-wheel bike.' She pointed to a small store on the corner. 'It was blue and it had a white basket.' It was the first bit of information she had offered since they left Virginia.

Max looked over at her, but her face was turned

away so he couldn't see her expression. Her voice sounded dreamy, lost in reverie.

'My father tried to teach me to ride it. I was eight years old.'

'How long did it take you to learn?' Daisy asked. She had been trying herself for a long time, and she still couldn't keep from tipping over.

'A long, long time,' Gillian said. 'Every time I got on I fell.' She paused. 'Robin was the one who finally taught me. And then I tried to teach Amanda but she wouldn't let me.' Her voice grew distant. 'Even then, Amanda wouldn't have anything to do with me.'

'How come?' Will asked. 'Didn't your sister like you?'

'No. She never did.' Gillian leaned her head back against the seat. 'I wonder whatever happened to Amanda.' She said it as if she were alone.

How odd, Gillian thought, as they drove through the countryside, that everything should be so unchanged. She had fully expected the passage of time to have left its mark here, as it had everywhere else in the world. But not so. It was all exactly as she remembered.

As they followed the narrow country road, now and again through the overhanging branches, she caught sight of the river and, beyond, the foothills, covered with birch and pine and maples.

Steadily, as she watched the passing landscape, she had a strange sense of being in a time-warp. Eighteen years had passed without her, and yet it seemed as if she had never left. You're coming home, the voice whispered. Can you stand it?

'Does Grandfather have a dog?' Daisy asked.

'He has two,' Gillian said, then realized that she

28

was talking about what used to be. Not what was now. She shivered, and went back to her private thoughts. How many times in my dreams have I done this, she wondered. How many times have I passed along this road and through the iron gate? 'We're here,' she said quietly, pointing. *Turn round. Don't go through with it. Go back.*

She clenched her teeth. She had come this far. Her only choice now was to go on. Face it.

Beyond the gate a long gravel drive led them along a shaded avenue of oak trees, past low field-stone walls covered with honeysuckle and old roses, through meticulously tended woodland gardens filled with mountain laurel and wild flowers and azaleas.

Gillian watched, mesmerized, caught somewhere between panic and wonder. I was born here, she thought. I lived here for thirteen years, and until this moment I never realized how much I loved it. How much I lost when I had to go away. How much my children have missed.

'There *is* a house around here somewhere, isn't there?' Max said, half under his breath.

She nodded.

'Holy cow, Mom,' Will said. 'Is this all private land?'

Gillian nodded again, her mouth bone-dry, part of her desperate to catch that first glimpse of Clairemont, the other part wanting to cover her face with her hands and hide. As they came over the crest of the hill, she caught her breath. Below them the forest ended, the walled gardens and shaded walks began, and in the next instant Clairemont stood before them. A magnificent structure of grey quarried stone, with gleaming mullioned windows, high-peaked gables and even higher chimneys.

'My gosh,' Max breathed, 'it looks like it belongs in the Cotswolds.'

'I know,' Gillian murmured, overcome by what she was seeing. How dearly she had loved this place. Her home. Her Clairemont. 'It was built exactly as my grandmother wanted it. And it's just the same now as it was then. Nothing has changed.' She felt Max's hand on her shoulder, and it seemed to her that it was the only thing holding her in place, keeping her from breaking into a million pieces.

He stopped the car. 'Gilly?' he said. 'What do you want to do? Do you want to go back to Virginia?'

She turned to him, open-mouthed, torn between elation at being home again and fear of what she had to face here, and suddenly something told her to turn round, to get away from here at once. But the warning came too late. The front door had opened and she could see Robin coming through the garden and down the stone steps, quickly, opening the car door, taking her hand, pulling her towards him, hugging her. 'Gillian. My dear sister,' he said warmly. 'Welcome home.' His open display of affection was so out of character that she was taken aback, but somehow she managed an answering smile. And somehow, though her insides were trembling, she managed to make the appropriate introductions.

Then, with Robin on one side, Max on the other, and the children tagging along behind, Gillian went up the stone steps, and at the top she stopped, transfixed. The formal garden leading to the front entry stretched before her, its ingenious patterns unchanged, its sculpted yews and boxwoods exactly as she remembered them. In an act of moral courage, she forced herself to look up at the west wall, up to the mullioned windows high above the entrance. The last place she had seen her father that awful day so long ago.

But it wasn't the same. Today there was no evidence of life behind the dark glass. No shadowy outline of a broken man, happy to see her go.

Or was he standing there? She blinked. Had she seen movement? Was her father watching?

You never should have come back. You never should have come back. She heard the same words in her head, over and over. And in spite of the warmth of her brother's welcome, she was filled with fear. A deep, irrational fear that had nothing to do with her own feelings of guilt.

Desperately she turned to Max, but he wasn't looking at her. He was looking at a lovely dark-haired woman who had just stepped through the front door and into the garden.

Robin held up his hand. 'Lenore. Come and welcome Gillian home.' He turned to Gillian. 'You remember Lenore?'

Gillian stared. Lenore? Her cousin, Lenore? Still here at Clairemont after all these years? Impossible. And yet, as the woman came along the brick walk, Gillian knew it was no one else. Lenore looked as she had eighteen years ago. Like Clairemont, she was unchanged. 'But what is she doing here?' she asked with an air of bewilderment.

'She is my wife,' Robin answered.

'Your wife?' Gillian couldn't believe her ears. 'You married our cousin?'

Robin smiled a cool, faintly patronizing smile. Unlike his earlier greeting, this was a smile that Gillian remembered. 'Have you forgotten?' he said. 'She is your mother's niece, not Father's. That makes her *your* cousin. Not mine.'

'Gillian,' Lenore said in a soft, resonant voice. 'How wonderful that you've come.' For a moment she paused, seeming unsure of herself. Then she reached out and took Gillian's hand. A shy smile touched her lips. 'I am so happy. You've come home.'

Gillian opened her mouth to speak but no words came out. This was all too much. Too much. And then she felt Max put his arm around her shoulder. 'We're very pleased to meet you, Lenore,' he said smoothly. He turned. 'Daisy. Will. Come and meet your aunt.'

Will stepped forward, his cheeks on fire. Standing there in front of him was Sigourney Weaver. At least she looked like Sigourney Weaver, with dark curly hair and white skin and greenish eyes that sort of slanted up at the corners. She was so beautiful that Will was speechless. He knew he was smiling a stupid smile but he couldn't seem to wipe it off his face. Nevertheless he managed to pull himself together. 'It's nice to meet you,' he said.

Lenore took his hand. 'I'm very pleased to meet you too, Will,' she said. The sound was soft and musical, like wind chimes. 'You are a very handsome young man. And very well mannered.'

Then she turned to Daisy. 'We're all so happy to have you here at Clairemont. Dickon hasn't been able to talk about anything else for weeks. He's off on his horse right now, but he should be back any minute.'

Will watched as Daisy shook Aunt Lenore's hand, but like the dork she was she didn't say a word. Typical. Will was hoping she would have sense enough to ask who Dickon was, but she didn't. And then his uncle interrupted. 'Let's go in,' Robin said, taking Gillian by the arm. 'Everyone's inside waiting to welcome you home. Grace and Theo and Peter. You remember Peter?'

Then the door into the entrance hall opened and swallowed them up.

Chapter Three

They're all here to catch a first glimpse of the prodigal daughter come home to roost, Gillian said to herself. Dimly aware of her children standing right behind her, she stood just inside the front door, white-knuckled, clutching Max's arm, staring at the faces of those who had gathered in the front hall to welcome her to Clairemont, then past them to the magnificent painting of her grandmother hanging to one side of the wide, curving staircase.

She was overcome by another rush of nostalgia. So much was the same. How many times had she run across this Oriental carpet and up the stairs to her own room? How many times had she stood at the tall, paned windows and looked down into her mother's rose garden? Would that too be the same?

'We're happy to have you home, Miss Gillian.' The sound of the voice snapped her back. A plump, white-haired woman had stepped forward. 'On behalf of the entire staff, welcome.'

'Grace.' Gillian said the name, although for the life of her she couldn't imagine why. Twenty years ago Grace had been one of the kitchen staff. A rail-thin young woman with red hair and a sharp tongue. Gillian frowned. This couldn't be Grace.

'You remembered,' the woman said with a stiff smile.

'Grace is our housekeeper,' Lenore said.

The housekeeper? 'But where is Jocelyn?' Gillian did not mean to ask. The question just came out.

'Jocelyn died a long time ago,' Robin said quietly.

Gillian felt a touch of panic. How could she be so stupid? Things *had* changed. She took a deep breath and pulled herself together as one by one the servants stepped forward to be introduced. A few faces she recognized. Most were strangers. They are the ones who came after, she thought grimly. They know you only by reputation.

Finally the ordeal ended and Robin dismissed the staff. 'Max, Gillian, I'm sure you must be exhausted,' he said, touching Gillian on the shoulder. 'Lenore will show you to your rooms. Although I'm sure you can find your way blindfolded.'

Gillian looked away towards the staircase. Her mouth went dry, and her words came out unexpectedly sharp, brittle. 'Where is Father?'

Robin squeezed her hand. 'It's all right, Gilly. He's in Europe and he won't be back until Sunday, so you have a little time to catch your breath. To prepare.'

Gillian was tremendously relieved. At the same time she felt a small tug at her side.

'Mom,' Daisy whispered, 'are we going to stand here forever?'

Lenore, who had been waiting quietly off to one side, stepped forward. 'The children will be staying just down the hall from you, Gillian,' she said. 'Daisy is in the rose room, and you, William, are in the blue.'

Will flushed. His aunt definitely was Sigourney Weaver.

'We'll give you a chance to get unpacked,' Robin said, glancing at his watch. 'What do you say to cocktails in the drawing-room at seven?'

Lenore put her hand on his arm. 'The children should be down for supper at six.' Her tone was almost apologetic. She turned to Gillian. 'But you needn't worry. We'll send Dickon to fetch them when it's time.'

'That's very thoughtful of you,' Max said. 'And needless to say, we're all looking forward to meeting Dickon.'

Gillian felt weak. Who was Dickon? Had she heard the name earlier? She wasn't sure but she didn't dare ask. *You should never have come back. Never.*

'Would you like me to show you to your rooms?' Lenore asked.

'Just take the children,' Robin said. 'I know Gillian would prefer to be on her own. Like the old days.'

'Of course,' Lenore nodded.

'You two go along,' Max said to Daisy and Will. 'Mom and I will be along in a minute.'

Gillian was numb. Was she really capable of making her way by herself? Would she remember? She watched until they had all disappeared up the stairs. Then she took one step forward, and for a moment she thought she was going to fall on her face. Max reached out and held her steady. 'Easy, Gilly,' he whispered gently. 'You're doing great.'

'I don't know what's the matter with me,' she mumbled. 'I feel . . . I feel disembodied.'

'You're tired, sweetheart. That's all,' Max said. 'It's been a long, tough day.'

'The worst.' She turned and went through the wide archway, stopping at the foot of the stairs. To the right the wide corridor continued, leading to the west wing. She remembered how she used to run its length, stopping to glance at her reflection in every Venetian mirror along the way. Never again, she thought. What used to be is over. She passed her hand over her eyes, about to begin a slow, cautious ascent to the first floor when she heard a soft, shuffling sound behind her. She turned.

In the shadow just to one side of the library door she could see someone standing. A woman.

'Let's go, Gilly,' Max said. 'You're not the only one who's tired. I'm beat.'

'Wait.' She reached out and took hold of the balustrade to steady herself. 'Lenore?' But it couldn't be Lenore. She had just seen her cousin disappear up the stairs. It must be one of the servants, and yet somehow she knew it wasn't. 'I'm sorry,' she said loudly. 'Do I know you?'

Instead of responding the woman turned abruptly and vanished down the corridor.

Max took Gillian by the hand. 'Come on,' he said softly. 'I need to sit down. My back is killing me.'

Her breath came out in a short, shallow gasp. 'But I *know* her.'

'Then I'm sure you'll see her again.' He turned and led the way up the stairs. At the top he stopped. 'Now it's your turn,' he said. 'Lead on, my love.'

She went to the left through a short gallery filled with paintings, and into a narrow hallway with doors on both sides. 'This is the west wing,' she said quietly. 'Where all the children slept. Robin and Amanda and me.' She stopped. 'This was my room.' She lifted her hand, then dropped it to her side. 'You open it, Max.' She hesitated for a moment, then followed him in.

Her first reaction was one of panic, that somehow she had taken a wrong turn and had ended up in the wrong room. One where she had never been before.

The floor was carpeted in forest green, the walls covered with bold French tapestries. A double canopy bed stood between the windows, hung with yards and yards of rich floral chintz. On the opposite side of the room the same fabric covered a sofa and two chairs, and in between there was a massive bouquet of apricot tulips and white narcissus.

Gillian stared. This is a hotel room, she thought. It isn't mine. And then she saw their suitcases standing beside the bed. She hadn't made a mistake. She had simply expected the impossible. That for eighteen years they had kept her room exactly as it had been left. But they hadn't. Even the hanging shelves on either side of the fireplace were gone. The shelves that had been filled with angels. Ever since she could remember, people had given them to her. For birthdays, for Christmases, sometimes just because. Crystal angels, porcelain angels, the Cherubim, the Seraphim, the Archangels. Where are you, she wondered. Where have you gone?

Max took off his jacket and sank down on the sofa. 'I guess some things around here have changed after all.'

'Yes,' she said dully. 'It's been a long, long time.' She looked across the room towards the windows. From those windows she had an unobstructed view of her mother's rose garden. In June it had always been a blaze of colour: pink tea roses and purple hybrids and clusters of crimson floribundas and trellises covered with ramblers and brick walks winding through rows and rows of cabbage roses and low-growing miniatures. When she was very young her mother had taught her the names of every one. In English and Latin.

Footfalls echo in the memory, down to the passage which we did not take.

She held her breath. Were her ears deceiving her?

38

Was she actually hearing her mother's voice? She kicked off her shoes and hurried across the soft carpet, parted the curtains, looked out.

What she saw made her gasp.

The brick walks were still there. And the stone walls that had enclosed the garden. But where roses had filled every inch of space, now there was nothing. Nothing but clumps of grass. Ornamental grass whose colours ranged from blue to green to gold, but it was grass nonetheless.

Gillian's insides trembled. Her mother's rose garden had vanished. But why? Why hadn't they taken care of it? Surely even now they all knew what it had meant to Claire. Hadn't anyone cared?

Stunned, she was about to turn away when something caught her eye. A movement in the garden below. A stirring. Something, *someone* was coming through the tall grass. Mesmerized, she watched. Any moment she would see who it was.

The grass parted.

Gillian stared.

And saw . . .

Nothing. And that frightened her out of all proportion. Who had she expected to see?

The sound of Max's voice brought her back to reality. 'I'm surprised you didn't know about Robin and Lenore,' he was saying. 'Who exactly *is* she?'

Gillian turned away from the window. Enough of this absurdity, she said to herself. Don't look out there again. She crossed the room and sat down next to Max on the sofa. 'Lenore is my cousin. My mother's niece.'

'I know. I heard Robin. But you didn't know he had married her?'

Gillian shook her head. 'Robin never told me

anything about his life here at Clairemont. And I never asked. In all these years our telephone conversations have never amounted to anything more than how-are-you-fine-how-are-you. I didn't want to know and he didn't tell me.' She paused. 'When you come right down to it, I never did know much about Robin. He's a very private person. Always was. When I was a child I always considered him one of the grown-ups, even though he was only five years older than me.' She grew pensive. 'He was never very close to any of us. Except Father. And not openly affectionate even with him. But he loved Clairemont. He used to pretend that he owned it. That he was the master and Amanda and I were his servants. But deep down I don't think he ever felt as if he really belonged here. Clairemont was my mother's, and no matter how sweet she was to him, he never believed she loved him the way she loved her own children.'

'You and Amanda?'

She nodded.

'And did she?'

'No. She didn't love anyone the way she loved us.'

'How old was he when his own mother died?'

'Three years old. Just a baby really. She died of tuberculosis. The next year Father married my mother and came to live with her at Clairemont.' She broke off abruptly.

For a moment there was a strained silence. Begin with the easy stuff, Gillian said to herself. Tell him about Lenore. Then maybe you'll be able to work your way up to the rest. She looked at Max, saw his familiar I'd-love-to-ask-but-don't-dare expression. 'There are lots of things I can't talk about. Yet,' she said softly. 'But I'll tell you what I know about

Lenore. If you're interested.'

He took her hand. 'I'm interested.'

She pulled her legs up under her and settled back. 'Lenore's father was in the diplomatic service. He had a good job but they lived a nomadic sort of life, constantly moving from one country to another. In the early seventies he was assigned to the embassy in Jordan, a time when there was a great deal of unrest in the country. Some kind of civil war. So Lenore's mother sent her here to Clairemont.'

'Lenore's mother and yours were sisters?'

Gillian nodded. 'But after my grandmother died they had little to do with each other. I think it was because Clairemont was left solely to my mother. She always felt guilty for it even though it wasn't her doing. I think that's one of the reasons why she took Lenore in so graciously. Anyway, Lenore lived here for two years. I don't know if she ever went back to Jordan.'

'Did you spend a lot of time with her while she was here?'

'No. She was the same age as Robin. She had very little interest in me.' She grimaced. 'Probably because I was a spoiled brat. I do remember though that she was one of the few who got along with Amanda. In fact, as far as I know, she was the *only* one.'

'Speaking of Amanda, whatever happened to your sister? Do you have any idea?'

Gillian felt suddenly overwhelmed by her lack of knowledge. She knew so little about these people, her closest relatives, her family, her only sister. Why hadn't she ever asked about them? Why had she stayed hidden all these years?

But the answer was clear. Because her father wanted nothing to do with her.

41

Max put his arms around her. 'Cheer up,' he said. 'You've made great strides, my darling. You've said more about your family in the last hour than you have in the last twelve years. You're not there yet but you're on your way. I'm convinced of it.'

Gillian rested her head on his shoulder but she didn't speak. For some reason, instead of feeling better she was feeling worse. Increasingly apprehensive. And she didn't know why. It wasn't the full-blown fear that had taken hold of her earlier, but with each passing moment she was feeling more and more uneasy.

'There is nothing here that can hurt you, Gilly,' Max said, sensing her mood. 'Don't forget. We can always pack our bags and get the hell out.'

'You sound just like Robin.'

'Why?'

'The last thing he said to me on the phone was exactly that. Come to Clairemont, he said. See if you like it here. If you don't, you can get the hell out and never come back.'

Chapter Four

Amanda's journal. 16 June.

I saw my sister today. Her name is Gillian and I hate her. There's nothing really strange about that. I've always hated her and now that I've seen her again, I know I still do.

Robin told me she was coming and I said to myself, Amanda, be open-minded about this. After all, she's been gone a long time. And so I gave her the benefit of the doubt.

I shouldn't have.

I stood in the dark and watched her go up the stairs. As if she had any business doing that. For what she is, she should never have been allowed back in this house at all. Never. I should have told Father not to let her come.

Some say Father doesn't know I exist. I have to admit they are right. But that's the very reason I care about him. When I attract attention it's always troublesome. I dislike people who don't leave me alone. People who interfere in my life. Like that obnoxious Mrs Comstock at the garden centre. 'May I help you, Amanda?' She always says it in that whiny voice of hers. As if I didn't know what I was doing.

I always know what I'm doing. Precisely what I'm doing.

Amanda closed her journal and set the pen back in its holder. It was 7.15. Another forty-five minutes until dinner. And then she would have to see Gillian face to face. She wondered whether she should be pleasant like Lenore told her to be, or if she should let her sister see how she really felt about her. She snarled at her reflection. 'That's what I think of you, Gillian. Would you leave Clairemont if you knew how much I still hate you? I believe you would.'

She crossed to the closet and looked in, wondering what she should wear. Something appropriate for the occasion. Something conservative. She might decide to be pleasant, but she was certainly not going to wear anything festive. She took out her purple gauze skirt and grey blouse. She lay them on her bed and went to draw her bath. She had been working outside in her 'rooms' all day and she was in need of a good cleaning.

Amanda loved baths. They made her skin feel so soft. Velvety. Like the petals on her pansies. She turned on the water and poured in a capful of Chanel. Then she went back into her room, but before she had a chance to rid herself of a single piece of clothing, a knock came at the door.

How rude, Amanda thought. She decided not to answer. She sat back down at her writing-desk and folded her arms across her chest.

'Mandy?' A soft voice. Lenore's. Lenore was the only one who called her Mandy.

Amanda felt the anger draining away. Lenore was the only person in this world she really loved.

'Mandy, please unlock the door.'

Amanda rarely did anything she didn't want to do. It was one of her rules. After all, she was twenty-eight years old. Old enough to make up her own mind. But she decided to open the door because she

44

wanted to talk to Lenore. Amanda's *impatiens wallerana* were ready to be potted, and this morning she hadn't been able to find the moss baskets. It was a distressing omen, one that she needed to discuss. And also she wanted to talk about getting rid of Gillian as soon as possible.

Lenore was smiling when she stepped into the room, but it was a puzzled smile. 'You didn't come down to welcome your sister, Mandy. You promised me you would. What happened?'

For a moment Amanda hesitated, considering. Then she said, 'I decided it wasn't a good idea. Why should a person have to welcome a person they hate?' She studied Lenore's face, waiting for some sign of disapproval, but Lenore's expression didn't change. She seemed curious. Nothing more.

Lenore put her arm around Amanda. 'But what if you discover that you don't hate her any more?'

Amanda pulled away, then reminded herself not to be angry with Lenore. After all, bringing Gillian back was none of her doing. It was all Robin's idea. 'But I *do* hate her,' she said stubbornly. 'I'm going to have dinner in my room.'

'Of course you may do whatever you like. But you know I'll miss you terribly. And so will Robin.'

Amanda didn't know why Lenore said such a ridiculous thing about Robin. Maybe because somehow she hoped Amanda would believe it. 'Your husband is a despicable person. And now with Gillian here, that makes two of them. She should go away and he should go with her.'

'Mandy,' Lenore said gently, 'things will get better. You'll see. But you mustn't be impatient. You know what happens when you lose your patience.'

Amanda pulled away. She had made a bad mistake.

45

She shouldn't have told Lenore anything about how she felt. From now on she would have to be very, very careful. She smiled. 'I've changed my mind. I don't want you to miss me so I'll come and sit beside you at dinner.'

'I'm so pleased,' Lenore said with relief. 'And now . . .' She paused, tipping her head to one side. 'Do I hear water running?' In the next instant she was at the bathroom door with Amanda right behind. Just as the water began to spill over the rim of the tub Lenore bent down and turned it off.

Amanda frowned. She didn't care about the water. It wouldn't be the first time she had flooded the bathroom. What concerned her was what she thought she heard. She thought she heard Lenore say damn. Amanda hated to hear foul language. People ought to be careful what they say. And to whom they say it. 'Are you upset with me, Cousin Lenore?' she asked quietly.

Lenore didn't reply, but when she turned round she was laughing. 'Of course not, silly. I could never be upset with you.' Softly she patted Amanda's cheek. 'And now you'd better hop in the tub before the water gets cold.' She glanced at her watch. 'You haven't much time. Dinner is at eight. By the way, we're eating in the tea-room.' Then she left.

Amanda undressed, but before she got into her bath she went back to her writing-desk and opened her journal. She picked up her pen and made the following entry.

I forgot to tell Lenore about the moss baskets. She wants me to sit beside her at dinner and I will, even though it's in the tea-room. And then I'll decide what to do about Gillian.

46

At ten minutes before eight Amanda went downstairs. As she passed the drawing-room she heard voices, but she didn't look in. She knew whose they were. They were having cocktails, and Amanda found that habit distasteful even when the drinkers were people she didn't hate, never mind Robin and Gillian. Amanda was twenty-eight years old and she had never had an alcoholic beverage. Nor did she ever intend to. It was another one of her rules.

As she usually did, she went through the library slowly, running her fingers along the top of the mahogany table. She loved that table, the feel of its wood. It was where she always did her jigsaw puzzles. Whenever she had time, that is. She had no time now. In spring and summer her 'rooms' needed all her attention. Her puzzles would have to wait until after the leaves fell.

She went out through the side door, along the short corridor and into the tea-room, a place that Amanda found especially unpleasant. Not because of the room itself, but because of the corner cupboards with their locked doors. Where Father kept what was left of her mother's collection of precious Rose Mandarin.

The table was set for dinner and, frowning, Amanda walked round it and stood in front of one of the cupboards. The shelves behind the glass were full of Chinese porcelain. Tea sets and platters and shrimp dishes and brush pots. Part of the collection used to be displayed on the mantel in the library, but one night a few months ago it had fallen to the hearth and smashed to bits. She wasn't sure why. Perhaps it was because she had finally wished hard enough.

Amanda stared, remembering how much she wanted to smash every bit of it. But she didn't dare.

Years ago she had tried. She had broken the fruit compote on the sideboard, but Robin had warned her never to do it again. 'Do you want to stay here at Clairemont?' he had asked in that cold, sinister tone of his. 'Or would you prefer to go to Havensport?'

Havensport. The hellhole that tried to pass itself off as a *health clinic*. From the time she was eight years old she had been carted off every week to visit Doctor Robert. But Amanda knew that his real name wasn't Doctor Robert at all. It was Doctor *Rabid*. She had seen a rabid raccoon once and he was the spitting image of the creature. With little blobs of saliva that gathered in the corners of his mouth, and a walk that was more like a queer lop-sided shuffle. Back and forth, back and forth. *Well, Amanda, how are we today?* Talking to her as if she were a *baby*. Trying to insinuate himself into her life. Putting her in the playroom, arranging the toys for her, *watching* her. *Release therapy*, he called it. It was supposed to help her correct a *disordered behaviour*. Which was absurd, because there was nothing *disordered* about Amanda. Nothing at all. And she had handled those sessions the same way she handled every other disruption in her life. She refused to participate.

But that hadn't dissuaded her mother. She never accepted Amanda's independence. She made Amanda come with her *every week*. It was one of the reasons – there were too many others to even think about – why Amanda hated her mother. She *always* made Amanda go with her. *Every single week*. To see the drooling Doctor Rabid.

That was bad enough. But just before her mother died, she had been planning to send Amanda to Havensport, not for the usual loathsome visit with the doctor, but for an *extended stay*. Amanda had overheard the doctor planning it with her mother.

And then, hallelujah, before they could put their heinous plan into action, her mother died and Amanda was saved. She never heard the word Havensport again until the day she broke the fruit compote and Robin threatened to send her there. So she never touched the Rose Mandarin again. She broke plenty of other things but never that. But when Father dies, she thought, I will do it. I will destroy every single piece. It won't matter what Robin says. Unless . . .

She shuddered. Unless Gillian interferes. Somehow she had never considered that possibility before. But now that her sister had returned . . .

Behind her she heard voices. She put everything else out of her mind. She sat down quickly at the end of the table where she always sat when there were strangers coming to dinner. From there she could observe without having to converse unless she wanted to.

The first one to come into the room was Robin.

Robin.

What an arrogantly handsome man her half-brother was. He looked just like Father. And how uncaring, how selfish he was, qualities that must have come from his mother. Yet Amanda couldn't be sure about that. She had never known Robin's mother. It wasn't until after the woman died, Father had married Claire and then added two more children to his family. Of the three, Amanda thought, watching the door, there was only one worth having and that is me.

Following right behind Robin was Gillian's husband Max. Such an odd name. But then he must be odd to have married *her*. Amanda narrowed her vision the way she did sometimes when she didn't want to see everything at once.

'Ah, Amanda,' Robin said, baring his teeth in a forced smile which didn't fool Amanda for a minute. 'I'm glad you're here. Have you met Max?'

Amanda knew he wasn't truly smiling, so she pretended not to hear.

'I'm delighted to meet you, Amanda,' Gillian's husband said in a bland, offensive manner. 'It came as a pleasant surprise to learn that you were still living here.' He came round the table and held out his hand.

Amanda ignored the gesture. She never shook hands with anyone. It was unsanitary. Another of her rules. But she forced herself to smile in a cordial way. After all, if she was anything at all, she was cordial. 'Unlike other members of the family,' she said politely, 'I have lived here all my life. This house belonged to my mother.'

At that point her head was turned away from the door, but all the same she knew that Lenore had come in. Lenore and Gillian. Her older sister. Her *only* sister. She heard Gillian's voice, then a breathless kind of gasp. 'Amanda.' And in the next instant she was standing beside Amanda's chair.

Slowly Amanda looked up and stared. Fine lines were visible around the corners of Gillian's eyes and her face was pale. Otherwise she looked just the same. Older but no wiser. She looked just like Mother.

Amanda turned away without speaking. The rest of them could behave like fools, pretend that Gillian was welcome, but not she.

Lenore sat down next to Amanda at the end of the table. 'Come and sit here, Gillian,' she said, pointing

50

to one of the places across from Amanda. Better there than beside me, Amanda thought. But then Lenore knew that Amanda liked to have the whole side of the table to herself. Even when Father was at home no one in the household ever sat next to Amanda.

'I'm so happy to see you, Amanda,' Gillian said. Her voice shook and she reached across the table. Clearly she wanted to touch Amanda's hand, but Amanda kept her hands tucked firmly in her lap.

After a minute Gillian pulled back. 'How have you been?' she asked. And then, 'Are you happy?'

Amanda wasn't going to answer, but she decided that she ought to be polite. At least on the surface. 'I'm very happy,' she said levelly. She would have to try her best not to be rude. If she was, Gillian would retaliate just like always. And Amanda would suffer.

'Amanda is constantly happy,' Robin said coolly. 'As long as she gets her way. You learn that very quickly when you have to live with her.'

'Hush, Robin,' Lenore said. She always stuck up for Amanda. 'Let's enjoy the evening, shall we? Dickon is entertaining the children, so we can all relax.' She rang the dinner bell. 'It's your favourite appetizer, Mandy. Maryland crab.' She smiled.

Amanda smiled back. There was no reason to be angry with Lenore. She loved Lenore. It was for her sake that Amanda had decided to come down for dinner. But now that she thought about it, why should she allow Gillian to force her into hiding? It was Gillian who ought to be hiding after what she did.

Amanda looked around the table. In this difficult encounter she had tried her best. She had shown herself to be charming and pleasant. To no avail. As usual, Robin was sneering openly at her. He did it all the time, trying to make her out to be a fool. But tonight she suspected he had a different motive. Tonight he seemed intent on impressing Gillian with the difficulties of living here at Clairemont with Amanda.

She stared at him, keeping her face immobile so that he wouldn't see that she was watching. What was going on in his diabolical mind, she wondered. Why had he asked Gillian to come back? Just to show her how unpleasant it was to live here? That made little sense, but as she thought about it, it suddenly occurred to her that for once, without even being aware, Robin might be doing something good. Perhaps left to his own devices, he would drive Gillian out.

As for Gillian – Amanda snorted in disgust – she was behaving as if Robin didn't matter, as if she were interested only in her sister, but she was *so* transparent. She had never cared about Amanda. She had always done precisely what she wanted to do without ever having to answer to anyone. Gillian, the favoured child, Claire's darling. It had always been Amanda's lot in life to play the role of the bad seed, spawn of the devil, while Gillian played the saint. Until she made the fatal mistake, Amanda gloated, and rightly paid the price.

Amanda took a good look at her sister sitting so quietly across the table, and she felt a tide of anger beginning to rise in her throat. On the surface, Gillian looked so . . . so innocent. So fragile. But underneath Amanda knew she was a viper. Robin's motives might be suspect, but not Gillian's. She had come back to Clairemont for one reason. To reinstate herself as the family jewel. To make Amanda's place worth nothing. The youngest sibling. A household pet who must be kept in tight control.

One of her favourite quotes came into her head. *Thou call'dst me dog before thou had a cause. But since I am a dog, beware my fangs.* She tipped her head back and glowered. Beware my fangs, she whispered to herself. Indeed, since you think I am a dog, beware my fangs.

Chapter Five

Daisy knew from the very first moment that there was going to be trouble at Clairemont. Her brother was going to try to leave her out of everything. She could tell because sometimes it was like there was a radio inside his head and she could hear what he was thinking. Like just before they went into the fifth grade, she knew that he was going to start ignoring her at school. And she knew why. He didn't want any of his friends to think he liked her. She knew the change was coming before it ever came. Because she had heard him thinking it. And from then on, when they were alone it was all right to do things together, but never any more at school. She didn't really blame him for it, because sometimes she felt the same way. She and Will had lots of differences. He loved popcorn, she hated it; he liked snakes, they terrified her; he was a show-off, she was shy. But deep down, it didn't change how they really felt about each other. Even though they never discussed it, they knew they were more than merely brother and sister. They were twins. That meant that no matter what their complaints about each other, they weren't supposed to blab.

But lately Daisy was finding it harder and harder to keep her mouth shut. Since she and Will turned eleven he seemed really short-tempered and much quicker to make fun of her, and one of these days she was going to forget they were twins and tell her mother all about how mean he was. But not yet, because there were still some things she did that she trusted *him* not to tell. Like last week when she and her friend Nan called Mia's Restaurant and ordered all that pizza to take out. Just as a joke. She and Nan had laughed and laughed about it, but then Will found out. He said it was a dumb thing to do, but he never told. And he never told about her spilling the iodine on the upstairs hall carpet. Later he told Daisy that it was because he wanted some tattle insurance. She was to respond in kind if the need ever arose. She agreed.

Anyway, this afternoon Aunt Lenore told them that Dickon would come to get them for supper, and when Will asked who Dickon was she said, 'Why, he's your cousin', surprised that he didn't know.

'Our mother didn't know either,' Will said. 'Because she would have told us if she had.'

Aunt Lenore didn't seem at all upset about it. 'It's your uncle's fault. He never tells anyone anything.' She smiled. 'But it makes no difference. When you meet Dickon, it will seem as if you've known him forever.'

'I'm sure we'll get along just fine,' Daisy said, even though she knew right then that there was going to be the usual trouble with Will. Whenever he met someone for the first time, Will always tried to separate himself from her. Like he was older, even though he wasn't.

Back home it wouldn't have mattered. Back home Daisy didn't mind going her own way. But here at Clairemont, for some reason, she didn't want to be left alone, and to prevent that, she knew she was going to have to watch her brother like a hawk.

When Dickon came to get them for supper, he went to Will's room first, and if Daisy hadn't heard the two boys going down the corridor she would have been left behind. Even when she caught up with them, Will ignored her. But Dickon didn't, and Daisy fell in love with him almost the minute she saw him. He wasn't the only boy she ever had a crush on, but she knew for certain that he was going to be the last.

Dickon was thirteen years old but he looked a lot older. He had straight dark hair and startling blue eyes and a deep grown-up-sounding voice, and when he talked he seemed even older. 'How old are you?' That was the first question he asked, and Will said twelve.

You liar, Daisy thought, but she didn't correct him. She didn't want Dickon to know that they were just barely eleven.

They headed down the back stairs. 'Do either of you ride horseback?' he asked. 'At three every afternoon I go exploring. If the weather's good, that is. We have lots of horses and some very interesting trails around here.'

Daisy had never ridden, she said. But she would love to learn.

'You would not,' Will said. 'You'd clunk over in a fit if you ever got up on a horse.'

'I would not.' She gave him a kick.

'I'll teach you both if you like,' Dickon said.

'I'd like,' Will said.

'Me too,' said Daisy.

They ate supper in the kitchen, a huge, airy room with white-tiled walls and cushioned chairs painted blue, and shelves full of books and pottery and spice

56

jars. The cook, Mary, served them soup and sandwiches, then left them alone.

Normally, Dickon said, he ate with the family in the dining-room, but tonight his mother thought it would be better if the three of them ate by themselves. So they could get to know each other.

'I think it's weird that our mother didn't know you were alive,' Will said.

'It's probably because my father never told her.' Dickon laughed a little. 'My father discusses only what interests him. I don't happen to qualify.'

Daisy couldn't believe that. How could a person's father not be interested in him? She didn't want to ask but she hoped that Dickon would see the sympathy in her face.

'Geez us, Daisy,' Will said sharply, 'don't start bawling, for Chrissake.'

Daisy reddened and kicked him again under the table. Hard.

'Cut it out or I'm going to kick you back.'

'You wouldn't dare.' She said it but she knew he'd do it if she gave him half an excuse.

'Why don't you get lost, Daisy-dork?' he said. 'Dickon and I have things to do.'

Dickon looked from one to the other with a half-smile. 'My mother told me to keep you two busy. Not to let you spend any time alone while you're here. So I guess you'll have to put up with each other no matter what.'

Daisy gave Will a withering look, then turned to her cousin. 'Will and I get along just fine.' Except when he's being an a-hole, she thought. She didn't say it though.

'Have either of you seen *My Father's Glory?*' Dickon asked.

'Not yet,' Will said. 'Is it rated R?'

Dickon shook his head. 'But it's supposed to be pretty good. I have the video. We can go into the games room after supper and watch it if you like.'

'Cool.' Will paused. 'Do your parents screen all your tapes before you watch them?'

'No. My mother trusts my judgement. My father doesn't give a damn. I watch whatever I decide on.'

Daisy felt a tingle of nervous excitement. They never got to watch *anything* unless their parents approved. In the next instant her brother said, 'It's no sweat at our house either. We watch whatever we want.' Another lie but again Daisy let it pass.

They finished their supper and were served chocolate brownies topped with Cherry Garcia ice cream. From then on none of them had much to say, Will and Daisy because they were too busy eating their dessert. Dickon didn't touch his and seemed lost in thought.

'Don't you like Cherry Garcia?' Daisy finally asked.

Dickon shrugged. 'It's all right, I suppose. I just don't want it right now.'

Daisy put her fork down. She still had half of hers left and she wanted to eat every bit of it, but she certainly didn't want to look like a pig.

She and Dickon waited until Will finished his. Then Dickon said, 'Before we watch the movie, do you want to see my spiders?'

Will went wide-eyed. 'You collect *spiders*?'

Dickon nodded. 'I have seventy-eight species.'

Daisy made the most awful face, and she was glad her brother wasn't looking at her. Not that it mattered. He didn't have to see her expression. He knew how she felt about spiders. But to her surprised relief he didn't mention it.

'Where do you keep them?' he asked Dickon.

'Downstairs. In the old store-room.' Dickon put his napkin beside his plate and stood up. 'I think you'll find them very interesting.'

Will got up and followed their cousin, leaving Daisy to bring up the rear, but at the kitchen door he turned. For a minute he looked as if he was going to say something nasty about how she hated spiders so why was she coming, but again he surprised her. 'Don't be such a snail,' he said, pushing her out of the room.

She smiled to herself. This was another reason why she never told on her brother. Because when the going got tough for her, somehow he knew it and laid off.

The walls on both sides of the narrow stairway leading to the cellars were made of stone painted white, and it made everything seem bright, clean, not at all intimidating. But once she stepped off the last step onto the damp concrete floor, everything changed. This part of the cellar was dark and windowless, and above her head the ceilings were low and arched. Like in a church.

Dickon turned lights on as they went, and at first Daisy was able to keep calm. She followed the two boys through a door and into a chilly room filled with ceiling-high wooden racks, stacked from top to bottom with wine bottles resting on their sides. What was behind them she couldn't tell, but the darkness there was thick, musty-smelling, inhabited, she was sure, with unnamed, unseen creatures. Heavy oaken beams crisscrossed the ceiling, and in between, lengths and lengths of copper pipes seemed to stretch on forever.

'That's where the furnace is.' Dickon pointed off to the right but he didn't go in that direction. Instead he turned left and went down some curved steps and through a narrow doorway which led into a large square room.

Once inside the door he reached up and pulled a cord, and a light hanging from the ceiling went on. It was so dim Daisy couldn't see clearly. Even so, she saw more than enough to make her wish she had stayed upstairs.

The room was filled with rows and rows of glass cages, one stacked on top of the other, some filled with dirt, others with small plants. And although she couldn't see them, she knew what lived inside.

Will said, 'Wow!'

Dickon spoke in a very professorial tone. 'There are two groups of spiders in the world. The *Araneomorphae* and the *Mygalomorphae*. On the right-hand side and to the rear are the *Araneomorphae*. The true spiders.' He pointed to the far end of the room. 'I have only eleven mygalomorphs. Tarantulas and trap-door spiders. I keep them over in that corner. Come on. I'll show you my favourites.'

'Are any of them poisonous?' Will asked, wide-eyed.

'Some,' Dickon nodded. 'I have seven *lycosa raptoria*. Wolf spiders. And I have eleven black widows.'

Dickon and Will moved into the room, but Daisy didn't. She stood frozen beside the door, her flesh crawling, neither looking to right nor left but staring straight ahead. And suddenly she had to go to the bathroom. Whether she really had to or not she wasn't sure, but it was like when you played hide-and-seek. Just when you found the perfect hiding-place, all of a sudden you had to go to the bathroom.

Not that there was anything perfect about this place. Just imagining what was scurrying around inside the cages made her sick with fear. 'I'm going upstairs,' she mumbled and, without waiting for an answer, she turned and fled back the way they had come.

Along the way, though the lights were still on, somehow it seemed darker. Thicker with shadow. And it was clammy-cold. Her sneakers made soft, shuffling sounds on the concrete but, except for the thumping of her heart, that was the only thing she heard.

She slowed down. Was there something ahead, lurking behind one of the doors, waiting for her? Something that always hides in cellars just beyond the range of light?

Or worse, was the something behind her? Following her? Keeping just out of sight?

She glanced back over her shoulder.

Nothing. But that didn't mean nothing was there.

She didn't dare glance towards the creepy place where Dickon said the furnace was. Instead she quickened her pace and, looking straight ahead, hurried through the low-arched doorway leading to the wine cellar.

There she stopped. Before taking another step she had to be sure she was going the right way. At the moment nothing was more frightening than the prospect of getting lost down here. Not even spiders.

Ahead, the rows and rows of dusty wine bottles all looked alike in the dim light, and they seemed to stretch endlessly and she didn't remember which aisle they had come down. Each row was closed in so you couldn't see from one to the other, but they all seemed to go in the same direction. She counted the rows. Nine in all. So if she went between the fourth and fifth, she should come out at the stairway. Or at least close to it.

One. Two. Three. Four.

She paused, took a deep breath, then with growing trepidation began to walk down aisle number five. On each side the racks of wine towered over her, reaching almost to the ceiling. She guessed there must be hundreds and hundreds of bottles stored here, maybe thousands, and if all of a sudden one of the racks tipped over . . .

You should have stayed with Will, she thought. Spiders are nowhere near as scary as this. 'Don't be stupid,' she said out loud. 'There's nothing to be worried about. Just find the stairs.'

And then it happened. Something that raised every goose-bump on her body. From behind, she heard a sound. A soft rustling. Like a lady's skirts sweeping along the floor.

Daisy whirled round. 'Mom? Aunt Lenore?'

No answer, but the swishing sound came nearer.

Daisy felt a sharp stab of panic, and she had to cross her legs tight to keep from wetting her pants. Her first thought was to turn and run but, terror-stricken, she couldn't move. 'Who's there?' The rustling stopped and everything was still, but it didn't make her any less afraid, because now she knew she wasn't alone. She was being watched.

She wanted to close her eyes tight, but she knew that if she did whoever it was would come and grab her and take her away. So, shivering violently, she kept them wide open.

And to her growing horror, slowly materializing out of the darkness, stretched towards her, came a *pair of hands*. Mangled, broken hands, all blood and bones and purple flesh, attached to the grey, shadowy arms of a woman.

Daisy opened her mouth to scream but nothing came out.

There followed a cold, dead, tomb-like silence, and then a whisper, grey as the spectre herself. *Go home, Daisy. Go home.* And incredibly, as if the whisper itself were doing it, the bottles of wine began to come free of the rack, one after another, smashing to pieces on the cellar floor.

More frightened than she had ever been in her life, Daisy managed to do two things. She shut her eyes tight and she let out one single blood-curdling scream.

As suddenly as they had begun, the bottles stopped falling.

'Holy shit!' Will's voice.

Shaking wildly, Daisy squeezed her eyes open.

Will and Dickon were standing at the end of the aisle, staring in disbelief. 'Holy shit, Daisy,' Will said, picking his way through the shattered glass. 'What did you do?'

Unable to speak, Daisy could only shake her head. Then she burst into tears.

Chapter Six

Amanda left the tea-room immediately after the dessert was served, and Robin took advantage of her absence to make it clear how he felt about his younger half-sister. 'Amanda is as mad as a hatter,' he said bluntly. 'It's impossible to deal with her. If she's displeased she can make Clairemont a most unpleasant place to live. Which she does with extreme regularity.'

Gillian could hear disgust in his voice coupled with resignation. As if he hated the situation but knew it would never change. 'Has she ever lived anywhere else?' she asked, reaching for her coffee cup with an unsteady hand.

'No,' Robin said. 'Though it should come as no surprise. Her options have always been limited. Either she stays here at Clairemont where she can function on her own terms or . . .' He shrugged. '. . . or nothing.'

'Exactly what *is* wrong with her?' Max asked.

'It's hard to say.' Robin lifted his shoulders in a gesture of puzzlement. 'I think she's a psychopath. Which is really a junkyard term for a whole collection of mental disorders. All of which, in my humble opinion, belong to Amanda.'

'What do the doctors say?' Gillian asked.

Robin raised an eyebrow. 'Doctors? She hasn't been near one for eighteen years.'

At that point Lenore told him to hush and the

subject was dropped, but Gillian couldn't put Amanda out of her mind. Was she really what Robin had said? A psychopath? And if she was, why weren't they seeking help? Gillian shuddered, remembering Amanda's frozen face across the table. A twenty-eight-year-old woman who seemed barely into her teens. A frail, thin person with huge dark eyes and skin so pale she looked as if she had never been outside a day in her life. There was a strange childish quality about her voice, so youthful that when Gillian closed her eyes she could hear the child Amanda. Her little sister. A child, she remembered, who could be touchingly sweet at times, utterly unmanageable at others. A child who had caused their mother anxiety beyond description. Robin's words echoed in her mind. *I think she's a psychopath.* Was that really what she had become? Or had she been one from the beginning?

Gillian stared into her empty cup. No matter what Amanda's problem, Gillian thought, she never committed the crime that you did. And Robin may have forgiven you but Amanda hasn't. But then what else had she expected? Robin had never suffered the way Amanda must have. Claire was not his mother.

And then, as if the atmosphere weren't already charged with tension, Robin began talking about sleepwalking, talking to Max and Gillian as casually as if he were discussing the weather. He said he had installed locks on the windows and doors in her bedroom just in case she hadn't outgrown the dreadful habit. But even if she had, he certainly hoped that being here at Clairemont wouldn't trigger a recurrence. Clearly he had no idea that she couldn't bear the mention of the word, never mind the memory that still devastated her.

Lenore knew, though. Gillian could see it in her face when once again she told her husband to hush. Gillian was very grateful to her for that. Lenore seemed a very kind, thoughtful person. How sad that Gillian had never been close to her cousin all those years ago when they had lived at Clairemont together.

Once Robin realized that he had upset Gillian by bringing up the sleepwalking business, he withdrew, talking very little, and after a few awkward moments Lenore suggested that they all retire.

Robin stopped Gillian at the door. 'I'm sorry if I offended you,' he said quietly. 'But sleepwalking is something you can't afford to ignore. Considering where you are. Maybe it was a mistake for you to come back here.'

Gillian felt a stab of panic. Why was Robin saying this? Did he know something she didn't? Had he let her come all this way knowing that it could prove to be disastrous? 'Do you think it was a mistake?' she asked, feeling chilled to the bone. 'My coming here?'

'I'm a realist, Gillian,' he said quietly. 'I think you should face Father. For your own sake and for ours.' He paused. 'And then let the chips fall where they may.'

She saw the twins only for a moment when she went to their rooms to kiss them goodnight. Daisy was already asleep, but Will was in bed reading a stack of comic-books Dickon had given him. 'How come no one told you we had a cousin?' Will asked, curious.

She thought about it. 'I guess because I never wanted to hear anything about life here at Clairemont,' she said.

'Why?'

66

She bent over and kissed him. 'For a lot of reasons. I'll tell you all about it some day.' She paused. 'Did you two get along well with Dickon?'

Will nodded.

'Good. I'm sure you'll have a wonderful time while you're here.' *You will. I won't.*

She went back to her room and watched in silence while Max locked all the windows and the door. She prayed that she wouldn't walk in her sleep, but almost as bad, that she wouldn't lie awake all night, rigid with dread of what was to come.

Her prayers were answered. As soon as her head hit the pillow she fell into a deep sleep.

Will pulled the covers up under his chin. He hadn't told his mother what had happened earlier in the wine cellar. He didn't dare. When Dickon saw the broken bottles he freaked out. He warned them to play dumb. If anyone asked, he said, they should say they knew nothing about it. Otherwise Daisy would be in deep shit for breaking them, and so would Dickon for letting her go back through the cellar alone. His mother had made him promise not to let either of them wander around by themselves.

The whole time he was lecturing, Daisy was silent as a clam. The only sound that came out of her was an occasional hiccough. It wasn't until Dickon had gone to his own room that she exploded, talking so fast that Will could hardly understand her. She told him about the bloody hands and the eerie creature who owned them. And about the terrible whispering voice telling her to go home.

He couldn't believe his ears but, worse than that, holy shit, he knew that she was telling the truth. Daisy had a vivid imagination and sometimes she exaggerated. But when she did, he could always tell. This time he knew as sure as anything that Daisy had really seen someone with gross, mangled hands. Someone who had smashed dozens of wine bottles just to scare the shit out of her. But who had done it? And why?

'Who do you think it was?' he asked, shivering in spite of himself.

'I don't know. How the heck would I know?' Will could see that she was getting ready to cry again. 'Maybe . . . maybe it wasn't a person at all,' she mumbled.

'Aw, Daisy, give me a break,' he groaned. 'Things are bad enough. Let's not start talking about ghosts and shit like that.'

She looked really angry. 'You didn't see her, Will. I did. So explain to me how a real person could have hands like that.' She shuddered.

'Geez, Daisy. Haven't you ever seen those things that the stores sell every halloween?'

'These hands were *real*,' she said between clenched teeth.

'They couldn't have been, or we would have seen the blood all over the floor,' he said, trying to be reasonable. The last thing he wanted to do was get into a fight over this. Fake hands or not, Daisy had a perfect right to be scared. Whoever had frightened her was a sick person. Someone he sure as hell didn't want to run into.

'Do you think we should tell Mom?' Daisy asked.

Will thought about it for a minute, then shook his head. 'Even before we got here she was nervous about coming to Clairemont. This would be the frosting on the cake.'

'So what *do* we do?'

'I guess we try to find out who it was.'

68

'And what good will *that* do, I'd like to know.'

There was a long silence. Finally Will said, 'I think we should find out as much as we can about the people around here. We can ask Dickon.'

She looked wary. 'You aren't going to make me sound like some a-hole sissy girl who makes things up, are you?'

'I'll be very careful what I say,' Will promised. And he meant it. What had happened to Daisy was bad enough. He would never make it worse by making her look stupid.

Will lay in bed and thought about switching on the light. When she left, his mother had turned it off and closed the door behind her. He hadn't asked her not to. He would never let anyone know he was still afraid of the dark. And no one did. Except Daisy.

He decided he'd better leave the light off. Someone might see it and then they'd know.

Outside the window he could hear the sound of the wind and he shivered even though he wasn't cold. He wished he had brought his crab shell with him. It was his lucky charm. The one he used at home to keep himself safe.

He tried not to think about what had happened, but it kept creeping back into his mind. Geez us, that was a scary thing. But there wasn't much they could do about it. They certainly couldn't tell their parents. At least not yet.

He shivered again. It sure was frightening. It sure was. 'I wish I'd remembered to bring my crab shell,' he said to himself. 'Tomorrow I'll see if I can find something else to bring us good luck.' Then he went to sleep.

* * *

When Gillian awoke the next morning there was a chill in the air. Common in the early part of June, but somehow she perceived it as a bad omen. *We are not happy to have you here at Clairemont.*

After breakfast the twins went off with Dickon to the tennis courts, Robin disappeared into his study, and Lenore made herself scarce. 'We thought you might like this time to reacquaint yourself with your childhood home,' she had said in a hopeful tone.

'It will give you a chance to get your sea legs under you before Father gets back,' Robin had added. 'Once he arrives, you'll need all the strength you can muster. Even in the best of circumstances, he's difficult to get along with.'

That had made Gillian even more uneasy. Robin seemed convinced that she was in for a rough ride. So again she wondered why he had encouraged her to come back to Clairemont. She was just about to ask him when he was called away to the telephone.

This has been a bad start to a bad day, she thought. The one bright spot was that Amanda had not appeared at the breakfast table.

'Let's take a walk round the grounds,' Max said when they were finally alone. 'It's a glorious morning.'

'That's the best idea I've heard in years,' Gillian said, suddenly desperate to be outside in the warm sunshine.

'Maybe later we can play some tennis.' He took her arm and together they left the house, talking as they went.

'What does Robin do for a living?' Max asked

'He's a financial consultant. And that's all I know.' She threw up her hands. 'Though that should come as no surprise to you. You know I don't know anything about *anything*.'

'I wonder if he works here at Clairemont.'

She shrugged.

'My guess would be that he doesn't,' Max mused, thinking out loud. 'To hear him talk about the place, it isn't hard to see that he can't wait to get away.'

'It isn't Clairemont he wants to escape from. It's Amanda. If she weren't here I don't think he'd be so negative. And if what he says is true, Amanda is here to stay.'

Max nodded. 'I think you're right. But why do you suppose your father hasn't insisted she get some psychiatric help?'

'Again, I don't know.' She hesitated, then continued. 'I do know one thing for sure. Whatever is happening here, it's none of my business. I don't belong here any more. And once I've faced my father, whether he forgives me or not, I'm leaving Clairemont and I'm never coming back.'

She led the way down a short flight of steps and onto the terrace. The wrought-iron benches that she remembered as a child were still there, lined up along the edge of the flagstones, but now, instead of the old wicker furniture, the centre of the terrace was filled with an infinite variety of herbs and low shrubs, all planted in a large raised bed in perfect geometric patterns.

Gillian sat down on one of the benches and Max sat beside her. 'This is really something,' he said.

'It's called a knot garden. It takes a tremendous amount of planning and an equal amount of work to maintain it.' She grew pensive. 'My mother never had the time for such a thing. Her passion was her rose garden.'

'Where was that?'

'I used to have a perfect view of it from my

71

bedroom window, but when I looked yesterday, all the roses were gone. Every single one.' She still found it hard to believe. Clearly, from what she had seen so far, someone cared a great deal about the gardens at Clairemont. So why hadn't they preserved the one that had mattered so much to her mother?

'Want to show me where it was?' Max asked.

She didn't try to hide her distress. If anything had been looked after, it should have been the rose garden. But for some reason it had been forgotten. She shook her head. 'I don't think I want to see it again. Not the way it looks now.'

Max took her hand and squeezed. 'Let's go down to the tennis courts and see how the kids are hitting 'em.'

Seeing the children was just what she needed to pull herself out of this trough of despondency she was slipping into. She let him pull her to her feet. 'It's that way.' She pointed. 'At least, it used to be.'

They left the terrace and followed one of the flagstone walks through an opening in the hedge, and found themselves in another small garden, this one square in shape, filled with beds of pink begonias and pink geraniums, enclosed on all sides by banks of pink rhododendron just past their prime. The paths were strewn with fallen petals.

'Fantastic,' Max said. 'It's like a house. One incredible room after another.'

'I don't remember any of this,' Gillian said. 'I'm not even sure we're going in the right direction. Maybe we should go back.'

'Let's see what's over there.' He pointed to an opening beyond the hedges.

Gillian watched him disappear. She was about to follow when all at once something stopped her.

Footfalls echo in the memory/Down the passage which we did not take.

She tipped her head to one side, listening. The fragment of verse had come clearly, but was it in her mind? Or had someone else spoken it? Someone she knew? She turned.

You shouldn't be here.

Unnerved, she looked back towards the terrace, but she couldn't see over the hedges. Couldn't see if someone was coming.

She put her hand – ice-cold – on the back of her neck where it had begun to tingle with apprehension. Was someone nearby? Someone who had spoken to her?

And then quite clearly she heard another sound. A rustling. As if someone in a long dress were coming along the path on the other side of the hedge.

Weren't they?

She forced herself to take a deep breath, to tell herself to be calm. There was no one around except Max. But even her denial frightened her.

Behind her on the path the fallen petals stirred.

'Who is it?' she whispered. Who is it? Who is it? Who is it? An echo whispering through the garden.

No answer.

And then something completely unexpected. The fragrance of Persian lilac. As if her face were suddenly buried in a mass of flowers. So familiar, so comforting, *so terrifying*. And at the same time from behind, a hand on her shoulder.

Horrified, she spun round.

'Gilly! What's the matter? What is it?'

She began to shake uncontrollably. How could she explain to Max when she didn't understand herself? How could she have thought her *mother* was there?

Max put his arms around her and pulled her close. 'Gillian,' he said sternly, 'the time has come. We have to talk. Serious talk. You have to tell me what happened. I don't mean just now. I mean what happened here all those years ago to make you leave, to estrange you from your family.'

She looked at him, feeling a slow tide of misery beginning to engulf her. 'What good will it do except to make you hate me too?'

Gently he put both hands on her shoulders and brought his face so close to hers that she could see nothing but his eyes. 'You silly, silly girl,' he said softly. 'I don't have to tell you but I will. Nothing, *nothing* you have ever done or ever *could* do would make me stop loving you. You are the very best thing in my life.'

'In praise of simple comforts?' she asked.

'In praise of simple comforts.'

She fixed her eyes on his and felt the tide of misery ebbing away. Max loved her and he meant what he said. He would never stop. No matter what.

No matter what?

She pushed the doubt aside and threw herself against him, holding onto him with a fierce new determination. She needed help. She had come this far alone but now she desperately needed help. She was slipping away. Losing her grip. *Imagining things.* The time had come when she had to admit the truth while she could still recognize it. 'I'm going to tell you, Max,' she said firmly. 'Every single thing.'

'Good girl,' he said. 'Let's not waste another minute. Let's get to it.' He put his arm around her and together they walked back to the house.

74

Chapter Seven

The sight of her sister walking unrestricted through her gardens set Amanda's tooth to throbbing, and she knew it was going to require another trip to the dentist. How dare she, she thought, livid with rage. These gardens belong to *me*!

She watched as they came down off the terrace and disappeared into what Amanda called the library. That was the place where she had set her knot garden. She called it the library because all the herbs planted there were Shakespearean. The wormwood and the columbine and the marjoram and the mint. It had taken her years to achieve the perfect effect. She had selected every plant with great care, starting some from seed, ordering others from Mrs Comstock. Through the summer she nurtured them as if they were her children, and in the autumn, before the first frost, she moved the more fragile plants indoors, taking great pains to mulch the hardier specimens. And she had been marvellously successful. Almost every day during the summer there was a harvest of one kind or another. Snips of mint for afternoon tea. Sprigs of lavender to use in her sachets. Great bunches of hyssop.

She moved as quietly as she could through the library, checking to make certain that nothing had been disturbed, then continued on where she couldn't be seen. Thank heaven she had come out to work early this morning. There had been a great deal of weeding and clipping to be done, none of which she could have attended to had she known Gillian was going to *intrude*. Like it or not, Amanda would have had to have hidden until they had left.

Just outside the pink sitting-room she paused, taking great care to keep out of sight. She couldn't hear what they were saying because they were speaking in low, muffled tones. As if they thought someone might be spying. And then she heard Max say quite loudly, 'Let's get to it.'

She watched until they were out of sight.

Let's get to it, he had said. How abominable, Amanda thought. She knew what he meant by it. There was only one thing he could have meant. The two were going back to the house to perform the sex act. She shut her eyes and swept the thought from her mind. Another human function that Amanda found incredibly distasteful. Perhaps at night in the privacy of one's marital bed it might be tolerated. Indeed, she supposed it was necessary if the human species were to survive. But at eleven in the morning?

But then, she thought, what else could anyone expect from Gillian? Promiscuity was exactly what had led her sister down the path to disgrace in the first place. A well-deserved disgrace at that. She grimaced.

When she was sure they were out of sight she went beneath her ivy-covered trellis and took a careful look around the pink sitting-room to make sure they hadn't touched her flowers. Then she hurried back to the potting-shed. Lenore had found the missing moss baskets, but Amanda still had to prepare her *impatiens wallerana* for hanging. 'Just the perfect touch in my garden bedroom,' she said. 'The arched-top canopy will be the ideal spot.'

She was almost finished when Lenore appeared in the doorway. 'Aren't they lovely?' Amanda asked, holding up one of the baskets. 'This one is my prize. I'm going to hang them all later this morning.'

'You've done a splendid job, Mandy. As usual,' Lenore said. 'But are you going to be finished in time to join us for lunch?'

Amanda kept her tone level. She had no intention of going anywhere near Gillian. Anywhere near *any* of them. 'I think not. I'm taking a picnic basket with me up to the grove. I have a great deal of work to do in my living-room. The tulips need to be thinned out and the geraniums have to be set before the end of the month.'

Lenore put her arm around Amanda's shoulders. 'I don't know where you find the strength. Look at you. You're no bigger than a minute.'

'Size is no measure of ability, Lenore,' Amanda responded coolly. 'If one wants something badly enough, one can always find a way.'

'You've proven that a million times over,' Lenore said, hugging her. 'Your gardens are masterpieces of horticultural art.'

Amanda smiled. Lenore was always so appreciative of her efforts.

At the door her cousin turned. 'Will you be riding with me at three?'

Amanda hesitated. Sometimes in the afternoon she and Lenore met at the stable and rode together all the way to Sharon. It had been one of her favourite pastimes. But then Dickon had come home for the summer and he had to be included. It was the one thing Lenore would not budge on, even though she knew that Amanda disliked the intrusion.

I hate all children, Amanda thought, feeling the black waves of anger begin to lap around the edges of her mind. Lenore loved her son and that made Amanda even more angry. There was only one thing that enabled her to endure it. She knew that Dickon was growing up. The time was fast approaching when he would be gone from Clairemont for good.

'I hope you'll ride with me today,' Lenore said but this time she put the special sweet look on her face. The look that said she knew Amanda would be pleased by what she was about to say. 'Dickon won't be joining us. He's busy entertaining Gillian's children.'

Amanda *was* pleased. 'You have chased my gloom away,' she said, laughing. 'This is going to turn into the most splendid afternoon. I just know it.'

They took turns playing against one another. First Will and Dickon, then Will and Daisy, now Dickon and Daisy. Not that Will had had a chance against his cousin. Dickon was a much better player than him. But Dickon hadn't been trying to clobber Will or anything. Once he had shown Will his best serve, he didn't use it any more. He settled back and played just hard enough to keep the ball moving, and it was fun even though he won every set.

On the other hand Will had played as hard as he could against both Dickon *and* Daisy. He hated it when she beat him. It wasn't often but it was often enough. Like today. She won two sets out of three. Now it was her turn to play against Dickon.

Will hoped Dickon wasn't going to be a dork and let Daisy win on purpose. Although, on second thought, maybe it might not be such a bad idea. After what happened last night, Daisy needed some cheering up. This morning she had tried to act normal but Will knew that inside she was very, very nervous. And he didn't blame her. He was, too. Even in the broad light of this sunny day it freaked him out to think about those bloody hands and whispered threats from a nameless, faceless someone.

He still hadn't figured out what to say to Dickon, but he knew some questions had to be asked. But first he definitely needed to find a good-luck charm.

He thought about what they had seen earlier on the way to the tennis courts. Up on the slope. They had stopped to stare at a group of peculiar-looking plants growing on the side of the bank.

'Aunt Amanda puts her cacti here every spring,' Dickon had said. 'You ought to see the operation. She hires an army of gardeners just to haul the plants out of the greenhouse and set them in just the right spots. Then in September she hires another army to haul everything back inside. It's a real circus.'

Will had stared. There were hairy plants and spiny ones, some small, others almost three feet in diameter.

'Those are called Sea Urchins.' Dickon pointed. 'They have beautiful flowers but they only bloom at night.'

Will had been fascinated. Cacti had always intrigued him, and he wished they could spend a little time just looking at the dozens of different plants but Dickon seemed in a hurry to move on.

From the top of the hill they had headed down a shady walkway and were almost at the tennis courts when Dickon stopped again. 'These are her succulents. They're all weird but that one right there is the weirdest of all. It's called Mother of Thousands. It grows its own children on the tips of its leaves.'

79

'Neat,' Will said, and he made a mental note not to forget that plant. Maybe it was just the thing he was looking for.

Now, since he had nothing else to do but watch Dickon and Daisy play tennis, he decided to go back and look at that plant again. He paused for a minute outside the court. Daisy had just made a great serve. 'Nice shot,' he mumbled. Then he turned and made is way up the walkway towards the place where he had first seen the Mother of Thousands.

Once he passed into the shadow of the trees the air grew much cooler. And very quiet. So quiet, in fact, that he couldn't even hear the thud-thud of the tennis balls any more. He felt a sudden chill along his backbone. Don't be a nerd, he said uneasily to himself. There's no one here but you.

He was almost to the crest of the hill when he stopped. There it was. Right where he remembered it. The curious-looking plant which had intrigued him earlier. It had long greyish-green leaves shaped like tubes, with tiny teeth all along the edges. It was exactly what he had been looking for. Something unusual. Something lucky.

With a last furtive glance over his shoulder, he left the path, careful not to step on any of the other plants, and without a moment's hesitation, he bent down, snapped off one of the tubular leaves, and stuck it in his pocket. A lucky charm for sure, he said to himself.

Feeling instantly secure, he turned round and was almost back on the path when, all at once, for no reason, his legs shot out from under him and he fell to his knees. 'Shit,' he said and scrambled to his feet. Mortified, he looked around to make sure that no one had seen him, then down at the ground to see what he had slipped on.

The path was clear of any kind of debris. No rocks, no moss, no slippery wet leaves.

'Shit,' he said again, and threw another nervous look over his shoulder. But this time what he saw made his heart stop dead in his chest.

About fifteen feet behind him, at the edge of the trees where the path ended, a figure was standing. A grey figure in a long grey gown. He couldn't see her face, but he could see her hands stretched out towards him, beckoning. Grotesque hands with sharp, jagged bones and rotted flesh and red, red blood. And then she spoke to him in a low, terrifying whisper. 'Come here, William.'

He jerked back in utter horror. *She knew who he was! And she wanted him to come closer!*

Just once before in his life had he ever been this frightened. But that was while he was watching a horror movie and he had known it wasn't real.

This was real!

Unable to speak, to scream, to howl in protest, he shook his head wildly, then whirled round and began to run, stumbling back down the hill in blind flight. So blind that he almost smashed head on into Daisy.

'What the heck are you doing?' she panted, jumping out of the way. Like Will, she was breathing hard. 'What's the matter?'

Somehow he managed to control himself. 'I just wanted to look at those plants again,' he gasped. He felt her eyes boring into him, trying to read his mind, and just then Dickon came running up. 'What're you two doing? You aren't mad at me for winning, are you?'

81

Daisy flushed. 'No. I just wanted to see what my brother was up to.'

Dickon turned to Will. He had a small trace of a frown between his eyebrows. 'I have to ask. You didn't touch any of the plants, did you?'

Still badly shaken, Will shook his head. Fat lot of good it had done him to pick the damn thing. The leaf hadn't been in his pocket one minute when all hell had broken loose.

'Because that's one rule that everyone has to follow,' Dickon was saying. 'Never touch any of Aunt Amanda's plants. Never. Or she'll flip, and I mean *flip*.'

Aunt Amanda, Will thought, his eyebrows flying up. Maybe that's who it was. Wearing some kind of fake rubber hands, trying to scare the shit out of me just like she scared Daisy.

Daisy must have read his mind because out of the blue she asked Dickon a very critical question. 'What does Aunt Amanda look like?'

'Why do you ask?' Dickon answered, surprised.

'I don't know. Just wondered, that's all.'

'Well, she looks like the wicked witch in the Wizard of Oz. Only she's a lot younger and she has blond hair.'

'A witch? What do you mean, she looks like a witch?' Will mumbled, keeping his eyes glued to the ground.

'You'll see what I mean when you meet her. Come on. Let's head back. It's almost lunchtime.'

For a short distance no one spoke. Then Daisy said, 'Does she live here at Clairemont all the time? Aunt Amanda, I mean.'

'Of course,' Dickon said. 'Where else would some- one like her go? She can't live alone.'

'How come?' Will asked, almost breathless to hear the answer. From what Dickon was saying, it was almost a sure thing that Aunt Amanda had been the one with the bloody hands.

Dickon answered in his most educated tone. 'Because she's insane. She gets to stay here instead of going to an asylum where she belongs because Clairemont belonged to her mother. Your grandmother. And when she died she left it in some kind of trust. I don't know any of the details. But I do know that Amanda gets to live here for as long as she wants. As for my own family, we live here now because Grandfather has full use of the place until he dies, and he wants my father with him.' He paused, kicking angrily at a clump of ferns, but when he spoke again his voice was full of enthusiasm. 'When Grandfather dies we'll find another place to live. I can't wait. I'd love to have our own house. We wouldn't have to be so careful about what we did. We wouldn't have to live with Aunt Amanda.'

'I like Arlington,' Daisy said. 'I'm glad we don't live here.'

Will knew right away that Daisy had said the wrong thing because Dickon threw a startled look in her direction. 'Aren't you having a good time? Is it something I've done?'

'I like it fine,' Daisy said quickly. 'I just like Virginia better.'

'Me too,' Will said. 'Besides, our mother isn't very comfortable here.'

Dickon nodded. 'I know.'

It was Will's turn to be startled. 'How do you know that?'

Dickon flushed, started to say something else, then seemed to think better of it. 'My mother *loves*

Clairemont,' he said, changing the subject. 'But that's because she gets along with Aunt Amanda. *Nobody* gets along with Aunt Amanda but her. Not even Grandfather. Aunt Amanda's got a real screw loose. You'll see what I mean.'

Yeah, Will thought, shuddering. We already have.

They went through the wrought-iron gate into a beautiful walled garden filled with flowers. 'Aunt Amanda thinks all these gardens are her rooms. Like in a house, only it's a house without a roof. We're walking through her living-room right now. Over there' – he pointed – 'is her dining-room, and beyond that is the water garden.' He chuckled. 'Aunt Amanda calls it her *salle de bain*. That means bathroom.'

'You mean she goes to the bathroom outdoors?' Will was incredulous. Their aunt really was off the wall. He was still scared, but with each passing moment he was becoming more and more sure that she was the one.

Dickon threw up his hands, laughing. 'I don't know. I've never seen her do it. But knowing what a goonball she is, she probably does.'

They went up a short flight of steps onto a patio and Will's eyes opened wide. Right in front of him was a huge swimming-pool. 'Wow!' he said.

'This is one of the only spots outside the house that doesn't belong exclusively to Aunt Amanda,' Dickon said. 'In fact she never comes outside on this side of the house.'

'How come?'

Dickon shrugged. 'Nobody ever told me, but I think it's because she tried to drown herself here once.'

'Holy shit,' Will said. That bit of information only added to his growing conviction. If their aunt was capable of *that*, she was capable of anything.

'She did it on purpose?' Daisy asked, wide-eyed.

'Yep. Too bad she didn't succeed.' He bent over and stuck his hand in the water. 'Anyway, she never uses the pool.'

There was a moment of awkward silence, and then Will squatted down next to Dickon and stuck his hand in the water too. 'Holy cow, it's really warm.'

'It's heated. We can swim whenever we want. Maybe after lunch.' Dickon stood up, walked round the side of the pool, and headed towards the house.

'I'm starved,' Daisy said, following.

'Me too,' Will said. He stood up and followed the others. Maybe now they would meet their lunatic aunt face to face. And then, scared or not, he and Daisy would figure out how to fix her good for what she'd done to them.

But what about what *you* did, said a small voice in the back of his head. What about the Mother of Thousands? What if that lady was really Aunt Amanda and she saw you pick her plant?

Will stuck his hand in his pocket. The leaf was still there. But was it worth keeping? After he'd picked it he'd gone through hell, so how could it possibly be lucky?

He thought about throwing it away but then changed his mind. Wait and see, he said to himself. Who knows? Maybe it was like finding the Holy Grail. Maybe the plant had been protected by some kind of secret spirit. And he had managed to sneak past it and pick the magic leaf. And as a result, maybe it would bring him the best luck in the world.

Maybe.

And – he shuddered – maybe not.

In any case he was hungry. Time enough to worry about all that after lunch. He took a deep breath and followed Dickon and Daisy into the orangery.

Chapter Eight

When they came in from the garden a message was waiting for Max. Call your office. Urgent. So he had. Now, almost forty-five minutes later, he was still on the phone.

Gillian sat at the table in the orangery and looked out across the patio to the swimming-pool. With each passing minute she could feel her courage ebbing away. She had come inside filled with determination, finally ready to tell Max the whole terrible story. Every detail. The secret that she had kept all these years hidden in the deepest, darkest recesses of her heart. But now, the longer she waited, the weaker her resolve.

You'll never go through with it, said the voice in the back of her mind. You haven't the strength. Put it off for now.

She stood up. Then sat back down. Even as she told herself to run away, to hide, to tell Max nothing, she knew she had no choice. Something strange was happening to her. Something destructive. She still felt the old shame but underneath it she had discovered something else. A fear. But a fear of what? Where had it come from? Was it in her mind? She didn't know. But it was making her imagine things that weren't real. Like this morning, when she thought that someone was coming into the walled garden. When she thought it was her *mother*.

White-knuckled, she gripped the arms of the chair with renewed courage. She *had* to tell Max what had happened all those years ago, and pray that with confession this inexplicable fear would disappear. She could live with the shame but not the fear.

She glanced at her watch. 11.50. Where the hell *was* he? She tapped her fingers on the table. *Hurry, Max. Before I lose my nerve.*

A sudden flurry of activity outside on the patio caught her eye. Her nephew had come into view, followed right behind by Daisy and Will. She had met Dickon at breakfast and she had liked him immensely. A very poised, polite young man. And clearly eager to make them all enjoy their visit. She wondered how much he knew about what had happened here at Clairemont all those years ago. And worse, whether he would tell her children.

She could hear the chatter of young voices and, although she couldn't make out what they were saying, they all seemed perfectly happy. At least *they* aren't afraid here, she thought.

Watching them, Gillian felt a rush of affection. How much she loved her children. How easy it had been to push aside her own self-loathing when such precious little people loved her so dearly. Without reservation, without conditions. She was their mother. Anything she had been before or had done before was of no concern to them. Their curiosity about her past life was minimal, if it even existed at all.

A minute later Dickon came in. 'Hello, Aunt Gillian,' he said. 'Are we having lunch in here?'

'No, we aren't,' Lenore said from the doorway. 'Everything is set up in the dining-room. Why don't you children get washed.' She waited until they disappeared, then turned to Gillian. 'I don't mean to pry,' she said hesitantly, 'but you seem uneasy. Is something wrong?'

Gillian shook her head. Her talk with Max would have to wait. 'Everything's fine,' she said. 'I'm just waiting for my husband to get off the phone. Then we'll join you for lunch.' She half smiled. Lenore was trying so hard to keep things on an even keel. 'I don't think there is anything anyone can do to make things easier,' she said honestly. 'I have to get over the jitters and get used to the house and all of you by myself.'

Lenore gave her a sympathetic look. 'It will all work out. You'll see.' She paused, and Gillian could see that she was deliberating about something. 'I have to ask,' she said finally. 'Does your husband know? About what happened?' She hurried on without waiting for Gillian to answer. 'Because if he doesn't, I think Robin and Amanda and Father should be aware. Just so they don't say the wrong thing.'

'He knows.' Gillian didn't know why she lied. She should have told Lenore the truth. But she didn't know which was worse, the lie or the truth. Now you're absolutely going to have to tell him, she thought. You have no choice. If you don't, he's going to hear it from someone else. Even if she begged, Amanda would never keep her secret. Nor, she surmised, would her father.

'I'm relieved,' Lenore said. 'Robin seemed to think that Max didn't know.' She sat down across from Gillian. There was something tentative about the way she arranged herself. As if she wanted to say something more but wasn't sure how to begin.

Gillian waited, apprehensive.

'I'm not sure whether this is the time or the place,' Lenore began, her voice faint, sounding as nervous as Gillian felt. 'But I need your help.'

Gillian's anxiety lessened and she leaned forward slightly, holding out her hand. 'I'd be willing to do almost anything to help anyone at this point. But what could I possibly do that would be of any benefit to you?'

Lenore met her gaze directly. 'It's Dickon.' Tears came into her eyes. 'I can't seem to help him. And I thought . . . I *hoped* that maybe you could. Would.' She turned away. 'I know it's selfish of me to bring it up. I know how you hate the mention of the word.'

The feeling of apprehension came back in a rush. What was Lenore talking about?

Lenore's next words tumbled out. 'My son walks in his sleep.' She looked back at Gillian, her face pale, drawn. 'I've taken him everywhere for help but to no avail. With Dickon, locks don't keep him safe. Somehow he always manages to get out. And when he does, I can't reach him. Can't get through to him at all. It's been a misery for all of us.' Her voice drifted off. 'I just have to hope that he never hurts himself. Or anyone else.'

Gillian was aghast. To imagine that her nephew was enduring the same destructive malady that had tormented her for as long as she could remember was unbelievable. 'Oh, Lenore,' she whispered, 'how could such a thing have happened? Lightning isn't ever supposed to strike twice.'

Lenore shrugged. 'Who knows? Some of the doctors say it may be a genetic flaw. Others say he may be suffering from some terrible stress. Others do what I'm doing now. They shrug.'

Gillian held up her hands in a gesture of helplessness. 'But what can I do for him?' A bitter taste had come into her mouth. 'You know I've never been able to help myself.'

Lenore seemed desperate. 'Talk to him. Explain what can happen if he is foolish. If he ignores my warnings. He refuses to discuss it with me. He thinks I'm making a big fuss over nothing.' She shook her head. 'He doesn't realize. He just doesn't realize.' She hesitated for a moment. 'There's one more thing that frightens me more than all the rest combined. Twice in the past month I've . . . I've found Dickon in the grist mill.'

Gillian gasped. 'Surely . . . surely you've told him . . . about me,' she answered. 'Surely he knows what happened there.'

Lenore shook her head. 'I've thought about telling him. As a last resort. But I never have. I didn't feel I had the right. But when I heard you were coming home, I hoped . . .' She reached out and grabbed Gillian's hand. 'Think about it. You don't have to promise anything right now. Just think about it.'

At that moment Max stepped into the orangery. 'I thought I'd never get off the phone.'

'You're just in time,' Lenore said, composing herself, brushing the tears from her eyes. 'We were getting ready to go in for lunch.'

Gillian made herself smile. 'It's hell to be indispensable, Max. You can't even take a vacation.' She was smiling but her voice sounded hollow.

He looked at her. 'You okay?'

She nodded. 'What took you so long?'

He made a face. 'The Muldare mess.' One of his most important clients.

'You can tell us all about it over lunch,' Lenore said. 'Robin will be most interested.'

'I'm afraid it's pretty much a bore,' Max said. 'A crisis situation, potentially catastrophic, but all the same a bore.'

Gillian barely heard him. She could think of only one thing. Dickon. Poor ignorant Dickon. He's just like I was, she thought. He doesn't know what he's capable of doing. But he has to know. He deserves to know. So he will never be as stupid as I was. And spend the rest of his life paying for it.

Numb, she stood up and followed them out.

Chapter Nine

Once outside the last of the walled gardens, everything changed. They weren't in a forest exactly because there was no underbrush. But the trees grew close together and the path they followed was covered with pine needles.

Dickon and Will walked ahead, Dickon's gun slung over his shoulder. Daisy lagged behind, dreading what lay ahead.

After lunch she had hoped she would have a chance to talk to Will alone. Find out what had happened this morning up on the hill. He had been so scared and she had known it without even reading his mind. He was petrified. But why? She hadn't had a chance to ask because right after lunch Dickon invited them all to go swimming. But then Aunt Lenore said the pool had to be backwashed, so then Dickon asked if they wanted to go crow hunting instead.

Will thought it was a fantastic idea, but Daisy didn't. After all, it was her greatest ambition to become a veterinarian, someone who wanted to save animals, not kill them. She couldn't imagine anything worse until she thought about staying behind.

After lunch everyone else disappeared, leaving the three of them still at the table, talking about little things, nothing very important. Until Daisy asked Dickon the question that ruined everything. 'Do you have a dog?' It was the wrong thing to ask.

Dickon's face froze. 'It's the one thing I've always wanted. One thing my mother has refused.'

'How come?' Will asked.

'Aunt Amanda hates dogs. She says all they do is lick and sniff and try to eat the food off your plate. Not to mention the fact that they love to roll around in the flowers.' And that's when the subject came up about hunting. 'I've always wanted a black labrador,' he said. 'Everyone says they make superior hunters.'

'What do they do?' Will asked.

'When you shoot a bird, they go and retrieve it.'

Will had never gone hunting before and he couldn't wait to try it. But Daisy found the whole subject sickening. She decided right then and there that she wasn't in love with Dickon any more.

From then on Daisy sat numb and dumb while the two boys discussed the ins and outs of killing birds and animals. Killing anything except mosquitoes or house-flies turned her stomach. She never even squished spiders unless they were in her bedroom. But she kept her mouth shut. After last night's fright the worst thing that she could imagine was to be left alone.

Besides, she desperately wanted to talk to Will, to find out what had scared him this morning. And whether he thought the person who had frightened her so badly was really Aunt Amanda. She couldn't ask those questions if she stayed behind.

So now she found herself trudging along behind them, praying that at least the poor crows would have sense enough to stay out of sight.

Once they started down the hill they moved a lot faster and her side began to ache. At one point a small grey rabbit darted across the path, but Dickon paid no attention. Lucky rabbit, Daisy thought. Dickon isn't looking for you.

At the foot of the slope they paused for a minute while Dickon tied his shoe. Then they were off again. Daisy could hear the sound of running water, and in a few minutes they came to a stream.

'Salmon Brook,' Dickon said. 'We'll cross it up here a little way.'

The stream was shallow in some spots, but in others the water flowed swiftly, spilling over rocks, forming deep, swirling pools. They moved up along the bank until they came to a narrow wooden bridge made out of logs, and in the middle Dickon stopped, pointing upstream. 'From here you can just make out the old grist mill,' he said.

Daisy squinted. Just where the brook curved out of sight she could see a low stone building.

'What's a grist mill?' Will asked.

'It's where they used to grind corn to make meal.' He turned and continued across the bridge. 'I'm not allowed to go near the place.'

'How come?'

'I'm just not, that's all.' He stopped again and looked up towards the mill. 'But I've been there,' he said, his face clouding over. 'It's where your grandmother died.'

'Our grandmother?' Will asked, stunned.

Dickon flashed him an apologetic look. 'I guess you didn't know. Well, anyway, that's where she died. But that's all I know about it,' he added quickly.

There was a long silence while they all stood motionless, staring up the stream. 'What happened to her?' Daisy asked finally.

'You'd better ask your mother,' Dickon said. Then he shifted his gun to his other shoulder and walked off the bridge into the woods.

Will threw Daisy a look of complete bewilderment. It was the first time either of them had ever heard their grandmother mentioned. They knew she was dead. That was all. 'Did Mom ever say anything about this to you?' he asked.

Daisy shook her head.

'Me neither,' Will said. 'I wonder why?'

'Maybe Dad knows. When we get back let's ask him.'

Will nodded. He was about to follow Dickon but, before he could, Daisy reached out and grabbed his arm. 'Wait a minute,' she said.

'What's the matter with you?' he asked, annoyed.

'There's something I need to know. And you aren't going to like it but I'm going to ask anyway. What happened to you this morning?'

'No big deal,' he said, but she knew he was lying. 'Maybe I'll tell you about it later. When we're by ourselves.' He turned away. 'Come on. Let's catch up with Dickon.'

Daisy opened her mouth to protest but, before she could get one word out, Will took off. She had no choice but to follow.

They caught up with Dickon on the other side of a low stone wall, and without any further conversation they continued on their way until they came to a vast open field filled with bushes covered with small green berries. 'Blueberries,' Dickon said. 'They'll be ripe in a few weeks.'

'Too bad we'll be gone,' Will said.

'Yeah, really,' Daisy mumbled. She could tell from her brother's tone that he wasn't the least bit sorry about leaving. And she wasn't either.

Dickon put his finger to his lips and took his gun

in both hands. Slowly they moved to the edge of the field, then stopped.

Daisy saw the crow just before Dickon fired. One minute it was a huge black bird flying up into the sky, and the next it was a mass of feathers falling like a stone.

Daisy couldn't bear it. She just couldn't. Without considering the consequences, she whirled round and ran all the way back, across the bridge, through the trees, not stopping even to take a breath until she reached the top of the hill and could see the line of hedges that enclosed the last of Aunt Amanda's gardens.

Then she slowed to a walk. She would never go hunting with anyone again. Never, never, never. Nothing was so terrible. Not even being alone in the darkest, scariest cellars at Clairemont.

Not even seeing broken, bloody hands? something whispered.

Her heart stopped and she froze, looking fearfully in every direction.

She saw no one.

Still filled with trepidation, she made her way down the slope and followed the hedge until she came to a small arched opening. A tiny grey chickadee flew up right in front of her and into the garden beyond. Daisy took a deep breath, then followed.

She found herself in the most beautiful place she had ever seen. Except for the brick walk that wound through the centre of the garden, masses and masses of pansies were planted everywhere. Violet and yellow and dark, velvety red. And at the end of the path a series of wide grass steps led up to a large square patch of greenest grass with tall ivy-covered posts at each corner and beams across the top which came to a point in the middle.

Daisy was awe-struck. It reminded her of a canopy bed except there wasn't any canopy. It was all open to the sky. This must be Aunt Amanda's bedroom, she thought, smiling. And Dickon doesn't know what he's talking about when he says she's crazy, because anyone who could create something so beautiful must be a truly wonderful person.

She was so enchanted by what she saw around her that she didn't notice the shadowy figure come through the opening in the hedge and start up the path. It wasn't until she heard a deep, menacing growl that she jerked her head round to stare.

A woman was coming towards her, moving with a weird sort of loping gait, low to the ground. Like a hound-dog. When she reached the grassy steps she stopped, but she stayed hunched over and drew her lips back from her teeth. *And then she began to snap them together hard. As if she was about to bite Daisy!*

Daisy was beyond fear. Her mouth fell open in utter disbelief, and instinctively she threw her hands up to defend herself. She took two faltering steps backward, then turned and ran as fast as she could out of the garden, trampling the pansies underfoot as she went.

She did not look back.

Chapter Ten

Sparks of rage were flying out of her mouth. All the mythical monsters she had ever read about came rushing into her mind. Cerberus. Cyclops. Minotaur. Hydra. None so vile as the child who had just invaded her *bedroom*. Still snarling, Amanda watched until she disappeared, then turned and hurried up the steps to her bed. She knelt and inspected her grass quilt. It was *matted down* and some of her precious violas had been *crushed underfoot*.

She moaned low in her throat. The sight of it made her weak with fury. She lay on her back and closed her eyes tight. Black waves washed over her, making it hard for her to breathe. How much do I have to suffer, she wondered, before I can stop the pain? How many more injuries must I endure before I say *enough*?

She rolled over onto her stomach. She had never asked for anything in her life but to be left *alone*. To be allowed her *own* space, her *own* place in the world. But even as a child she had been forced to *share*. Not just with things but with *herself*. Come here, Amanda. Talk with me. Her mother's voice. Intruding. Always intruding. Making her go to *school* of all things. Making her join in. Showing her off when company came to call.

How she hated her mother.

And Gillian. Let's play dolls, Amanda. Let's go

picking berries. Let's get our sleds and go up on Thorn Hill. *Let's. Let's. Let's.*

No peace for Amanda. No rest. No solitude. No aloneness. No splendid isolation. Nothing but intrusion until she was ten years old. And then her mother died and Gillian went away. And then Amanda was happy. No more school. No more questioning faces. No more intrusions. She was given the right to live in her own world in her own way. No one bothered her any more. *No one.*

Father never forgave Gillian for what she had done and so he sent her away and *that was good.*

Father got Amanda a private tutor. He never asked about her progress, and *that was good.*

She ate dinner with Father and Robin and Lenore only when she felt like it. Father never required her presence for anything, and *that was good.*

The only bad thing was the rose garden. Remembering made her even more angry. She buried her face in the grass, feeling the cool dampness of the earth. When Father gave her permission to design her own gardens the first thing she did was rip out all the roses. That had been a near-fatal mistake. Father had never paid any attention to anything she had done before, but *that* he noticed, and he was *furious.* He was going to send her to Havensport but Lenore saved her. Sweet, sweet Lenore. The one who told Father that it was too late to save Claire's roses, and too late to save Gillian, but not too late to save Claire's only other child. Amanda. The gardens, Lenore told him, would keep Amanda happy forever.

Father never interfered with her gardens again, and *that was good.*

The only thing she hadn't done that she *desperately* wanted to do was to destroy her mother's Rose

100

Mandarin. The tips of her fingers itched to open the china closet in the tea-room and *break every piece*. But she had learned not to infuriate Father. She had escaped punishment once. She knew better than to risk it again. She would have to wait until he was dead.

For a long time now she had dreamed about Father dying. She loved to imagine what it would be like to live alone. She opened her eyes and looked up at the sky. It was a pale, transparent blue almost the colour of her own eyes. She watched as one small cloud scuttled across the sun. A solitary cloud. Vastly alone. The way she wished she could be. Solitary. Not answering to anyone for anything. Not vulnerable to *invasion*.

I hate children, she thought blackly. Almost more than anything else I hate children. How dared that girl be allowed to invade *her* world? *Her* gardens? *Who* had allowed it?

I have died and gone to hell. She stiffened her body as if she had been laid out in a coffin.

How long she lay dead she didn't know, but when she came back to life she suddenly felt the urge to go to the Play House. *Her* Play House. The one place where she could be assured of absolute aloneness. She could do all of her thinking there. All of her planning. She would stay there and figure out what to do even if it took forever.

Watching Max, waiting for him to wake up, Gillian felt the beads of sweat come out on her forehead. The time has come, she thought. No more waiting. Lenore had asked for her help. And she would give it willingly. She would talk to Dickon. Warn him. Tell him what sleepwalking had done to her. And perhaps, if any good came of it, it would ease her own pain a little.

But first she had to tell Max. Right after lunch they had come upstairs but, instead of talking, they had made love, because, in spite of all her resolve, she needed a last bit of comfort. Something to remember if the worst happened and he stopped loving her.

Afterwards Max had fallen asleep, but she had stayed awake, pacing back and forth, going over everything word by word, working out every detail so he would understand. Don't tell him any bullshit, she told herself. Tell the truth. *All of it*.

She waited for him to wake up and finally he stirred. He opened his eyes to see her sitting beside him on the edge of the bed.

She felt her heart jump. After all these years of hiding, this is it, she thought. She put her head down, resting it on his chest. 'It's time,' she said.

He lay still for a minute, then put his hand on her hair, smoothing it the way he always did when she was upset.

She stayed where she was. 'Don't ask any questions, Max. Just let me say it all while I can.'

'I'm listening,' he said softly.

She began at the beginning. 'I've always been a sleepwalker. Always. When I was little my parents put a huge padded playpen around my bed so I couldn't wander away and hurt myself. But as soon as I was able to climb over that, they had to put locks on all the windows and doors.' She took a breath. 'But those came only after many, many episodes. Like the time I climbed up on the roof of the west wing and my mother had to come after me to bring me down. No one else dared. She was the only one who could manage me. And that frigid night when I walked all the way to the Crossings and spent the next week in the hospital.' She shuddered. 'With sleepwalkers, you learn the hard way. Like you did.'

He nodded but didn't speak.

'My mother was the most watchful, concerned mother in the world, and she took care of me the very best she could. She asked for only one thing in return. After I was sent to bed, I was never to sneak out of my room. I was never to ask to spend the night with any of my friends. It was too dangerous, she told me. And I promised I wouldn't. But I didn't mean it. I thought she was being ridiculous.' She was surprised at how calm she sounded. Inside she was screaming.

Then she told him about Cameron Stokes. The boy she fell in love with on her thirteenth birthday. Afterwards she never thought about him again. Didn't dare. 'Cameron Stokes,' she echoed, and suddenly she felt a deep sadness for the foolish child she had been. A selfish, foolish child, but a child all the same. Until this moment she had never realized how very young she had been when it happened. Only two years older than Daisy.

She sat up, stunned. 'God, I was so young. Why didn't I ever realize it before?' Not that it changed what she had done. It didn't. But God, she had been *so* young. She clasped her hands together and closed her eyes tight, the way you do just before you get to the top of a roller-coaster. Just before you go over. She took a deep, desperate breath. 'I killed my mother.' The words fell like stones. She let all the air out of her lungs and repeated them. 'Eighteen years ago I killed my mother.'

There. It was out. She had confessed. But how had he taken it? Did he hate her? She opened her eyes.

103

Max was still looking at her the same way he always did. There was neither anger nor shock in his expression. Only a gentle kind of sympathy. He reached out and took her hand. 'What happened?'

She closed her eyes again. 'On my thirteenth birthday my mother had a party for me. It was a wonderful party. All of my friends were there, and that's when Cameron and I arranged to meet. Later that night. At the old grist mill.'

She kept her tone level, unemotional, trying to distance herself. Trying to pretend that it was only a story she'd heard somewhere about someone else. 'After all the guests left, I went to my room. But I didn't go to sleep. I broke my mother's most iron-clad rule. I sneaked out of the house and went to the grist mill to meet Cameron.'

Cameron. She could barely remember what he looked like, but she knew that everything about him had been irresistible. She had loved him beyond belief. It was the only feeble excuse she had for what she had done. She continued in the same flat tone. 'I went to the grist mill because I couldn't bear being without him, but Cameron never showed up. I waited and waited but he never came.' Slowly she shook her head. 'Poor, stupid Gillian.' She said it as if she were talking about a friend of a friend. Someone she never knew. 'Poor, dumb, stupid sap of a girl. She should have gone home. She shouldn't have waited. She shouldn't have.' Her voice faded away.

'And she fell asleep,' Max said quietly.

Gillian nodded. 'I don't have to tell you what she does when she's asleep,' she said bitterly. 'She climbed up the ladder into the loft, a very dangerous place even for someone wide awake, and that's where her mother found her.'

Max put his arms out to comfort her but she pulled away. She had to make him understand the depth of her pain. 'Don't, Max. Don't be sorry for me. I know I was stupid, young, ignorant. No excuse. No excuse. My mother *died* because of me. I *murdered* her.' She had never said it that way before and hearing it she let out a long, strangled moan. 'Oh, Christ. Oh, Jesus Christ.'

Max didn't speak for a minute but, when he did, his voice was calm, level. 'Gilly, don't stop now. Tell me the rest. How did it happen? What did you do?'

'She came up after me . . . I don't know . . . and she slipped and fell. She grabbed onto a beam . . . and I . . . and I . . .' She shook her head violently back and forth. 'She hung there, trying to get back up, and I stamped on her fingers. I stamped on them and broke every one. Every single one.' The words hit her like bombs. *You murdered her. You murdered her. You murdered her.*

She let Max hold her then, felt him smooth her hair, felt him kiss the top of her head, and they sat like that for a long time.

Finally Max spoke. 'Sleepwalkers are victims too, you know. You never meant to hurt her.' Then, 'I love you, Gilly.'

She made no response. She couldn't. What was there to say? She had told him the truth. Now he knew. He didn't seem to hate her, and for that she felt a deep sense of relief. But she felt no less guilty. She knew that if she was ever to let it all go she needed to do two more things. First, she had to talk to Dickon. Do whatever she could to help him. But more important, she needed to ask forgiveness from the one person who had loved her mother most of all. Her father. If he could forgive her, perhaps she would learn to forgive herself.

She heard herself crying. At the same time Max jumped up. 'It's Daisy,' he said.

Gillian looked towards the door, heard the knock, the tearful voice. 'Mommy.' In the next instant her child was in her arms, sobbing. 'I want to go home,' Daisy choked. 'Please. I want to go home.'

Daisy sat between her mother and father. She didn't tell them everything. She didn't tell them about Dickon's spiders or the bloody hands or about the crow. She didn't ask them what had happened to her grandmother. The only thing that mattered right now was the lady with the snarling face and snapping teeth. The lady she suspected was Aunt Amanda.

'What did she look like?' her father asked.

'She had long blond hair and white, white skin, and she was really skinny,' Daisy sniffled.

'Amanda,' he said, confirming Daisy's suspicions.

Her mother held her close, soothing, comforting. 'Don't cry, darling,' she said. 'It's not what it seems. Aunt Amanda would never hurt you.'

'But she was going to *bite* me,' Daisy said, shivering. 'You should have seen her. She looked like a wolf.' She twisted her face to show them what her aunt's face had looked like.

Her father threw her mother a funny look. 'It sounds as if Robin wasn't exaggerating.'

'Dickon said she has a screw loose,' Daisy said. 'And now I believe him.'

Her mother gave her a fierce hug. 'Aunt Amanda shouldn't have frightened you, Daisy. No matter what she was thinking, she shouldn't have done it.' She turned to Max. 'I have to talk to her.'

'Do *I* have to?' Daisy asked tremulously.

106

Her mother's voice was angry. 'No,' she said. 'Amanda is my sister. I'll take care of it. Okay?'

'Okay,' she mumbled. But it wasn't okay. She didn't want to spend another minute here at Clairemont. She might be able to forget the spiders and the dead crow. But there were three things she'd *never* forget. First, the terrible bloody hands. Second, the awful person that was Aunt Amanda. And third and most frightening of all, the fact that now Daisy knew that the first did not belong to the second.

Chapter Eleven

Gillian was outraged. She knew her position here at Clairemont was tenuous and she knew why. But this was not about her. This was about her child. Amanda had gone too far in her attack on Daisy. No matter what her reason, her behaviour was intolerable, and Gillian was going to tell her sister so in no uncertain terms.

She left Daisy with Max and hurried down the hall to Amanda's bedroom. She hesitated but only for an instant, then knocked.

No answer but she wasn't surprised. If memory served her, Amanda never answered a knock.

She opened the door and stepped inside. 'Amanda?'

She said the name at the same time she realized that this was no longer Amanda's bedroom. It looked more like an attic, filled with the oddest assortment of old, battered furniture and boxes and empty picture frames, one of which she recognized. It was impossible not to. Its gilded border had once enclosed a sweet, wistful portrait of her mother. The portrait itself was gone.

Looking at the empty frame, Gillian felt the same wrenching sadness she had felt when she had seen what was left of her mother's rose garden, and she cursed herself for having come back to Clairemont. Robin is right, she thought grimly. There is no place here for me. There never will be.

She backed out of the room, closed the door behind her and stood leaning against it, trying to figure out where Amanda might be. She should have realized that at the first opportunity Amanda would have changed bedrooms. Even as a child, her sister had always hated this room because it was in the west wing, where Gillian and Robin slept. Amanda had wanted as much distance between them as possible. She had asked their mother to move her somewhere far away, but Claire had refused, convinced that it wasn't healthy for Amanda to be apart from the other children.

In response, Amanda had constructed an elaborate series of booby traps in her room to ensure her privacy. The first victim was one of the upstairs maids. Eloise spent several weeks recuperating from a terrific blow to the head, and it was then that their mother decided to take Amanda to Havensport for the first of many treatments.

Poor Mother. Always trying to help Amanda. Always doing the wrong thing.

Gillian shuddered and walked quickly down the back stairs. She met Lenore coming up. 'Do you know where I might find Amanda?' Gillian asked.

Lenore seemed upset. 'I was about to ask the same thing. She said she would ride with me this afternoon but she didn't come down to the stables. It's not like Amanda.'

Gillian felt a wave of sympathy for her cousin. Not only did she have Dickon to worry about, she had Amanda as well. Still, Gillian didn't mince words. She told Lenore exactly what Amanda had done to Daisy. 'It took a lot of courage for me to come back to Clairemont,' she said bluntly. 'And I was prepared for almost anything. But not this.'

'Of course you weren't,' Lenore said softly. 'There is no excuse for what Amanda has done. The only thing I can say is that when you live with her you learn to expect the unexpected.' She put her hand on Gillian's arm. 'I am at fault. I told Dickon not to leave the children alone, but I must not have been emphatic enough. I didn't want anything like this to happen. And now it has. Please forgive me. You needn't worry. I'll see to it that Amanda behaves.' And without waiting for Gillian to respond, she disappeared down the stairs.

Gillian didn't follow. She stood where she was, once again painfully aware of how little she really knew about these people. Over the years she had been so consumed by her own feelings of guilt that she never stopped to wonder about what was happening to them. Did they care about each other? Were they happy? She didn't know, but Lenore had made one thing crystal-clear. Gillian was lucky. She wasn't responsible for anything that happened at Clairemont any more. Nor did she want to be. Robin was right. Living here was bad enough for him. For Gillian it would be unbearable.

She took a deep breath. There were only two things left to be done. To try to help Dickon. And to face her father. 'Then I'll leave Clairemont,' she said firmly. 'And never come back.'

Will couldn't believe what had happened to Daisy. And he couldn't wait to talk to her about it. She had actually seen Aunt Amanda!

As soon as he and Dickon had come back to the house, he went to look for his sister to see if she wanted to go swimming. He found her with Dad,

110

and to his surprise his father gave him holy hell for having left Daisy alone.

'But I didn't,' Will protested. 'Daisy left *us*. She got spastic and just ran away.'

'I didn't get spastic,' Daisy sniffled. 'I just didn't want to see the dead crow.'

'It was no big deal,' Will said. 'You're making a mountain out of a molehill.' But watching her, he could see that Daisy was really in the weeds. Even here with Dad she was still frightened. But why? And then she told him about what happened in the garden. Holy shit. It was unbelievable that any grown-up would behave like that. And he was more convinced than ever that the bloody hands did in fact belong to their aunt. But he decided not to bring it up in front of their father. Not yet. Not until he talked to Daisy.

Now, sitting next to her at the edge of the pool, he looked at her cautiously. He knew he had to be careful what he said because Dickon was standing right behind them. 'Was she really going to *bite* you?' he asked.

'I'm sure she would have if Daisy had given her half a chance,' Dickon said. 'She bit me once, and I was only four years old. I told you she was bonkers. I just wish Grandfather would put her away for good.' He turned and dived into the water.

Will waited until Dickon was across the pool. 'Was she the one in the wine cellar?' he asked under his breath. 'She was, wasn't she?'

Daisy turned and gave him an emphatic one-word answer which took his breath away. 'No!'

'I don't believe you. It *had* to be her. She probably has lots of disguises. Masks and stuff.'

Daisy grabbed his arm and squeezed hard. 'I knew

it. You saw her too. I don't mean Aunt Amanda. I mean the one in the grey gown. With the bloody hands. You saw her this morning. I know it, so don't lie.'

He shook her hand off. 'That hurts,' he said angrily. 'Cut it out.' He stood up.

'We have to talk about this, Will,' she insisted. 'I think we should tell Mom and Dad everything because I'm really scared. I want to go home.'

'Geez us. Give me a chance to think about it, will you?' Will said, and abruptly he turned away. He didn't want to discuss it, mainly because he wasn't sure *what* the hell to do, didn't know just how much he was ready to admit. He could feel Daisy staring at his back. 'Let's make a deal,' he said, over his shoulder. 'As long as we're here at Clairemont, you go wherever I go even if you don't want to.'

'What kind of a crummy deal is that?'

Will kicked at the water with his foot. 'It's not crummy. It means that you won't be by yourself.' He frowned at her. 'That's when you get scared shitless, isn't it? When you're alone? Nothing bad would have happened if I'd been there.'

'That's the dumbest thing I ever heard. You saw her too.'

'Didn't.'

'Did too.'

'Did not.'

'Aren't you guys coming in?' Dickon yelled from across the pool.

'I'm on my way,' Will yelled back. He ran to the diving-board and did his best cannonball flip into the water. When he surfaced the first one he looked at was Daisy.

She was still sitting where he had left her.

112

'Is it a deal or not?' he shouted.

'It's a deal,' she muttered, but she didn't look happy.

Will wasn't surprised. He wasn't happy either. He knew he was going to have to tell Daisy the truth about his own encounter. And soon. He was too scared not to. And he knew something else. They couldn't tell their mother about any of it. He didn't know why, but he knew she was already a nervous wreck. But that didn't mean they couldn't tell Dad. They could. And they would. The very first chance they got.

Chapter Twelve

Amanda's journal. 17 June.

> *My name is Amanda which means worthy to be loved. Which is all right, I suppose. But I have looked through every reference book in the library and I have never found one single person with that name who deserved recognition. I would much rather have been called Leonard even if it is a man's name. Leonard means strong as a lion.*
>
> *Which I am.*
>
> *The strongest most competent best person in the world.*
>
> *And soon they will all know it. They will leave my Clairemont. Because because because.*
>
> *Because I am the strongest most competent best person in the world.*
>
> *But troubled. Trouble trouble trouble.*
>
> *Something must be done.*
>
> *But what? What what what?*

Amanda put her head down across her arms. Lying here in her Play House on her soft feather mattress, she tried to arrange her thoughts in proper order. She knew that she could do it because this place was where she felt the most clear-headed, the safest, surrounded as she was by the things she loved most dearly. She carried them here every spring. Things that had lain dormant all winter long. Things like her blue and white porcelain tea set, and her jars of home-made pickles made from cucumbers out of her own kitchen garden, and her clarinet, and her most valuable collection of books.

And of course there was the portrait of her mother. The one that she kept hidden under her mattress. The one she looked at only when things got truly desperate for her. Then Amanda would pull it from its hiding-place and make small cuts in the canvas with her pruning-knife, flecking off little specks of paint. And then she would feel immeasurably better.

Now, she moved to the edge of her mattress, reached under and slid the painting out, surveying it with a critical eye. Since she had stolen it from its frame almost seventeen years ago, she had made two hundred and thirty-two cuts in the canvas, beginning around the edges, moving closer, ever closer to the face.

Someday the face would be obliterated.

But not yet. Not today.

She slid it back. Today she had other things to think about. That was why she had come to the Play House. So she could be alone. No one was allowed in her Play House except for spring clean-up and fall shut-down. During the summer months this was the one place no one came but Amanda herself. Here she could be *alone*.

And she needed to be alone to think properly. For one thing she was dealing with cruel and irrational people. *Selfish* people. Except for Lenore, of course. But Lenore was too naïve. Too trusting to be of any help.

'Amanda,' she whispered. 'Dear, dear Amanda. Noble Amanda. Brilliant Amanda. What will you do to put things back where they belong? To right the wrongs?' She rolled over and reached into her book basket. The place she kept her seven guides to successful living. She picked up the first one her hand fell on. The corners of the most important pages had been turned down for quick reference. She opened it and began to read aloud. 'Since love and fear can hardly exist together, if we must choose between them, it is far better to be feared than loved.'

She turned to the next underlined paragraph and continued. '. . . the lion cannot protect himself from traps, and the fox cannot defend himself from wolves. One must therefore be a fox to recognize traps, and a lion to frighten wolves.'

As usual the reading brought back the memory of her mother's voice, interfering as usual. *Don't try to do it yourself, Amanda. Let me help you.*

Amanda slammed her book closed. Of course she'd say that, of course she'd say that. *Let me help you.* But it was meaningless. Always when Amanda was a child her mother had tried to help. By *interfering*. It showed how little she had really known about her daughter.

And then there were other things her mother would say. *Suppose you try and explain it to me, Amanda. Why are you so unhappy?* As if she had been concerned. As if she had really been concerned. But she wasn't. If she had been she would have left Amanda alone. Anyway, the only one who had ever mattered to their mother was *Gillian*.

Gillian the saint, Gillian the angel, Gillian the *whore*. That's what she was and Amanda had always known it. She had actually seen her sister *lick her lips* when there were boys around. *Lick her lips*, of all the disgusting things. And still their mother wanted Amanda to spend all her time with *Gillian*.

That's when Amanda decided to join the convent, even though the Blackmarshes weren't Catholic. It wasn't the religion that attracted her. Not at all. It was the word that sometimes went with it. *Cloister*. She discovered it by accident when she was looking up the word *cloisonné*, and she had been instantly intrigued. Cloister meant a place of religious seclusion. To be cloistered meant to be shut away from the rest of the world – forever.

Amanda had never cared about religion or heaven but she liked to pray, even though she didn't know to whom she was praying. For Amanda, praying was more like making things happen with your mind. Anyway, she found out that in order to be admitted to the convent you had to show the nuns that you knew how to pray, and she could do that effortlessly. She made the decision to go. As soon as possible.

She never told anyone in the family about her plan to leave Clairemont. She wrote directly to the Order of Saint Ursula.

They were the ones, unholy wretches, who had contacted her mother!

Amanda remembered her feeling of outrage at having been betrayed. Her dream of splendid isolation was gone. Poof. Vanished. It was the angriest she had ever been at her mother. At the Catholics. At the whole world.

It was the only time she ever tried to kill herself. She tied her mother's antique flat irons to her ankles and jumped into the swimming-pool. But Lenore saved her. Amanda hated being saved, but Lenore hadn't done it to be mean. She was just doing what came naturally. Caring about Amanda. And in the end it turned out to be for the best.

Another of her favourite quotes came to her. *It is*

117

always darkest just before the day dawneth, and in that instance it was true. After her suicide attempt her mother made plans to send her to Havensport again. For an extended stay with Doctor Rabid, and Amanda didn't just hate the idea. She *loathed* it.

That was the dark.

The dawn came one week later.

Her mother died and Amanda never went back to Havensport or Doctor Rabid or any other such fool again.

Let me help you.

There it was again! Amanda sat bolt upright and listened intently. This time it didn't seem like a memory. This time she thought she was really hearing her mother's voice. But that was impossible. Her mother was dead. Ha ha. Ha ha.

She picked up her journal and once again, in her perfect Palmer Method handwriting, began to organize her thoughts.

This afternoon I frightened the child badly. An excellent display of strength on my part. From now on I will not weaken. I will prevail. But how? When?

Her pen stopped moving, arrested in mid-air, and all at once she was filled with uncertainty. She knew what she wanted. To be rid of Gillian. To be rid of them all. But how?

She placed the tip of her pen on the top line of a new page and stared, waiting for the creative juices to begin their flow.

Just as she had hoped, her hand began to move. But what she saw made her eyes grow round as saucers.

It wasn't her perfect Palmer Method handwriting any more.

It was her *mother's elegant script.*

Don't try to do it all by yourself, Amanda. I will help you.

Something had changed. For the first time in all these years, Gillian felt as if she was finally headed in the right direction. Not there yet. Not out of the rapids. Not safe on the bank on the other side of the river. Not yet. But on the way. She had told Max and now she would tell Dickon. Maybe it would keep him from making the same terrible mistake she had made when she was exactly his age. Thirteen.

It was late in the afternoon but still warm, and Gillian sat at the side of pool, watching her children. Constant activity! Climbing up the ladder, dripping wet, shivering, plunging back into the water, swimming across the pool, coughing, laughing, scrambling up the ladder to begin the process all over again, every move accompanied by shouts and laughter.

Daisy waved her hand and Gillian waved back. 'Watch this, Mommy.'

Gillian smiled. 'I'm watching.'

Daisy flipped off the deep end of the pool, and Will climbed out and came over to where his mother was sitting. 'Where's Dad?'

'He's on the phone.' Again. The Muldare case. 'He'll be out in a minute.'

Will shifted from one foot to the other, teeth chattering. 'I've got something I need to talk to him about.'

'Don't you think while you're waiting you ought to warm up? Your lips are blue.' Gillian held out a towel. 'Here. Wrap yourself up until he gets out here.'

'Okay.' Will sat down in the chair next to her.

'Aren't you coming back in?' Dickon yelled.

'In a minute,' Will said through chattering teeth. He sat fidgeting, clearly unsure about something, then turned to his mother. 'Did you talk to Aunt Amanda? About what she did to Daisy?'

'No. Aunt Lenore said she would prefer to handle it.'

Will nodded. 'I guess it's for the best,' he said seriously. 'Dickon says his mother knows Aunt Amanda a lot better than you do. He says it's best not to rile her up, and he was hoping you weren't going to yell at her or anything. After all, in two weeks we'll be gone. They have to *stay* here.'

Gillian looked at her son, concerned by what he had said. Clearly there was something about Claire-mont that made him uncomfortable. Was it only because of what Dickon had told him or was there more? 'It sounds as if you don't like it here very much.'

Will shrugged. 'It's okay. I'm just glad we don't live here, that's all. It's . . . it's kind of weird.'

'Because of Aunt Amanda?' Gillian paused. 'Or is there something else?'

'There *is* something else,' Max said, coming up behind them. 'I have to go back to D.C. tonight. I'm booked on the five o'clock flight.'

Gillian felt a surge of panic. Alone, could she face her father? Without Max to support her would she flounder? Keep calm, she told herself firmly. You can do it. You *have* to. You're a big girl now. Behave like one.

Will slid off his chair. 'Does that mean we're going home?' He sounded relieved.

Max shook his head. 'Not unless your mother wants to.' He stood looking down at her, and in the smooth planes of his face she could see concern.

She flashed a smile. 'We'll be fine, Max. You'll be back in a few days. Right?'

He hesitated. 'If you'd rather, I'll see if I can get four seats on that flight. We can all come back together as soon as I settle this mess.'

Gillian shook her head, determined now to see it through. And maybe help her nephew in the process. 'My father will be here in three days. I'll stay until then.'

The words were barely out of her mouth when right behind her she heard a voice. Where no voice could possibly be. Sharp, angry words. *Go home! Go home! Go home!*

Overwhelming fear engulfed her, and she jerked her head round, but even as she did it she knew no one would be there.

No one was.

She looked back at Will and Max, but neither seemed to have heard anything. 'Did you want to talk to your father?' she asked Will in as calm a tone as she could muster.

'I guess it'll have to wait,' he said glumly.

'You sure?' Max asked.

Will hesitated for a minute, then said, 'Yeah. I'm sure.' He took a deep breath, dropped his towel, and ran to the edge of the pool. 'Watch this dive, Dad.'

Numb, still frightened without reason, Gillian watched her son torpedo into the water.

'Gilly, are you all right? Are you sure you want to stay here alone?' Max asked quietly. 'The truth.'

She shook her head. 'No. I'm not all right. No. I don't want to stay here alone.' Her voice cracked. 'But I'm going to.'

Max did some quick mental calculations. 'I'll make

sure I'm back before your father gets home. I'll be gone for two days. Not a minute longer.' He paused. 'I'm not happy without you.'

She smiled a weak smile. 'In praise of simple comforts?'

'In praise of simple comforts.'

Gillian nodded and smiled and kissed him goodbye, murmuring a few words about seeing him soon and drive carefully and safe flight. And then he was gone.

She stood at the top of the stone steps and watched until the car disappeared round the curve in the drive. Then she turned and went back into the house.

The door closed quietly behind her.

And somehow, even though the house was full of people, she knew she was alone.

After dinner she tucked her children into bed – was it her imagination or did Will seem uneasy? – kissed them goodnight and went back to her own room. She locked the windows and the door and fell into bed. Tomorrow she would talk to Dickon. For now her only hope was to get through the night.

Chapter Thirteen

'Amen,' Daisy whispered finally. It had taken her a long time to finish her prayers, mainly because it wasn't something she did every night. In fact she hadn't felt the need to do it for months. Not since she broke her mother's pearl necklace. She had buried it under her socks in the top drawer of her dresser where her mother wouldn't find it. And every night she prayed that God would fix it. And every morning she opened the drawer to find the pearls exactly as she had left them, still unstrung.

Whether God was going to fix them or not she never knew, because before He ever had a chance to do a thing, her mother found them. And Daisy decided then and there that prayers weren't worth much.

Still, on this particular night, when she crawled beneath the covers, she prayed every prayer she had ever learned and a few she made up. But there was one prayer that stuck in her mind, one she kept coming back to, one she kept repeating over and over. 'Please, God, find an excuse so we will all have to go home to Virginia right away just like Dad. If You can arrange it, I'll love You forever and ever, and I'll never doubt You again. So if You can hear me, please, God, send us home. Amen.'

After she said it for the twenty-seventh time, she

decided to quit. If God hadn't heard it yet, she guessed He never would.

She lay on her back with her sheets pulled up to her chin and waited for Will. He'd promised he would come to her room after everyone had gone to bed and stay with her until she felt safe enough to be left alone. Not that she ever would. The only thing that would make her feel safe again was to get away from this fearful place. Get away from Clairemont. 'You stay in my room until I say go,' she had said to Will. 'Because if you won't do it, our other agreement about sticking together no matter what is off. Besides,' she added slyly, 'I can have the light on all night if I want because I already asked Mom and she said I could because I'm scared.'

As she had known it would, that bit of information clinched the deal, and she knew why. Will agreed because, in spite of all his protestations, he was just as nervous about being by himself at Clairemont as she was, especially if he had to stay in his own room in the dark just to prove how brave he was. Tonight maybe she would be able to get him to tell her what he'd seen this morning at the tennis court that made him so scared.

So she lay waiting, listening for him, and at one point she thought she heard him. Her door was ajar and there was a creaking sound somewhere down the hall. Here he comes, she thought, vastly relieved.

But nothing happened. Still no sign of him.

With a growing sense of dread, she sat up and looked at the clock. It was after ten. Her mother had said goodnight to her almost an hour ago, so how come Will hadn't shown up? Where was he?

She got out of bed, crossed to the book-case, and took a game of Monopoly off the shelf. It was their

W H SMITH 2566

WOMENS MKL   50 A
BOOKS   Exchange 4 99 A
TOTAL   3/5/94   5 49

TENDERED   6 00

CHANGE   0 51

06)83 (0129 R04 29/04/94

Please Call Again

Thank You For Shopping At

WHSMITH

Please Call Again

Thank You For Shopping At

WHSMITH

Please Call Again

own set brought from home, and the sight of some-thing familiar made her feel a little less uneasy. And it would give them something to do while they waited – she felt a cold shiver which began at the base of her spine and worked its way all the way up to the top of her head – *waited for what?*

She shoved the question back, knowing that if she let herself wonder about it, she'd be too scared to move. And then Will would come in and find her shivering and whimpering and acting like a real sissy, and then he'd never let her forget it. Besides, if she could just keep calm, sooner or later morning would come and maybe then Mom would tell them that she had decided to take them home. And then everything would be back to normal. And Will wouldn't ever know how *really* scared she was.

She sat cross-legged on the floor and opened the box. Inside the lid their permanent scores were inked in. Hers and Will's. The money totals and the dates they had played. The last game listed was 28 April, but there were no scores entered. She remembered why. Because Will had cheated and she had quit and he had claimed victory because he said quitters always forfeit.

'Will is a dork,' she muttered. She set up the board and began to sort out the mortgage cards by colour so that when her brother finally appeared they would have something to do. Something that would take her mind off her fear, at least for a little while.

The only sounds in the room were the click-clicking of the cards and the soft murmuring of her own voice as she read the street names out loud. 'Baltic and Mediterranean,' she said, putting them in one pile. 'Oriental, Vermont, Connecticut.' But in spite of her determination to keep herself distracted, she could still feel the chill at the base of her neck. A chill that kept reminding her that she was alone. And defenceless.

Please hurry, Will.

Please.

Will was cold. He found that strange because outdoors it was warm. Anyway, he pulled a sweatshirt on over his pj's, then opened his gym bag and began to gather the things he wanted to bring to Daisy's room, things that would keep them both busy. He knew Daisy was going to ask him what had happened this morning, but he wasn't sure how much to tell her. Should he let her know how freaked out he had been? How freaked out he still was? If Dad hadn't gone back to Virginia, he would have told him everything. But now Dad was gone, so maybe now the best thing would be to tell Daisy. But did he have to tell her everything? He wasn't sure. He'd wait and see what kind of mood she was in. There was no need to spill his guts if he didn't have to.

In the darkness he flicked on his pocket flashlight and checked to make sure his nine-stick gum wad was still in the bag. He had been chewing it on and off for more than a week now, and it was getting pretty stale. Almost time to throw it away and start a new one. He'd have to remember to ask Dickon if there were any stores nearby where he could buy some.

He made his way across the darkened room to the book-case where he had stacked Dickon's comic-books. He'd bring them along because he knew this was going to be a long night. He shouldn't have bragged to Daisy about how he could go without sleep for days. Now he'd need every little diversion to keep himself from falling asleep before she did.

He went back to his bed and felt around inside his gym bag to make sure his Nintendo Game Boy was there. It was. And his unopened package of cinnamon fireballs. He wondered how many Snickers bars Daisy still had. He knew she had brought six from home, but the question was how many had she gobbled up? But then on second thought he doubted that she had eaten any. When Daisy got nervous she lost her appetite. He was just the reverse. When he got spastic he ate everything he could lay his hands on. The eating machine, Daisy called him, especially when he sneaked ice cream bars out of the freezer and then blamed it on her.

The last thing he put in the bag was his Mother of Thousands lucky charm, carefully wrapped in foil. It certainly hadn't done him any good thus far, but maybe there was still hope. He picked up his bag, headed for the door, and opened it a crack.

He peeked out.

At the far end of the hall a light glowed dimly. Not bright enough to give him a feeling of security, but at least enough so he could see. The corridor was deserted. All the doors between his room and Daisy's were closed tight, but from where he stood he could see that hers was open a crack. She hadn't been lying. Her light was on.

On tiptoe he took his first few cautious steps, then stopped. A floorboard had creaked underfoot. It was no big deal, but he was so edgy that he almost bolted back into his room. You a-hole, he said to himself. You are one scared a-hole and it's time you did something about it. You need some moral support, so you have to tell Daisy everything. Right now.

He took a deep breath, set his jaw, and marched

127

through the doorway into his sister's room.

Daisy wasn't there.

He felt a flash of panic. 'Daisy?'

'Come on over here.' Her voice came from somewhere on the other side of the room.

Relieved, he dropped his bag on the chair and walked around the foot of the bed. Daisy was sitting on the floor, motionless, the game of Monopoly spread out in front of her. She stared up at him, white-faced. 'Where have you been?' She sounded out of breath.

'In my room, where do you think?' He settled down across from her and began to count his pile of money.

'I don't want to play,' she said flatly.

He raised his eyebrows. 'Why not?'

'Because I want to know what you saw this morning, that's why. And don't jerk me around, Will,' she said, deadly serious. 'I want the truth.'

Will swallowed hard, then held his hands out in front of him, curving his fingers into claws.

'You saw the same thing I did?' Her eyes squinched up and she stared at him without blinking. The way she always did when she wanted to make sure he was telling the truth. 'The lady with the bloody hands?'

He nodded.

'What . . . what did she do?'

'She wanted me to come closer.' He drew in a great gulp of air. 'She called me by name. She called me William.'

Daisy gave a quick convulsive shudder. 'Yikes!'

'It scared the shit out of me so I turned around and ran,' he said truthfully. Then he reached out and took her hand and squeezed it in a silent, honest sharing of panic. 'Are you sure the one we saw wasn't Aunt Amanda?' he asked finally.

'I'm sure.'

'But you told me you didn't see the grey lady's face. So how do you know?'

'I just do. And you will too, as soon as you see Aunt Amanda.'

Will didn't answer. For some reason he really wanted it to be their aunt. No matter how crazy she was, somehow he was sure they could deal with her. But now, as he thought about it, did it really make any difference? Would one person be less frightening, less threatening than two?

'If it was one person, and that one person was Aunt Amanda,' Daisy said, answering his question before he even asked it, 'it would make a *lot* of difference. At least we know that Aunt Amanda is real. A living, breathing person. She may be crazy and she sure is mean, but at least she's a human being.' She shivered. 'I don't know *what* the other one is. Do you?'

Will opened his mouth, then closed it. Tight. He had no answer. The truth was, like his sister, he didn't know. He didn't believe in ghosts or any of that supernatural crap. But then he had never been in a situation like this before. Where he had seen something with his own two eyes that he couldn't explain.

What if it is a ghost? What if the thing you saw is dead?

He looked over at his sister and knew without question that she was asking herself the same thing.

They both sat mute, and in the midst of the ensuing silence there came a sound. The opening and closing of a door somewhere down the hall. 'What was that?' asked Daisy, her eyes widening.

129

'I don't know.' Will jumped up, went to the door, and peeked out. *Just in time to see his mother disappearing round the corner at the end of the corridor.* 'Holy shit, it's Mom!'

Daisy jumped up. 'It couldn't be. She told me she was locking her door. She said she was going right to bed and if we needed her we'd have to knock real loud.' She followed Will out into the hall.

It was deserted. Not a sign of a living soul.

'Let's go,' Will said, grabbing Daisy by the arm. Together they hurried to their mother's room.

The door was closed tight.

'See?' Daisy whispered. 'I told you.'

'Yeah. But I'll bet it's not locked.' He reached out and turned the knob.

The door swung open without resistance.

Inside, the room was empty.

Will couldn't breathe. The worst had happened. His father was gone and his mother was walking in her sleep! What should they do? What, what, what?

'We have to follow her,' Daisy said in response. 'Bring her back without waking her, just like Dad said. And we have to do it quickly. Before she gets lost. Or hurts herself.'

Somewhere below, they heard a heavy door slam shut.

Without another word, the two whirled round and flew down the corridor after their mother.

Chapter Fourteen

The night was dark and chill, and the wind was blowing through the gardens, making faint, mysterious sounds as it passed, and for a moment Daisy was paralysed with fear. Even in the safety of her own room in her own house back in Virginia she hated the dark. Here at Clairemont it terrified her.

'Take my hand,' Will said, and she did. He squeezed hard. 'Don't let go,' he said. And Daisy knew he was just as scared as she was.

'Where *is* she?' Daisy whispered, peering through the gloom, trying desperately to see.

As if in answer, the clouds rolled past the moon and in the new light Daisy saw her mother, moving down the path that led through the gardens. Moving away from the house.

Neither Will nor Daisy called out to her. They knew better. Even though they had never seen her walk in her sleep, their father had taught them well. Just in case it were ever to happen when he wasn't around, they were to go after her, take her gently by the hand and, without waking her, lead her back to bed. Above all, they were not to let her out of their sight.

'Let's go,' Will said, and they went quickly, without any discussion, both fully aware of what they had to do.

'Where do you think she's going?' Daisy asked,

holding onto her brother's hand as tightly as she could.

'I don't know, but let's catch up before she leaves the gardens.'

They began to run, but somehow she always kept ahead of them, not hurrying exactly, but never hesitating, never looking back. She seemed to know precisely where she was going. And then suddenly, she began to run.

Within seconds she had disappeared.

Daisy and Will flew after her, coming to a dead end at the corner of the hedgerow. They looked to the right and to the left, but there was no sign of their mother. She had simply vanished.

'Mother!' Daisy wailed.

'Sshhh,' Will said. 'Don't start bawling. We have to find her. You go that way,' he pointed, 'and I'll go this.'

Daisy gasped and shook her head forcefully. 'No way. I'm not going anywhere by myself.'

Will didn't argue. In truth he didn't want to be alone any more than Daisy did. Together they turned to the right and headed up the slope along the back side of the hedge. At the very top they came to a stone wall and, just beyond, in the moonlight, they saw their mother running across the open expanse of meadowland.

Everything Daisy had ever learned from her father about sleepwalking was instantly forgotten. She didn't care if her mother *was* asleep. It didn't matter. What mattered was to catch her. If she and Will could do that, their mother would wake up and hold them close and keep them safe. 'Mother!' she cried, tears streaming down her face. 'Don't leave us!'

And even as the words left Daisy's mouth, her mother stopped dead in her tracks.

Daisy let out an explosive sigh of relief. 'See, Will? She heard me.' They climbed over the wall and began to run, two frightened children, wanting only one thing now. To find comfort, safety in their mother's arms. Comfort and safety. Two things their mother had never *ever* failed to give.

They could see her waiting for them at the edge of the trees and, not taking their eyes off her, they ran towards her as fast as they could.

And suddenly, in the middle of her stride, Daisy froze.

'What's the matter?' Will panted, almost crashing into her, pushing past. And when he saw, he froze too.

Their mother was still standing there. But she was no longer alone. *A grey shimmering figure stood at her side.*

'Geez us!' Will gasped. 'Holy geez us! It's *her!*'

Waves of mind-shattering fear swept over them, holding them paralysed. Thunderstruck, they stood side by side, gaping open-mouthed, not knowing whether to keep going or to run away as fast as they could.

'Mommy,' Daisy whimpered, and took one faltering step forward. Her mother, her salvation, her lifeline, was right there within reach.

But what about the other?

Daisy let out a low moan. There was something so fearsome, so unearthly about the creature that Daisy couldn't look any more. And yet she couldn't turn away. 'Mommy,' she whispered. 'Come back.'

Will reached out and grabbed her by the arm,

jerking her round. 'We gotta get out of here,' he choked. 'We gotta get Dickon. Aunt Lenore. Somebody.'

And knowing that they had to get help, they fled. But they also knew that in their frantic flight they were leaving their mother behind. Alone. With *her*.

Everything was dark.

And so cold.

The only thing Gillian heard was the faint sound of rushing water. And then her mother's voice.

Footfalls echo in the memory down the passage which we did not take . . .

Gillian stirred, painfully coming to consciousness. Her sleep had been long and dreamless and yet she felt so tired. And her eyes ached as if she had been crying endless tears.

She opened them. And saw . . .

Nothing but blackness. As if the shades in her room had been drawn so tight that no light could penetrate.

She moved. And suddenly came wide awake. She was not in her bed. Not in her room. But where?

She sat up, pushing against the thick darkness, smelling the deep, damp smell of dirt and stone and rotting wood. And as her eyes adjusted, she was filled with a growing sense of horror. She knew she had been here before. In her worst nightmares, in her most anguished memories.

Above the sound of rushing water she heard a roaring in her head. 'This cannot be,' she choked. 'This cannot be.' And yet it was. She wasn't dreaming. She was not in some kind of drug-induced trance. She was not hallucinating. She was fully awake – *and she was in the grist mill*. In the same loft, high above the threshing floor, where she had come awake that horrifying night eighteen years ago.

Her mind slammed shut against the shattering memory, keeping it out, knowing that denial was her last defence against madness.

She moved her hand, feeling the rough timber under her open palm, and she began to crawl, inch by inch, towards the ladder, knowing it was the only way down. *Try not to remember the rest. Don't remember, don't remember.* But in spite of her determination, fragments of memory, brutal, blinding, flashed before her. The sound of that scream. Her mother's voice. The deadly, sickening thud of a body hitting the floor below. And then the silence. The awful, suffocating, bewildering silence.

Now, just as she had done that night all those years ago, she lay flat on her stomach and in utter disbelief looked out over the edge, down into the void.

The same dim light was filtering in from somewhere outside. A narrow sliver of moonlight. Faint, but enough for her to see. And there it was. Just as she remembered it. The lifeless, broken body. With the pool of blood spreading, so dark, so dark against the bleached floorboards.

Gillian felt the scream of horror rising in her throat, but all that came out was a sickening, rasping whisper. 'Mother.'

She pulled back and ground her face into the dirt, fighting for a last shred of sanity. *This cannot be. This cannot be. Oh God if there is a God oh God help me.*

'Mother?' She heard herself speak again, but this time her voice sounded far away, as if it had left her body and was floating free, away from this hellish place.

'Mother? Where are you?' Again, this time more frantic. And this time she knew it was not her own. It was a child's voice, reaching out, trying to pull her back from madness.

Gillian grabbed for it and held it tight. And through the swirls of mindless horror came the treasured images of her children. 'Daisy? Will?'

'Mommy?' Louder now. Clearer. And *real*.

'I'm here!' Gillian screamed, jerking upright, heart pounding the way it does when you crash awake from the worst nightmare. Her mind felt scraped raw, but she knew what she was hearing was *real*. And recognizable. The voices belonged to her children. Daisy. Will.

'Mommy, where *are* you?'

Gillian crawled to the ladder and inched her way down, and at the bottom she stood for a minute, face pressed against the rungs, afraid to turn round, afraid of what she might see. And in the next instant a weepy-eyed Daisy came flying through the door. And right behind her, Will. They threw themselves against their mother, pulling her to her knees, and over the tops of their heads Gillian could see Dickon, standing in the doorway, his face ashen, full of disbelief. 'You okay, Aunt Gillian?'

She nodded, half crying, half laughing, hugging her children tight, her mind a jumble. What had happened to her? Had she come here in her sleep? Of course she had. She had walked here all by herself. *But what exactly had she seen? Had it been real?*

She forced herself to look past them, past Dickon, to the place where only moments ago she thought she had seen her mother's body. Her poor, broken mother. A nightmare within a nightmare. But now,

136

the only thing visible was the dark shadow of the old water-wheel.

This is the end for you, Gillian, she thought, clenching her teeth. I know how you got here. And if you stay at Clairemont it will happen again. So this is the end. Father or no father, you cannot stay here another day. Another night.

'We're going home,' she said forcefully. She said it to her children. To Dickon. But most of all to herself. 'Tomorrow morning we're going home.'

Chapter Fifteen

Strange how sometimes Will's mood seemed to follow the weather. This morning it was overcast, gloomy outside, and so was he. He sat on Daisy's bed reading comics while Daisy scurried around the room putting the last of her things into a suitcase. But he wasn't reading. He was thinking.

They hadn't had a chance to talk about what had happened last night. He and Daisy had run all the way back to the house, woken Dickon up, and together they had raced back to the meadow where they had last seen their mother. Along the way, Daisy had tried to tell Dickon about the awful creature they had seen, but she had been so out of breath he couldn't understand her. And anyway, Dickon had seemed more concerned about the sleepwalking than anything else. It was weird how he seemed to know all about the disorder. Not only that, but he seemed to know exactly where their mother had gone. To the grist mill, he had said. And that's just where they found her, shaking like a leaf, but so ecstatic to see them that nothing else seemed to matter to her.

Neither Will nor Daisy had asked their mother a single question. Not about why she had gone to the grist mill. Not about the phantom lady they had seen standing next to her. Not about anything, because when their mother said they were going home to

Virginia, Will and Daisy both knew that their troubles were at an end. Asking questions would only rile things up. Telling their mother about that grisly spectre would have made her just as upset as they were. And if they never had to see that creature again, who cared anyway?

At their mother's insistence, he and Daisy had slept on the floor in her room for the rest of the night. To stand guard over her, Mom had said. To make sure she didn't sleepwalk again. And neither he nor Daisy had uttered a single word of protest. Daisy, because even though she didn't tell Mom about what they had seen, she didn't mind admitting that she was still scared shitless. As for Will, he had stayed with the two of them because, macho image or not, the last thing he had wanted was to spend the rest of the night alone. In his room. In the dark.

Even now, in broad daylight, sitting on Daisy's bed in Daisy's room, he couldn't help but shudder thinking about what had happened last night.

'We're never going to know who she was, are we?' Daisy mumbled, folding the last of her shirts, putting them away in her suitcase.

'No.' He frowned. 'And who cares, anyway?'

Daisy stopped what she was doing and glared. 'I do.'

'Why? We're going home. Isn't that enough?'

'Cripes, Will. Sometimes you're so thick. Don't you think it would be important to know? I mean what if that woman is a *ghost*? Don't you even care about *that*?' He could feel her eyes boring into him.

Scowling, Will got off the bed and headed for the door. 'What difference does it make what *I* care about? We're leaving this joint in one lousy hour. And that's the end of that, so why don't you just shut up?' Deep down, Will felt angry. He felt even angrier because he didn't know why. He knew none of this was Daisy's fault, but she wasn't making him feel any better by asking stupid questions that he had no answers for. 'If you're so curious,' he said in his most sarcastic tone, 'why don't you stay here and investigate. I'm sure they'd all love to have you. Especially that bloody old ghost.'

Daisy put her hands on her hips. 'You're a real a-hole, Will. You can't even carry on a half-way decent conversation without freaking out.'

'Who's freaking out? *You're* the one who's freaking out.'

'I am not.'

'Are too.'

Daisy stared for a minute in silence, clenching and unclenching her fists, and Will knew that as usual she was working herself up into a real spaz attack. And that's why, when she finally spoke, he was so surprised. Because instead of screaming at him like she usually did, her tone was hushed, very intense. 'We're lucky, Will,' she said. 'If you don't know it, I sure do.'

Startled, he stared back, trying to see inside her head. What did she mean? For one thing, he knew she wasn't being bratty. She was being deadly serious. 'What do you know that I don't know?'

She threw her hands up. 'I can't explain it. But I know it's true. We're lucky. Because our mother is still alive.'

Will was shocked. It was the last thing he had expected her to say. 'Geez, Daisy, how did you come up with *that*?'

She didn't even blink. 'I told you, I don't know,' she said quietly. 'But it's true all the same. Mom was in real danger. We're getting out of here just in time.'

Will felt a tight knot in his stomach. Was Daisy imagining? Or had she somehow sensed something he hadn't? He didn't know. But it really didn't matter, because they were going home. In less than one hour. But if they had had to stay . . . he pursed his lips and made a low whistling sound . . . well, that wouldn't have frightened him just a little. That would have frightened him a *lot*.

Gillian stood at the window and looked down for one last time at what once had been her mother's rose garden. The stone paths were puddled with rain, the grass silvery-wet, and up above, a veil of mist lying across the gabled roofs, grey, sombre. Like her mood. How had she made herself come so far, she wondered, only to be turned back at the last? To leave Clairemont without seeing her father? What force had drawn her to the grist mill last night, retracing steps that she had wished so desperately to forget?

But she knew the answer. Sleepwalkers have no choice. That hideous disorder had brought her to the edge of madness once before, eighteen years ago, and last night, if her children hadn't found her, this time she would have been lost forever.

But they had saved her. They had pulled her back in time. They had rescued her. And now they were all going home together.

She closed her eyes. 'Goodbye,' she whispered, and was about to turn away from the window when something in the garden below caught her eye.

There, in the midst of a clump of silver grass, was a single pink rose.

She blinked, then blinked again. Had it been there

all the time? Had she been so self-absorbed that she hadn't seen it? Or had it been placed there as some kind of farewell gesture? And as she stared, an indescribable something brushed against her cheek. Like the gentlest kiss. And she heard a voice. Not angry any more. Not threatening like before, but soft now. Loving. *Goodbye, Gillian.*

She didn't understand, didn't know how much of what she was feeling was real, how much was imagined. But one way or another she knew it didn't matter any more. She was leaving Clairemont and that was that. She felt the tears of sadness falling. 'Goodbye,' she said softly, and turned away.

Upstairs in the east wing, Amanda's slippered feet moved swiftly from one side of the room to the other, from one window to the next. She was watching. Waiting. Something was happening this morning but she wasn't sure what, and she knew she was going to have to stay hidden until she found out. For one thing, Lenore was looking for her. Amanda had heard her knocking on her bedroom door early this morning, and even though Lenore had never entered without permission, Amanda had hidden behind the armoire. She didn't know why she had done it. It must have been a sixth sense, because no sooner had she tucked herself safely away than the door had opened and *Lenore had walked in*. *Right into Amanda's own private bedroom*. She had stayed only a minute, but the damage had been done.

Amanda had been beside herself with rage. All these years she had trusted her cousin implicitly. Lenore had never deliberately violated the rules. But now she had. She had opened Amanda's door and come inside *without permission*.

Held prisoner under the blackest cloud, Amanda had stayed behind the armoire for a long time, not knowing if she would ever come out again. How had Lenore *dared* invade her privacy? And why would she ever do such a hateful thing to Amanda, for whom she claimed to care so deeply?

Unless . . . unless she had been persuaded by someone powerful. Unless she had been sent to get Amanda because that someone wanted to find the dog and chain it up.

Indeed, since you think I am a dog, beware my fangs.

She came out from behind the armoire. Her tooth had begun to throb, and she had to pull her eyebrows together in a fierce attempt to concentrate in spite of the pain.

It couldn't be Father who had sent Lenore. He was still away. And it couldn't be Robin. Where Amanda was involved, Lenore never did anything that Robin told her to do. It could only be one person. Only one person was powerful enough to order Lenore around.

Gillian.

Amanda's hands moved to her face to cover her eyes, to push the image of her hated sister away. She began to moan low in her throat. 'What more must I do to be rid of her? What more? What more?' Weak, she sat down on the edge of her bed to keep from falling.

Teach her a lesson. Teach her a lesson she'll never forget.

And suddenly, above the sounds of her own moaning, she heard the whirr of a motor approaching.

She rushed to the window. In the drive, just beyond the formal gardens, she could see the top of a car. But who could it be? And were they just arriving or were they leaving?

Could it be possible that *they* were leaving?

This was too much. She couldn't bear the suspense. She flew across the room and eased her way out into the hall, closing the door softly behind her.

Her slippered feet moved soundlessly along the corridor. I'm like a shadow, she thought. I can go where I want, and no one will ever see me, and they will betray themselves because I'll hear what they say. And then I'll know what to do about it.

She was almost at the end of the hall when all at once she froze mid-step. In that single instant, somehow she *knew*. They were leaving Clairemont!

Goodbye, goodbye, goodbye!

Just ahead she could hear the sounds of people talking. People coming from the west wing. People pausing at the top of the great staircase, moving down. A woman. Children.

She inched forward and, just inside the archway leading back to the east wing, she stopped again. From where she crouched in the shadows she could see them. Gillian and the two wretched children. All carrying suitcases. *All moving down the stairs.*

They are leaving and I am staying, she thought, ecstatic. Here I am where I belong. At Clairemont. My home, my rooms, my solitude. She hugged herself tight.

Down below in the entrance hall she could see Lenore and Robin, standing at the foot of the stairs. She couldn't see her brother's expression. Didn't want to. But Lenore's face was pinched and drawn.

'Don't be unhappy,' Amanda whispered to her cousin. 'You'll see. We'll all be back to normal in no time.'

And then to her horror she heard Lenore say, 'Gillian, please don't go.'

Waves of black began to creep in, threatening to destroy Amanda's fragile sense of well-being. Don't listen, she told herself. Don't listen. Don't listen.

But she heard all the same. Gillian's voice in response. And once again she was delirious with joy.

'I'm sorry, Lenore,' Gillian said. 'We're leaving Clairemont. We must.'

That morning, when Gillian had first told them she was leaving, Lenore had been inconsolable. She had begged Gillian to reconsider. Not to leave until she had seen her father. But Gillian had known there was more to it than that. Lenore had hoped Gillian would help her son. And she would. But not here. Not now.

As for Robin, he had been fully supportive of her decision to leave. As if from the first he had known that she would never find any peace here at Clairemont.

Gillian took Lenore's hand and held it tightly. 'I'll write to Dickon,' she said quietly, then turned away. She couldn't bear to see the look of dismay still evident on Lenore's face. But Robin was clearly resigned. Through the mask of cool reserve, Gillian could see obvious relief.

And as she stood there, from somewhere far behind, up the stairs, down some distant corridor, she felt a stirring, an echo, a whisper. Of relief? Of happiness?

Was it Amanda?

Or was it her mother?

For God's sake, Gillian, she said to herself, grow up. Your mother is dead. Face it. If you do nothing else, face that much at least. She is not upstairs. She is not in the garden. *She is gone.* Disgusted with herself, she turned towards the door where her children stood patiently waiting. 'It's time,' she said.

And again, as if in response, she felt the house stir around her. *Goodbye, Gillian.* Again, the same familiar voice. The echo of something whispered from afar. But this time she knew it was only a memory.

She held out her hand to Lenore. 'Good luck to you all,' she said softly, feeling hot tears sting her eyes. She knew it was over. She had wanted to see her father. Wanted to be forgiven, and now that would never happen. Never. But she had no choice.

Lenore took her hand and gripped it with a fierce intensity. 'Please, Gillian,' she said. 'I'll speak to Amanda. I'll make sure she never bothers any of you again. We'll make sure you don't have to sleep alone. I'll stay with you myself. Please. Don't leave without seeing your father.'

Gillian shook her head. 'I can't.' She turned to Robin and managed to smile. 'Come and visit, will you? If you ever get to Virginia?'

He nodded, smiling. He, at least, was far from despair.

With a final look around, Gillian took his arm and together they went across the entrance hall. At the door, she paused. For just an instant.

And in that instant the front door opened and William Blackmarsh stepped into the hall.

146

Chapter Sixteen

Stricken, they stood facing each other, father and daughter, and then Gillian jerked back as if she had been dealt a terrific blow. Until this moment she had never imagined what it would be like to see him again, never allowed herself to remember how much she had loved him.

She looked down at the floor, certain that if she looked at him she would see nothing but disgust. And beneath it, hate. And then she heard his voice. 'Gillian.' A broken sound. Suffering.

She raised her eyes, wet with tears, to meet his. And clearly, astonishingly, she saw a face devoid of anger and hostility. A face full of tenderness and sadness and all the things she had never dared hope to see.

'My dearest daughter,' he said, and he opened his arms.

Paralysis seized her. *Could it possibly be? Has he forgiven me?*

'Come here, Gillian.'

And suddenly she was his child again, and like that child, unhesitating, she went to him.

He held her gently, smoothing her hair, a father trying to do his best to give comfort. 'My precious daughter. My poor, precious daughter.'

What she felt in the shelter of his arms couldn't be described. She *was* forgiven. She was, she thought, for the first time in eighteen years, completely happy. And she cried.

Her father made no attempt to stem the tide. He let her tears soak the front of his shirt, let her cling to him, let her whisper the same words over and over. 'I am so sorry, Father. I am so sorry.'

And finally his response, full of unmasked regret. 'No, Gillian, *I* am the one who is sorry.'

Unable to fathom what she was hearing, she pulled back to stare. 'But . . . but I don't understand. Why? Why should *you* be sorry?'

'Come with me,' he said softly. 'Into my study. So we can talk alone. So I can try to explain. I know I can't begin to make this up to you. These lost years. But I have to make you understand why I behaved the way I did.' He turned to Lenore. 'Have Kate bring us tea.' And without a word to anyone else he held out his hand to Gillian.

She hesitated for a moment, only dimly conscious of the others. Her children, still standing by the door, staring in wide-eyed confusion. Robin, his face pale, equally stunned. Lenore, fingers laced together, smiling.

And her father, hand outstretched, hopeful, waiting.

'Lenore,' Gillian said, her voice husky with emotion. 'Please. Take charge of my children, will you?' Then she took her father's hand and together they disappeared into his study.

Daisy couldn't believe her eyes. One minute they were at the door, happy, ready to leave, and the next, a tall, grey-haired man she had never seen before walked in. And in the blink of an eye everything changed. Her mother was crying and the man was hugging her and then off they went, leaving Will and Daisy, their mouths hanging open, aghast. Surely this didn't mean they were staying here. *Did it?*

'Holy shit,' Will whispered. 'I hope this doesn't mean what I think it does.'

She gave him a withering look. 'Of course it doesn't,' she said under her breath. 'It *can't*.'

Their uncle was the first one to move. Like Will and Daisy he was clearly upset. Without a word to anyone he left the house.

'So, you guys,' Dickon said, stepping forward, a broad smile on his face, 'I guess this means you don't have to leave. At least not yet.'

'Why don't you take them down to the stables, Dickon?' Aunt Lenore said cheerfully. She turned to Daisy. 'You both like horses, I'm sure.' And without waiting for a reply she turned and hurried off after her husband.

Thank goodness she didn't wait, because Daisy didn't have a clue what to say. The truth was that she didn't want to see horses or anything else here at Clairemont. She wanted to stand right here next to the door and not move an inch until her mother came out from wherever she was and said let's go.

'Do you want to take your bags back upstairs?' Dickon asked.

'No way!' Daisy said vehemently. 'You must be crazy!'

Dickon flushed, and Daisy was mortified. She should not have spoken to him like that. 'I'm sorry, Dickon. I didn't mean to yell. It's just that things are so . . . so messed up. Anyway, I think we'd better leave our stuff right here. So we'll be all set to go when Mom finishes talking.' She threw an anxious glance towards the study door, then turned to Will for support. 'Right, Will?'

Will nodded but he didn't say anything.

'Well, anyway,' Daisy continued, shifting nervously from one foot to the other, 'I think we should stay right here by the door. In case Mom comes looking for us. Don't you think?'

Dickon took a deep breath. 'You don't want to stay here at Clairemont another minute, do you?' he said. 'You hate it here. But how come? I know that what happened to your mother last night was frightening. But it wasn't her fault. She's a sleepwalker and that's what sleepwalkers do.' He waited for a minute, then added in a low voice, 'I don't think that's the reason you want to leave. I think something else is going on. Something you haven't told me about.'

Daisy shot Will another pleading look. Why the heck wasn't he saying something?

This time Will got the message. 'Nothing happened worth mentioning,' he said quickly. 'We just got all set to leave this morning, that's all. Got everything packed up. And now we have to wait.' He shrugged. 'It's a pain in the butt to have to hang around and not know what's going on.'

Dickon looked sceptical but he didn't push. He simply shrugged. 'Whatever you say. It's your business, not mine. In any case, we might just as well kill some time while we're waiting. And since you haven't seen our horses, let's go down to the stables. When your mother's ready, she won't have any trouble finding us.'

When she's ready.

Dickon's words echoed through the hall, and Daisy felt a sudden hard knot in her stomach. What if the

150

worst happened and their mother never *was* ready? What if she decided to *stay*? What would they do? What *could* they do?

She looked over at Will and in his face she saw a reflection of her own fear.

'Let's go,' Dickon said.

With one quick, hopeful glance back towards the place she had last seen her mother, a reluctant Daisy followed Will and Dickon out of the house.

From her hiding-place in the shadows, Amanda watched in utter horror as the scene below unfolded. Father *embracing* Gillian! Calling her *dearest daughter*!

Circles of light within circles of light spun wildly in the air in front of her eyes, and she shrank back, shielding herself from the searing heat.

Dearest daughter. Dearest daughter. Was that really what he had said?

She dropped to her knees and buried her face in her hands, wishing she could fit her whole self inside them. Carry herself away. Somewhere far away. Where she could be alone. Where they would never be able to touch her again. What she had seen, what she had heard *could not be tolerated*.

But then, perhaps it hadn't happened at all. Of course it hadn't. She was imagining.

Stumbling to her feet, she moved once again to the top of the stairs and looked down into the hallway below. She felt as if she were viewing the scene through a window filled with panes of bubbled glass. The figures she saw were distorted, moving as if under water.

Her father with his hand outstretched.

Gillian, speaking, her words garbled, impossible

151

for Amanda to understand. Gillian, moving towards him. Like a spoiled child, taking his hand, *going with him*.

Amanda opened her mouth to scream. *Get out of here! Leave! I hate you hate you hate you! I want you dead!* But at the very last moment, just as the words were about to split the air, her mind grabbed them and pulled them back. Kept them locked inside her skull. Something warned her that if they flew out of her mouth, everyone would know she was there. They would turn and stare. *At her*. They would see *her*.

She retreated into the darkness at the end of the hall, sinking down behind the folds of draperies, and the blessed darkness held her safe.

Now they cannot see me. Now they will never know I was here. Never be able to blame me for what happens.

But what? What *is* going to happen?

Why are you so frightened? Why are you so upset? Gillian is leaving Clairemont. She said so herself. Nothing has changed. Just wait. Be patient. Wait.

She made herself as small as she could, a tiny ball of flesh and bone, and there she stayed for a long, long time, the shadows moving softly around her.

Everything else in the house was still.

And she waited for Gillian to be gone, and then she would be free to come out of her hiding-place. 'Gillian will be gone,' she whispered to herself, 'because Father hates her. We *both* hate her.'

But in response, echoes of his voice invaded her nest, flew in and around the draperies, attacking her. *My precious daughter. My poor, precious daughter.*

And in her mind's eye she saw the hand out-stretched. The father's hand.

But what lay behind that hand? A blow? A slap

across Gillian's despicable face?

Or had his hand been extended for another reason?

She gasped in disbelief. Surely not, she told herself. Surely it hasn't been offered in *forgiveness*. Father would never forgive Gillian. Never! He hates Gillian.

But what if he doesn't, a dark voice whispered. What if it is *you* he hates, Amanda. What if he has said to himself, how can I punish Amanda? How can I torment her? And he answers himself. I can be kind to Gillian, that's how. I can *forgive* her.

How cruel of him. How cruel how cruel. But how like Father to be so cruel.

And worse, now there was Lenore. *Smiling*. Faithless friend. Viper. Lenore, who knew how desperate Amanda was to be rid of them. Lenore, standing there, *smiling*. Instead of ordering Gillian out of the house, she stood there and *smiled*.

Amanda made herself even smaller, hugging her knees, pulling them as close to her chest as she could. I mustn't let them harm me any more, she thought frantically, clenching her teeth together. I must think of what to do.

Think, Amanda. Only *you* can fix things now. Think, my dearest, most intelligent, most beloved girl. Put things back in proper order. Return your home to its pristine state.

But how?

She closed her eyes, listening.

Around her, the house stirred, restless, waiting for her to do something, anything, to be rid of her sister.

She opened her eyes.

She stared.

In the corner of the hall, where the two walls of the house came together, she could see a spider about to take up residence, beginning to *spin its web*.

153

Her first reaction was one of outrage. She hated spiders. Not only did the creatures repel her, but they presented evidence of a slovenly, ill-kempt home. Another reason why she detested Dickon. He actually collected the creatures, had been allowed to keep an army of them downstairs in one of the storage rooms.

Shuddering, she took off her slipper and was about to deliver a death blow when, in a flash of inspiration, the answer came to her! A *miraculous* answer!

That's it, she thought, feeling the corners of her mouth curve up into a shining smile of delight. The solution to her problem was crystal-clear. If Gillian didn't leave Clairemont today – this very minute, in fact – she would be very, very sorry.

Because Gillian would be very, very dead.

Chapter Seventeen

The rain had stopped but it was still misty-grey and cold. Will zipped his windbreaker up and saw Daisy do the same. She was shivering and had been ever since they left the house. And Will knew it had nothing to do with the weather. Daisy would be shivering even if it were one hundred degrees outside.

In silence they shuffled along after their cousin, down the wide gravel path that curved round behind the gardens, a short distance to the stables. Under any other circumstances Will would have been full of interest, eager to try his mettle at riding. But not now. Now all he wanted to do was mark time. How many seconds, minutes, hours before his mother came looking for them?

Geez us, he thought bleakly, climbing up on the fence to stand beside Dickon and Daisy. Let's hope like hell it's not *hours*.

The three hung over the top rail, watching some horses on the other side of a small creek. 'That's one of the creeks that flows into Salmon Brook,' Dickon said.

Neither Daisy nor Will made any comment. Salmon Brook was not a pleasant place to think about. It flowed past the grist mill and that was the last place either of them wanted to be reminded of.

'Okay. What's going on with you two?' Dickon

asked suddenly, jerking his head round to frown at Will. 'You've got a real bug up your ass, so why don't you tell me about it?'

Beside him, Will felt Daisy stiffen, and when he turned to look at her, almost imperceptibly she shook her head, a silent warning to him to shut up. Earlier she and Will had agreed not to say anything else to Dickon. On their way to the mill last night Daisy had tried to tell him about the lady with the bloody hands, but she had been really out of breath and hadn't been very easy to understand. As a result, Dickon hadn't paid any attention to her. He had been concerned about finding their mother and that was all. And when they finally found her and she said they were going home to Virginia, there didn't seem to be any reason to bring it up again. After all, they were all getting away from Clairemont. No reason to leave Dickon with the impression that they were weirdo sissy freaks.

But that was before. Now Will wasn't so sure they were *ever* going to get out of here. When he had seen how his mother had reacted this morning, a prickle of doubt had crept into his mind. And now that prickle had grown into a full-blown fear. Fear that maybe they weren't going to leave Clairemont today. And maybe not tomorrow. And maybe – he shuddered – maybe not ever.

He glanced at Dickon out of the corner of his eye, sizing him up. His cousin had really helped them last night. Saved their mother from God knew what. And now, if his mother decided not to leave Clairemont, she wasn't the only one who would be in trouble. He and Daisy were going to need help *big time*.

'I have to talk to my sister in private,' he said to Dickon. He nudged Daisy and together they slid along the fence, not a very great distance, but far enough so Dickon couldn't hear.

'I think we'd better tell him what we saw,' Will whispered.

'Why? What good will that do? The only thing he'll remember about us is that we're sissies.'

'Okay, okay,' Will nodded, 'if we leave today that's exactly what he'll think. But what if Mom decides to stay? Then what happens? Don't we need to tell someone what's going on?' He shuddered. 'So it won't happen again?'

Her eyes locked with his and he knew without hearing it what her answer was. Inching sideways, they moved back to their original positions along the fence.

There was a short silence while Will gathered his thoughts together. He wanted to choose his words carefully, wanted to sound curious but nothing more. The last thing he wanted was for Dickon to know how frightened they had been. How scared shitless they still were. 'Have you ever seen anyone around here that doesn't look . . . normal?'

'Like what do you mean, "normal"?'

'Well, there's this person who wears a long grey dress. A lady.' He glanced over at Daisy for help, but she was staring down at the ground. He took a deep breath and continued. 'And her hands are all dripping with blood and ripped skin and shit like that.'

Dickon tilted his head to one side and gave Will a funny look, like he didn't know whether to laugh or what. 'Chill out, Will,' he said with a snicker. 'Give me a break. Bloody hands?'

'We're not stupid,' Daisy cut in, and her voice was sharp, impatient. 'We know what we saw. Whoever she is, she has hands that would make you sick. And she doesn't look human.' She held up three fingers. 'First I saw her in the wine cellar. Then Will saw her yesterday by the tennis courts. And we both saw her last night. Standing right beside our mother.' She narrowed her eyes. 'So what we want to know from you is if you've ever seen her. And if you have, who is she?'

The intensity of her tone silenced them both, and Dickon's face grew pale. He turned from Daisy to Will and back again. 'You guys are really serious,' he said, frowning. And then, as if something had just occurred to him, he put his hand to his head. 'Christ, this doesn't have anything to do with stories you've heard, does it?'

Will's eyebrows shot up. 'What stories?'

'Stories about your grandmother.'

Daisy stared. 'Our grandmother? What does she have to do with anything?'

Dickon slipped down from the fence and stood leaning against the post. He seemed upset with himself, silently berating himself for having opened his mouth.

Will slid down and stood beside him. 'We just told you what *you* wanted to know. Now it's your turn. Fair is fair.'

'It isn't up to me to tell you anything,' Dickon said, shaking his head, but he still seemed unsure, as if he hadn't quite made up his mind. 'Your mother should be the one.'

Daisy jumped down, her face ashen, her lips drawn tight across her teeth, and when she spoke she sounded just like a grown-up. 'We know our mother has a secret,' she said grimly. 'It has to do with something that happened here when she was very young. Something she can't talk about.' She stared at Dickon without blinking. 'But you know what her secret is. And you have to tell us. Right now.'

For a minute Will thought Dickon was going to tell them both to drop dead. Two bright spots of colour had appeared on his cheeks and he clenched his hands into tight fists. But when he spoke he didn't sound angry. Just nervous. 'Okay, okay. I'll tell you. But don't blame me if it only makes things worse.' He turned, climbed over the fence, and headed out across the pasture. 'Come on.'

'Where're we going?' Daisy asked, hurrying after.

'To the grist mill.'

Will gulped but he kept walking. Daisy stopped dead in her tracks. 'But why?' she wailed. The grown-up was gone. The regular old sissy Daisy was back. 'Why do we have to go *there*?'

Dickon turned. 'You wanted to know what happened,' he said flatly.

'I do. But why can't you tell us right here?' Daisy's voice was whiny as hell, but Will had to admit that he agreed with her. He didn't want to go to the grist mill either.

At first Dickon was unrelenting. 'If you want me to tell you about your grandmother you have to come with me.' But almost immediately he softened his stand. 'On second thought no one will ever find us there if they're looking for you. Forget it. We'll go down to the riding ring. Come on.'

Will and Daisy followed, keeping close together. Normally Will would have given her shit for being such a whiner, but he didn't because, except for that one little slip, Daisy had come through like a trouper,

159

and she had accomplished what Will had failed to do. She had persuaded Dickon to tell them everything.

There was a soda machine just inside the stable door with a box of slugs on the shelf right beside it. 'You want something to drink?' Dickon asked, dropping a slug into the slot.

'I suppose so,' Will said glumly. He really didn't want a soda. He wanted to go home. 'I'll have a Seven-up.'

'Me too,' Daisy echoed.

They took their sodas, followed Dickon outside, and sat down on one of the wooden benches that lined the riding ring, Will and Daisy on either side of their cousin.

Dickon opened his soda and took a long gulp. 'Before I begin,' he said, 'I want your solemn promise that you'll never say I told. Never.'

'Promise,' Will said without hesitating.

'Me too,' Daisy nodded.

'Shake on it.'

They did, and the story began.

After Dickon finished, Daisy and Will sat thunderstruck. Will was the first one to say anything. 'You mean she *stomped* on her mother's hands?' he mumbled. 'She . . . she *killed* her?'

Dickon nodded. 'But don't forget, she did it in her sleep. That's why she wasn't really to blame. But Grandfather didn't see it that way. He never forgave her.' He paused. 'Not until this morning.'

Daisy's face was pinched and pale. 'No wonder she didn't want to come back here. No wonder.' Her voice trailed off.

There was a long silence. Then Will said, 'But why did she go to the grist mill last night? Why would she ever want to go there again?'

Dickon shrugged. 'My mother says that sometimes sleepwalkers do the same things over and over. Things they would never do if they were awake.' He started to say something else, then thought better of it. 'Anyway, my mother feels very sorry for Aunt Gillian. She really wants to help her.'

There was another long silence, and this time it was Daisy who ended it. 'So why did you tell us all this, Dickon? What does this have to do with . . .' She stopped mid-sentence and slowly turned her head to stare open-mouthed at Dickon. 'You don't think . . . ? Do you? Do you think it's our *grandmother*?'

'Geez us,' Will gasped.

Dickon stared back. 'Now can you understand why I asked if either of you had ever heard the story? This lady you say you've seen sounds a lot like your grandmother, bloody hands and all.'

'But that would make her a *ghost*,' Will said, pouring the rest of his soda onto the ground. 'I don't believe in any of that crap. It *has* to be someone pretending.'

'Well, there's always Aunt Amanda,' Dickon said. 'Did this ghoul look anything like her?'

'No!' Daisy said emphatically.

Dickon looked at Will. 'You agree?'

Will shrugged. 'I never saw Aunt Amanda so how could I tell?'

'You haven't met her?' Dickon was incredulous.

Will shook his head.

Dickon jumped to his feet in a sudden burst of excitement. 'Holy shit, it's the only reasonable explanation. It makes perfect sense. Aunt Amanda has always hated your mother and she wants to get rid of her.' His eyes were sparkling. 'And if we can just prove she did it, then everything will be just great. We'll tell my mother and father and grandfather and they'll *have* to get rid of her. And then Clairemont will be the best place in the world to live. For the first time in my life, I'll be really happy here.' He whirled round. 'Come on. We'll track her down and, when we find her, you can both take a long, careful look. And then we'll know for sure.'

'It's not Aunt Amanda,' Daisy said softly, shaking her head. 'It's not.' But neither of them paid any attention, and it suddenly occurred to her that maybe she had been wrong all along. After all, a costume and make-up could change the way anyone looks. Couldn't it?

The two boys broke into a trot, jogging back along the drive towards the house.

Daisy brought up the rear. Maybe you were mistaken, she said to herself. Maybe it really *is* Aunt Amanda.

But somewhere deep inside, another part of Daisy was still silently shaking her head. That part knew without a doubt that the lady with the bloody hands was not their aunt. That part knew that the lady with the bloody hands was not a living human being.

Chapter Eighteen

Her father's hand covered hers, his voice full of love, his eyes full of tears. 'How much you look like your mother,' he said. 'How happy I am that I have you back.' And his words were echoes of her own thoughts. *How happy I am that I have you back.*

'I was a blind, arrogant, selfish man. I still am, but for one difference. Now I am ashamed. So ashamed.' He grimaced, his face twisting into a mask of pain. 'Though I'll never know what brought me to my senses. Even when I allowed you to come back to Clairemont, in my mind it was an act of boundless generosity. I never thought that what I had done to you was wrong. In fact, before I left for Europe I had decided not to come back until you were gone. I even called Robin and told him not to expect me.'

'But you *did* change your mind,' Gillian said softly.

'I did.' And then he told her the most incredible thing. While in Paris he'd had a dream, he said. Claire had shaken him awake. She was weeping, but as happens in so many dreams, it was a distortion. Instead of from her eyes, the tears were falling from the tips of her fingers, and she had begged him to come back to Clairemont before it was too late.

Gillian gasped, remembering her own dream.

Her father gripped her hand. 'I woke up with a start. As if struck by lightning, I knew what I had done to you. I can't explain it. I just knew. So I came home at once. Thank God, I came home.'

They sat quietly together for a long time, talking, reliving all those torturous years, confessing to each other their deepest feelings of grief, guilt, remorse. Gillian, for having been so selfish, for having disobeyed, for having ended her mother's life. William Blackmarsh, for not having understood his own child's despair, for having banished her to a lifetime of exile.

Raw-edged, they listened to themselves and to each other. And Gillian's teeth finally stopped chattering, her sobbing gasps finally faded away. 'I love you, Father,' she said simply.

He leaned over and touched her gently on the cheek. 'I love you too, Gillian. I'm going to spend what's left of my life making it up to you,' he said. 'And I'm going to begin right now. I have a great deal to tell you, but I'd like Robin and Amanda to hear it as well.' He patted her hand. 'You wait right here.' He stood up and went out into the hall.

Gillian didn't move. She had listened to her father with absolute concentration, trying to absorb every word. He hadn't needed to forgive her, he said, because there was nothing to forgive. The fault was his. He had abandoned his thirteen-year-old child to face the loss of her mother alone. 'If your own Daisy had done what you did, Gillian, would you punish her the way I punished you?'

That question had left Gillian breathless, because she knew that the answer was an unequivocal no.

Still, her own sense of guilt was not diminished. She would always feel it. Deeply. No matter what her father said. The difference was that now she felt *forgiven*, filled with the most incredible sense of wholeness. At long last she was going to be able to rediscover what it meant to be a Blackmarsh. To have a father. To have a family. Oh, Max, she thought, smiling to herself, wait until you hear. Just wait until you hear.

So lost was she in her own euphoria, she did not realize that Robin had come into the study until she heard him clear his throat. She looked up to see him standing at the window, his back turned, staring out across the gardens. 'Robin?' she said in a tremulous voice. 'Can you believe what has happened? Can you believe that Father has forgiven me?'

He didn't move. 'No. It's the last thing I expected.' He sounded upset. No, not upset. *Angry*.

With a jolt Gillian came down from the clouds. Was it possible that Robin hadn't wanted their father to forgive her? That he had hoped she would never be accepted, never again be a welcome part of the family?

'Go in and sit down, Lenore,' she heard her father say. 'This is something you should hear.'

Together, Lenore and William Blackmarsh came into the study, Lenore crossing quickly to sit beside Gillian. William moved behind his desk, unlocked the middle drawer, and took out a sheaf of papers.

Robin stayed where he was, silent, stiff-backed, his face turned away.

Gillian started to get up, to go to him, but Lenore pulled her back. 'Pay no attention to Robin,' she said softly, her own face alight with relief. 'Welcome home, Gillian.'

Gillian sat back down and put Robin out of her mind. She didn't know why he seemed so angry, or if she had simply imagined it, but for the moment, the wonder of what had happened to her was all-consuming. Her father loved her. He was truly happy to have her with him.

'Where is Amanda?' William Blackmarsh asked, looking over at Lenore.

'I sent Grace to fetch her,' Lenore said. 'She should be along any minute.'

He made no comment. An air of intense concentration took over, and he leaned forward and began to shuffle through his papers, crumpling some into balls, throwing them into the waste basket, putting others aside in a neat, deliberate pile. 'There,' he said finally, bringing both hands down hard on the desktop. 'Your futures are assured.'

At that, Robin pivoted slowly round to stare at his father, his face a frozen mask. 'Do you intend to let us know what you have planned?'

'I do.'

Gillian heard Lenore take a quick breath. 'Don't you want to wait for Amanda?' she asked very quietly.

'It isn't necessary,' her father-in-law replied. 'Amanda has never been in charge of her own affairs, nor will she ever be. That's one of the things we need to discuss. What to do about Amanda. But first things first.' He picked up the pile of papers. 'This is a complete inventory of my assets, the sum total of which I had fully intended to leave to Robin and to Amanda.' He flipped through them, then dropped them back on the desk. 'But now I have changed my mind. Tomorrow I will contact my attorney. My will needs to be changed to reflect the following: at my death my estate will be divided into three equal shares. One is to go to you, Robin. One is to be placed in trust for Amanda's benefit. And the third will go to my dearest Gillian.'

Robin made a sound low in his throat.

Once again Gillian looked over at him, but his face was still hidden in shadow.

William Blackmarsh did not seem to notice. He continued. 'And therein lies the question. Which one of you wants to take care of Amanda? Which one of you should I appoint to oversee her trust fund?'

'You know I will,' Robin said sharply. 'We've already discussed that issue.'

'That was *before*,' his father snapped back, fixing Robin with a cold stare. 'Before I came to my senses. Before I realized how much harm I had done to Gillian.' He grew pensive. 'And you, Robin, are the one to whom I owe the debt of gratitude. You are the one who brought Gillian back to Clairemont so I could see her again.' His voice cracked with emotion. 'The moment I saw her I knew what I had done. Thank God there is still time for me to make amends.' His next words were probing and his tone had changed, become faintly accusatory. 'That *is* why you wanted her to come home, isn't it, Robin? So I would realize what I was doing to her? So I could right the wrong? So she would know that Clairemont was once again her home?'

Silence.

Stunned by the unmistakable tension between them, Gillian looked from father to son and back. What had happened between them? Was she responsible? In her euphoric state had she missed the obvious?

'Of course I'm delighted that Gillian has been welcomed home,' Robin said. 'But I see no reason to bother her with details.'

'Don't be absurd. This is no longer our decision to

167

make,' his father said curtly. 'Gillian is the one who must decide.'

My God, Gillian thought, decide what? What is all this about? Decide what? The only thing that she was absolutely sure of was that her father cared about her. The rest was a muddle. *Oh Christ, if only Max were here*.

Her father stood up and came round the desk, not looking in Robin's direction. Only at Gillian. And when he spoke it was as if she were the only one in the room. He bent over and took her hand. 'When your mother died,' he said quietly, 'she left Clairemont to me. For use during my lifetime.' He paused. 'But before I continue, let me show you something.' He drew her to her feet.

Leading her past Robin to the window, he and she stood side by side, looking out across the sculptured gardens to the meadows and the rolling hills beyond. 'You see all of that?' He waved his arm.

Gillian nodded.

'It was your mother's second most cherished possession. Do you know what the first was?'

Gillian closed her eyes, feeling the hot sting of tears.

'Her most cherished possession was you.' He touched her gently on the arm. 'Gillian, look at me.'

She opened her eyes to see her father's eyes, so blue, so like her own, so filled with love for her. 'I want you to read this.' He reached into his jacket pocket and pulled out an envelope. Inside was a pale-blue piece of stationery, folded neatly, with her mother's monogram at the top.

Gillian took it, and through a mist of tears she began to read.

My dearest child, my Gillian,

This letter is to be delivered to you immediately upon the reading of my will. Wills, alas, can only provide instruction. They do not always reflect intent, and sometimes, even in the best of circumstances, they leave painful questions unanswered.

I lie dead, Gillian. My will has been read. You know its contents. But I hear your painful question: Why, Mother, did you not leave Clairemont to both of us? To me and to Amanda?

And here is my answer.

You and Amanda are my two most precious possessions and I love you equally. But you are the only one with strength of purpose, you are the only one with the ability to stand on your own, the only one capable of making responsible decisions. And because of these special gifts, Gillian, you should be free to plan a life apart from your sister. Amanda must never be a burden to you because of something I've done. Were I to leave Clairemont to both of you, it would be tantamount to sentencing you to a lifetime of entanglements. It would bind you together whether you liked it or not. I fear that in the last analysis it would make you hate each other.

That I cannot, will not do. Clairemont is a jewel to be treasured. It must never be viewed as a prisoner's chain, holding two unwilling people captive.

I hope you understand, Gillian, that no matter how much a mother might wish it, things cannot always be equal. In the end, decisions must be made regardless. I have made mine.

Know only that I love you both. I make no demands upon either of you except that you try to be happy.

With deepest love,
Mother.

Gillian stood where she was and stared down at her mother's elegant script, watching it blur as her tears dripped one by one onto the paper, running across the lines, smudging the words.

'Do you understand?' her father asked.

Numb, Gillian nodded. Her mother had left Clairemont to Amanda because, even all those years ago, she had known that Amanda would never survive away from this place. And that to leave it to both of them would do nothing but create a terrible snarl. And Gillian wept. Not for the loss of Clairemont. She wept for the loss of her mother.

Her father handed her his handkerchief. 'Here, Gillian. Blow your nose.'

She did.

He put his arm around her. 'Now you can understand why I must talk to you. All of you. Before I die and the transfer of Clairemont is complete, there are decisions that must be made.'

'I have already told you, Father,' Robin broke in, 'that I will take care of Amanda.'

'I know that, Robin,' William said, his arm still around Gillian's shoulders. His tone softened. 'And I am grateful to you. No. More than that. Proud of you for having accepted my burden as your own. But now that Gillian has come home, I have to know her intentions. How she feels about her sister.'

Gillian swallowed hard. What was her father asking? That she take charge of Amanda after his death? But why would he ask such a thing? Surely he knew that if Amanda loved anyone it was Lenore. And surely he knew that once Clairemont was Amanda's, Gillian would never be welcomed here again. 'What is it, Father?' she stammered. 'Amanda and I have never been friends. Once Clairemont is

170

hers, she will never want me here. So what can I possibly do for her?'

She felt him stiffen beside her, and she turned to look up at him.

His expression was one of surprise, puzzlement. 'Once Clairemont is Amanda's?' Then his eyes lit up. 'My dear Gillian,' he said, hugging her, 'you misunderstand. Read your mother's letter again. She wanted you to know why she was leaving Clairemont to only one of you. But that one is not your sister. Your mother didn't leave it to Amanda, Gillian. She left Clairemont to you.'

Chapter Nineteen

Your mother didn't leave it to Amanda, Gillian. She left Clairemont to you.

Amanda heard him say it but it was too late to keep her hand from turning the knob, too late to keep the door from opening, too late to keep them all from seeing her standing there, staring at them in horrified disbelief. *Clairemont was going to belong to Gillian?*

'Well, Amanda,' her father said. 'You've arrived just in time. Come in. We have some things that must be discussed.'

Amanda had a flashing image of a hooded executioner dressed in her father's clothes, who, having just condemned her to death, was now urging her to step forward quickly to the gallows. And her first instinct was to run away. To hide. But Lenore had already crossed the room, had taken her hand.

Dimly Amanda heard Lenore speak, but it was from a great distance, as if her mind had separated itself from her body and was observing them all from somewhere just above her father's massive mahogany desk. 'Come, Mandy,' she heard Lenore say. 'Sit with me and I'll try to explain what is happening.'

Amanda allowed herself to be led across the room to the sofa, and she sat down hard, her heart trying to pound loudly enough to drown out the echo of her father's words. But it was useless. She kept hearing them over and over again. *Your mother didn't leave it to Amanda, Gillian. She left Clairemont to you.*

Amanda felt dizzy. She focused on the pewter vase by the window. The one that had been filled only this morning with her own sunny yellow and white calendula. They were *wilting*. 'Who was in charge of watering my cuttings?' she asked, trembling.

Lenore patted her hand. 'Be calm, Mandy,' she said soothingly. 'I'll explain everything. There's nothing to be upset over.'

Nothing to be *upset* over? Nothing to be *upset* over?

She was acutely aware that there were people – Robin, Gillian, Father – standing over by one of the windows, but she didn't look at them directly for fear her eyeballs would blow out of their sockets. And she could hear Father's voice, droning on and on, saying something about what would happen when he died.

'That's when I'll break all the Rose Mandarin porcelain,' she said out loud, 'because that's when it will all belong to me. That's when Clairemont will belong to me.'

And the echo came again. *Your mother didn't leave it to Amanda, Gillian. She left Clairemont to you.*

Amanda put her hands up and pressed them against her temples, trying to keep her brain from melting down. Could it be possible? Had she really heard such obscenity? 'Lenore . . .' She began in a whisper but it ended in a scream. 'What is Father doing? Why are we here?' She jumped up, hands rolled into tight fists of rage, suddenly wanting to murder all of them. EVERY SINGLE ONE. 'What are you doing?' she shrieked at her father. 'Are you planning to give my home away? To *her*?' She pointed a threatening finger at Gillian.

173

'Take her upstairs, Lenore.' The voice of God. Hateful. Devious. Destructive. Sending her away. Not wanting her to hear. But she was not about to be dismissed. Oh no. She was going to hear *everything*. And then she would act accordingly.

Like the intelligent, well-mannered person she was, she drew her shoulders back and slowly, with great dignity, she folded her arms across her chest. 'I am not a person to be trifled with, Father,' she said firmly. 'I believe I have rights too.'

'Of course you do, Mandy,' Lenore said from her place on the sofa. 'Now come and sit beside me.'

'I believe I will,' Amanda replied calmly, and she sat down on the edge of the cushion next to her cousin, being careful not to touch her. With one hand she smoothed the fabric of her skirt, and with the other reached up to brush the hair away from her forehead. She didn't want to appear in disarray. If there was one thing Amanda detested it was disarray.

For the next several minutes Father held the floor and Amanda listened. Quietly. Without expression. On the surface she knew she was the picture of control. But inside . . .

Inside she was beginning the long, dark journey towards despair. Towards the dark, black dungeons of despair. And it was all because of what she was hearing. At Father's death Clairemont was to be *Gillian's*. A desecration beyond belief. And she, Amanda, darling girl, strong and brave, was once again to be the slave. Father's only question seemed to be one of ownership. To whom was Amanda to be indentured? To Robin? Or to Gillian?

She sat still and listened, trying to decide who was responsible for this monstrous plan. And the answer was clear. Only one person. Her mother. Alive, her mother had caused Amanda endless hours of torment. Eternal interference. And now she was striking the final blow from beyond the grave. Amanda was to be nothing more than a lap dog, a plaything for one of her siblings. To be fed, then chained at the foot of the bed. But whose bed?

Not that it really mattered. Like her calendula in the vase across the room, Amanda was wilting, dying. Clairemont was never to be hers. Her Play House, her sanctuary, would be razed to the ground. Her gardens would be ploughed under, her plantings massacred without feeling, without hesitation.

And then, in the final savage assault against Amanda and everything she stood for, Gillian would rip up the ornamental grasses and plant *roses*!

Father's voice droned on, but now Amanda was hearing less and less of what he was saying, until finally she heard nothing at all except the beating of her own heart.

She felt Lenore touch her arm. 'We're finished here, Mandy. Let me take you upstairs and draw you a lovely warm bubble bath. And then we can have lunch together.'

In a helpless stupor, unable to respond, Amanda followed. What difference did it make? To follow Lenore was no worse, no better than sitting where she was.

At Amanda's bedroom door, as was the custom, Lenore stepped aside. Whether from the inside or the outside, Amanda was the only one allowed to open her door. But now everything had changed. Corpse-like, Amanda stood, arms hanging limp at her side.

'Aren't you going to open it?'

Incapable of speech she shook her head.

Lenore turned towards her and put her hands firmly on Amanda's cheeks, drawing her face close. 'Do not despair, Mandy,' she said. 'You are always strongest when you are down. You know that. Don't forget your best-loved quote. It is always darkest just before dawn.'

Amanda sighed. No matter how desperate she felt, she could not tolerate a quote misquoted. 'It is always darkest just before the day *dawneth*,' she said.

Lenore nodded, then took Amanda's hand and placed it on the door-knob. 'Now. Please open the door.'

Sliding back into her stupor, Amanda did as she was told. She could barely remember where she was, who she was, who she had been. All she knew was that she was about to become extinct. Like a giant sloth. Or a triceratops.

But once she stepped onto her own exquisite Chinese rug and saw her lovely rose-coloured sofa with its meticulously embroidered cushions, each one done in flame-stitch by her own hand, she began to see things in a different light. She began to feel a faintest glimmer of hope. Lenore's words came back to her. *You are always strongest when you are down.*

'Come, my darling,' Lenore said soothingly, taking her by the hand, leading her to the sofa. 'Sit here and rest while I draw your bath. You know how much good it does you to relax in oodles of deliciously scented bubbles. And while I'm in the bathroom, you chase away that gloomy, depressed Mandy and bring back my brave, my noble girl.'

Amanda sat down and went limp. There was no point in hoping. What was done was done. Suicide was the only answer.

The sun was streaming through the window, and she let it warm her skin. Not that it made any difference. She was through with life. Lenore should not have saved her all those years ago. She should have been allowed to die. If she had, she wouldn't have to endure this savage cruelty. But it wasn't too late. She could still kill herself. Better death than to see Gillian living in her home. Taking over her *rooms*.

And suddenly she was filled with self-disgust. What was the matter with her? Why should she be the one to die when it was Gillian who deserved it? And the more she thought about it the angrier she became. Instead of behaving like a fool, paralysed by this profound sense of hopelessness, she ought to be filled with renewed determination to save what was hers. *And Clairemont was hers. No one was going to take it away from her. No one.* Father and Robin and Gillian had dragged her into hell, but she wasn't going to stay there. She refused to be annihilated. If anyone was to be annihilated it was that one. It was *Gillian*.

Goodbye, Gillian. Goodbye forever.

But first there was something Amanda had to find out. A critical detail. If she murdered her sister, was there any guarantee that Clairemont would be hers? Or in a terrible twist of irony would it pass to Gillian's wretched children?

Knitting her brows together, Amanda gave that question serious consideration. Who could she ask? Who might have the answer? Was it possible that Lenore might know? But if you ask, she told herself sternly, you have to be careful. You mustn't give yourself away. Not to anyone. Not even to Lenore.

She heard the water stop running, and Lenore came to the door, smiling. 'Your bath is ready, Mandy.'

Amanda went into the bathroom, slipped out of her clothes, and eased her way into the warm, exquisitely scented water. It soothed her battered spirit and she began to relax.

Lenore sat on the edge of the tub. 'There, my sweet,' she said, picking up the bath sponge. 'Shall I scrub your back?'

Amanda nodded and leaned forward. The timing was perfect. Lenore was preoccupied. Amanda would ask her question now. But carefully, so as not to arouse suspicion. She should sound bewildered, perhaps even a little muddled, as if she was too upset by what she had heard to be making any sense of it. And when she asked the question, she would stutter.

'Do you understand all of this, Lenore?' She put a confused look on her face. 'Because *I* don't. Not one bit of it.'

Lenore continued with her gentle scrubbing. 'What is it you don't understand, Mandy?'

'Well, for one thing, what would happen to Clairemont if Gillian weren't around? Not that I think she isn't *going* to be, mind you.' She lifted her hands in a gesture of concern. 'It certainly should go to her children. It would, wouldn't it?'

'No, it would not, my darling Mandy,' Lenore said, squeezing the water out of the sponge. 'According to your mother's will, if anything were to happen to Gillian – heaven forbid – Clairemont would belong to you. But of course you could always give it to her children if it pleased you to do so. Shall I rinse you off?'

Amanda nodded again, but she kept her face turned away so Lenore wouldn't see the radiant smile, wouldn't know that Amanda was elated. When Gillian dies, she thought, Clairemont will belong to the person most deserving of it. Clairemont will *never* belong to those horrid, wretched, snivelling children. Clairemont will belong to me! 'I love you, Lenore,' she said and, unable to restrain herself another minute, she burst into a joyous peal of laughter.

'I love you too, Mandy.' Lenore stood up and dried her hands. 'And now I must see to lunch. Will you be joining us?'

'I think not,' Amanda said, still smiling. 'I believe I'll have Kate pack a basket for me. Something special. And then I'll be off for an afternoon of gardening. But don't worry, dear Lenore, I *will* join you for dinner.'

So I can say goodbye to Gillian. Goodbye forever.

Amanda's journal. 18 June.

> *Sometimes we have to do things we dislike in the interest of the greater good. And as Patrick Henry himself once wrote, we are not weak if we make a proper use of those means which the God of Nature has placed in our power.*

'There,' Amanda said aloud. 'It's finished.' And she was pleased. She had successfully outlined her plan, and now all she had to do was bide her time until nightfall. There would be no further delay. This evening, the drama would commence. And shortly thereafter *it would end*. All of it. Finished. Forever.

In the meantime the afternoon was hers to do as she pleased. She would go to the kitchen and pick up her lunch basket. And then it was off to her gardens. She had a great deal of work to do outside. She had noticed a disturbing patch of botrytis, and she knew the infected begonias had to be sprayed.

But she felt tired. Perhaps a short nap would be in order.

She got up from her writing-desk and crossed to the sofa, careful to remove her shoes so as not to soil the cushions. She curled up and closed her eyes and was almost asleep when, as if in a dream, she heard her name called.

'Amanda.'

She sat up and listened.

'Amanda.' It was only a whisper, and yet oddly enough it came from somewhere outside the room. Beyond her closed door. A woman's voice.

She caught her breath. With her door shut tight, how could she be hearing it? And why did it sound familiar? It wasn't Lenore. It certainly wasn't Gillian.

Then who?

She stood up, crossed to the door, and was about to open it when she heard a new, a different sound. A swishing rustle, as if someone were moving briskly up and down the hall. Searching.

Searching for me?

Amanda leaned against the door, holding it shut tight. Despair, hate, anger and disgust were all emotions well known to Amanda. But not fear. She had never at any time in her life experienced fear.

Until this moment.

Now she was *afraid*.

But of what? Was someone searching for *her*?

And if so, why?

Heart pounding, she pressed her ear against the door and listened. And heard.

Grey, creeping silence.

Whoever had been out there was gone.

Or were they?

She stood for a long time, stunned. She had been *afraid*. She, the brave, the courageous girl. She had been really, truly frightened. But again she asked herself, of what?

And more important, was she to be kept prisoner here forever, hiding behind her bedroom door?

And suddenly she was angry. Why was she crouching here, shivering and snivelling like a wretched child? Open the door, she told herself sternly. There is nothing outside that can harm you. No one would dare.

Slowly she reached down, turned the knob, and eased the door open.

She peeked out.

What she saw had no place in the world as she knew it. Shades of light and dark, fragments of colour, so bright, so shatteringly bright, swirled around her, touching her, and without choice her eyes followed their movement to the far end of the hall.

The fear that had taken hold of her earlier was nothing compared to what she was feeling now. A spasm of nausea convulsed her, and she gaped in utter disbelief and horror.

For there, at the end of the corridor, in a circle of blinding light, stood her *mother*, wrapped in her long silver-grey dressing-gown, her bloody, broken hands stretched out in front of her. But she wasn't beckoning. She seemed to be holding the rotting flesh out to Amanda *for viewing*.

'This can't be!' Amanda shrieked. 'You are dead, you vile creature! You are dead as dirt! Go back where you came from!' And wheeling round, she threw herself headlong through her open door, landing hard on her knees, lashing out with one foot to kick the door shut behind her.

In the grip of a terror she couldn't begin to understand, she did the only thing she knew how to do. On her hands and knees she crawled to the armoire and hid behind it. And there she stayed, lost in some nether world, thinking for the first time that maybe Doctor Rabid had been right all along. That maybe she really was a raving lunatic.

Chapter Twenty

Somewhere far down the hall someone had turned a radio on, and beyond it Gillian was vaguely aware that a telephone was ringing. But they were merely peripheral sounds. The only thing she was really hearing was her father's voice. 'Come along, my dear,' he said, taking her arm. 'We'll all have lunch together in the summer room and you can introduce me to my grandchildren.'

Still caught up in a kind of delirium, Gillian could only nod. Her brain was reeling. There was so much to sort out. Someday Clairemont was to be hers. But what on earth was she to do with it? What did her father expect of her? And what about Robin? Was he really as angry as he had seemed? Was she fooling herself into believing that the worst was over? Would she wake up with a start to find herself back where she started, unforgiven, hopelessly doomed?

She desperately needed to talk to Max. He would be able to tell her what to do. He would know whether they would ever want to live here.

And then a flat, business-like voice broke through into her consciousness. 'Telephone for you, Miss Gillian. It's your husband.'

Her father smiled and pointed to the phone on his desk. 'I'm sure you want to tell him everything, and you can do it here in private.' He patted her on the shoulder. 'I'll wait for you in the summer room.'

Gillian couldn't get to the phone quickly enough. She picked up the receiver and gripped it tight. 'Max,' she said, breathless. 'Oh, Max, wait until you hear.'

'Are you all right?' He sounded so far away.

'I'm fine. Fine.' Without being aware, she started to cry.

'Gilly!' Alarmed. 'What is it?'

'My father is here.' And the rest came out, words tumbling one after another. She didn't pause, didn't ask if he understood. It didn't matter if he did. Listening to herself, *she* understood. It *was* real. All of it was real. Now all she had to do was figure out how to handle it.

'Well, I'll be damned,' Max said, laughing. 'We're finally there. At the end of the tunnel.' And he sounded so pleased, so relieved, so much like himself, that she couldn't help but laugh too.

'My darling,' she said, 'the only thing that would make me happier is if you were here. I need you.'

'Simple comforts?'

'Simple comforts. When are you coming back?'

'Things are moving in the right direction. Two steps forward and one step back. It looks like the day after tomorrow.' A pause. 'Okay?'

She groaned. 'Damn.' And then she remembered that in a very short while she was going to be introducing her father to her children. To Will and Daisy. Something she had never dared hope to do and, in spite of the fact that Max wouldn't be here until Friday, she felt happy. 'We're having lunch together today. Me, my father, and Daisy and Will. He's finally going to meet his grandchildren. I cannot believe how excited I am.'

She spent the next few minutes trying to explain to

184

Max how dramatically her life had changed since yesterday, and how much she wanted him to be here to share in all this goodness. She didn't mention what had happened last night at the grist mill. She didn't mention it at all. That part was behind her. Over. Finished. Why upset him now? Why upset herself by remembering?

Later, much later, she wondered if things would have been different if she had.

'I'll call tonight,' Max said. 'So you can tell me how the kids like their grandpa.'

Finally they said goodbye, and she set the receiver down with a soft click. She stood for a moment, then turned quickly and headed for the door. Somewhere outside, she could hear the sounds of her children's voices, and she wanted to catch them before they went into lunch. Before they saw their grandfather. She wanted to prepare them. And she wanted to watch their faces. *Children, I'd like you to meet your grandfather.*

'Gillian.'

She stopped. Someone had spoken to her. Someone in the room behind her. She turned.

Robin was sitting in a chair by the window.

'Where did you come from?' she asked, smiling.

'I'd like to talk to you,' he said quietly.

'But Father . . .' She made a nervous gesture with one hand.

'I know he's waiting. But this is important. Please sit down.' His face was pale, his shoulders hunched over as if he were carrying a great burden.

Something is wrong, Gillian thought. Something is terribly wrong. 'What is it, Robin?' She went back across the room and sat down stiffly in the chair opposite his.

He was painfully direct. 'After Father dies, what do you plan to do with Clairemont?'

Gillian stared at him, her mind a blank. What was he asking? 'I don't understand.'

'Do you plan to make this your home?'

She spread her hands in a gesture of complete bewilderment. 'That's an impossible question for me to answer right now, Robin, and you know it. So why are you asking it?'

His eyes frosted over, became opaque, and he drew his lips back in a thin, tight line. 'I am asking you to sell your interest in Clairemont to me. You may name your price.'

For a moment she thought he was joking, and she almost laughed. But the sudden flash of anger that came across his face stopped her and she drew back, stunned. 'Are you serious?'

'I have done my best for you, Gillian,' he said sharply. 'I encouraged you to come back to Clairemont so you could see for yourself how very little there is left here for you to enjoy. I knew you'd hate it. I was right in that assessment, was I not?'

It was as if Gillian had been sitting in a dark room and someone had suddenly lifted the blinds. Finally she had a clear view of Robin's motives, and in a curious way she felt relieved. *This* was the real Robin. *This* was the way her half-brother had always operated. 'So *that's* why you wanted me to come home,' she said. 'You weren't interested in making me happy. You hoped I would be miserable, didn't you? You wanted me to go back to Virginia and never come here again.' She spoke slowly, deliberately, as if she were putting pieces into a puzzle. 'No wonder you were so angry at Father just now. Before he came home everything had been working perfectly,

186

hadn't it? I was leaving Clairemont this morning with full intentions never to come here again.'

Almost apologetically she shook her head. 'How terrible for you, Robin. And how unexpected. Before Father left on this last trip, not only was he leaving half of his estate to you, but he was going to put you in full control of Amanda. And after he died, I would have sold Clairemont to you in a millisecond.'

She fell silent, but when he started to speak she held up her hand. 'I'm not finished, Robin. I'm sorry, but you'll have to hear the rest. You were right. I haven't been happy here. In fact I've been really, truly frightened. Part of it was my own fault, I admit. My own childish imagination.' She paused, carefully considering her choice of words. 'But I think that someone else at Clairemont has been adding to my discomfort. Trying to drive me away. Was it you, Robin? Was it?'

Robin ignored the question. 'You have no reason to keep Clairemont,' he said in a cold, brittle voice. 'You never loved the place the way I do. The way I always have. For you, Clairemont is full of bitter memories. And it always will be.'

Gillian felt a rush of anger, but she made an effort to control herself. 'This was really not a good time to bring this up, Robin. I don't know what I'll do after Father dies. Maybe in a few days, a few weeks, a few months, I'll know better. Maybe after he decides what to do about Amanda . . .' Her voice drifted off.

'Didn't you pay any attention to what he said?' Robin asked sharply. 'His attorney will be here tomorrow morning and Father intends to change his will. He wants you to decide whether or not you're going to take care of Amanda after he's gone. Whether or not you are going to come here to live.'

He sat erect and riveted her with an icy stare. 'I am offering to save you the trouble of dealing with Amanda. I am offering to buy Clairemont from you. I am offering to keep Amanda here where she is happy, and oversee her affairs for the rest of her life. If you agree, you will be free to turn your back on this place with a clear conscience and never look back. What more can you ask?'

What more can you ask?

Gillian heard the question asked clearly the first time. But when she heard it repeated she could see that Robin's lips had stopped moving. Her breath caught in her throat. Was she doing it again? Was she imagining? Her heart began to pound and she turned her head to look behind her. Was someone else in the room?

What more can you ask?

Again, the question. And now the faintest scent of flowers filled the air. Persian lilacs? Was it the fragrance of her mother's Persian lilacs? Impossible. And yet . . .

She looked back at Robin and she knew from the stunned look on his face that he too had heard, he too was wondering if they were really alone. 'Robin?' she whispered.

He shuddered.

'Who . . . who is it?'

Without answering, he got up and crossed to the door but didn't open it. Instead he turned round and leaned against it, frightened eyes scanning the room.

And suddenly, all around her, Gillian felt motion. Cold, cold air, moving against her. Touching. Insistent. *What more can you ask? Leave Clairemont now!*

Her throat ached from the cold. It hurt to breathe, and she put her hands up to cover her mouth. What

188

is happening? she thought wildly. I am so afraid. Her only salvation was Robin. Seeing him leaning against the door-frame, as frightened as she was, kept her from going mad.

And at that moment the door burst open.

And there stood Lenore, smiling. 'Here you are,' she said cheerfully. 'I've been looking everywhere. The family is waiting in the summer room.' She reached out a hand to Gillian.

Trembling uncontrollably, Gillian stood up and somehow managed to get to the door. She didn't look at Robin.

'Are you all right, Gillian?' Lenore asked, frowning. She turned to her husband. 'Did you say something to upset our Gillian?' She was angry. '*Did you?*'

For a moment he didn't answer, and when Gillian looked at him the fear she had seen in his face was gone; now he seemed nothing more than annoyed. 'Lenore,' he answered in an impatient tone. 'I think you really ought to learn to mind your own business.' With that, he left the room.

Chapter Twenty-One

A yellow-winged butterfly fluttered across the surface of the water; too close, Daisy thought, watching. But at the last second, a current of air lifted it up and it flew away across the top of the garden wall.

'Did you see that?' Daisy mumbled to Will, who was sitting on the edge of the pool not too far away.

He shrugged. 'Big deal,' he said without looking up.

Daisy slumped back in her chair and went back to the task of picking at the cuticles on her fingernails. It was something she did whenever she got nervous and, boy, right now she was nervous. They were *both* nervous. In fact they were scared shitless, because they both knew they were doomed.

Just before lunch their mother, all excited and happy, had introduced them to their grandfather. That part hadn't been scary at all. Their grandfather had seemed very pleased to see them, especially Will. But Daisy hadn't felt offended. She was sure that the special attention was paid because Will was named after his grandfather. William Blackmarsh Norlund.

Anyway, everyone was together in the summer room – everyone but Aunt Amanda – and there was plenty of conversation. Grandfather asking them a million questions, and Aunt Lenore telling him about the new cook, and then Dickon started talking about hunting-dogs.

Uncle Robin wasn't very talkative and neither was their mother, but the others talked so much that Daisy almost forgot how anxious she was to get away from Clairemont. Forgot about it, that is, until her mother leaned over and said, 'Daisy, have you and Will unpacked your things?'

At that, Daisy almost fell out of her chair. The worst, *the worst*, had happened. They weren't going home.

'I . . . I thought we were leaving,' she stammered.

Smiling brightly, her mother shook her head. 'Your father is coming back the day after tomorrow to spend a few days and then we'll all go home together.'

'But what about last night?' Daisy whispered.

Her mother patted her hand. 'It's already forgotten, Daisy. You and Will needn't worry about me any more. Tonight and tomorrow night Aunt Lenore is going to sleep in my room with me. To make sure I don't do anything stupid and wander away like I did last night. And then your father will be here and everything will be just fine.'

Will didn't hear her, but right after lunch he pulled Daisy aside. 'What were you talking about with Mom? What did she say? Are we going home?'

'No, we aren't. So now we have no choice. We *have* to tell her what we saw last night. We *have* to ask her about our grandmother.'

Will nodded and looked over his shoulder. 'Let's tell her right now. Where is she?'

'She said she had to talk to Dickon,' Daisy said glumly.

'What'd she want to talk to him about, for cripe sake?'

191

'How the heck would I know?' Daisy said. She felt nervous as a cat, but she was exasperated too. With her mother and now with Will. 'Anyway, she said for us to wait for her out by the pool, that when she came out she'd explain everything. So why don't you just shut up.'

And surprisingly, he did.

They went out onto the patio and sat in silence, trying to keep calm, wondering how long it would be before their mother appeared, and wondering how exactly they were going to tell her about what they had seen last night. Not that it was going to make any difference how they said it. She was going to be awfully upset. First, she had been real nervous about coming here, then she cheered up like magic, and now she was going to hate it again. 'She seems so happy,' Daisy mumbled.

'So?'

'When we tell her, it's going to wreck everything.'

Will turned around and glared. 'So what are you saying? That maybe we shouldn't tell her anything? You must be nuts.'

Daisy stopped picking her nails and sat up straight. 'If Aunt Lenore is going to be with her all night, then maybe everything will be all right. Maybe nothing else will happen.'

'Maybe not to her. But what about us?'

There was another long silence.

Daisy slapped at a fly that was buzzing around her head, and Will went back to paddling his feet in the water.

'I wonder if that woman really is Aunt Amanda,' Daisy said finally. 'If she is, then all we have to do is tell on her and we'll all be safe. And just think about Dickon. He'll be ecstatic.'

Will pulled his feet out of the pool and stood up. 'Too bad she didn't show up for lunch.'

'I wonder where she is?'

'Probably messing around in one of her gardens.'

'Probably.'

Will stuck his hands in his pockets.

'What're you looking for?' Daisy asked.

'My good-luck charm.'

'You have a good-luck charm? Can I see it?'

'No.'

Daisy slumped back in the chair. 'Big deal. Fat lot of good it's done us anyway,' she said darkly.

'It's not supposed to work for *both* of us, stupid. Only me.'

'Yeah? Well, what's it done for you, I'd like to know?'

'I'm still alive, aren't I?'

Daisy didn't answer.

Another silent spell.

This time Will was the one to break it. 'Want to see if we can find her?'

'Who?'

'Geez us, Daisy. Aunt Amanda, of course.'

'We're not supposed to go anywhere. We're supposed to wait right here for Mom.'

'We don't have to go far. We can just look around in the gardens closest to the house.' He smirked. 'So when you start bawling someone will hear you.'

Daisy ignored the last part. 'I'm not sure I want to go,' she said, but after she thought about it for a minute she said okay. Their only hope now was to figure out if Aunt Amanda and the grey lady were one and the same. And then they'd really have something to tell Mom.

So off they went, following the brick walk that

curved round the side of the west wing, Will plodding along in his bare feet, Daisy right behind, not allowing him to get more than one length ahead. 'This is stupid,' she muttered. 'I don't know why we're bothering. We'll never find her.'

Will didn't answer, and they kept going until they came to the end of the walk.

To the right, a vast expanse of green lawn sloped down towards a long line of hedges. To the left, and behind the house, a series of wide steps led to a narrow path filled with white stones, a path bordered on both sides by rows and rows of pink and white flowers.

'Let's go this way.' Will pointed to the left.

Daisy nodded. The stone path was prettier but, more important than that, it was shaded by the house itself. And that meant that help was well within shouting distance.

'Ouch,' Will groaned, picking his way along. 'These stones are sharp.'

'You should've worn your sneaks.'

Will ignored her and kept moving, not daring to walk off the path for fear he would trample the flowers banked on both sides.

Daisy couldn't help but be impressed. There were flowers everywhere. And dragonflies. And bumblebees. A jumble of exotic colours and sounds.

And suddenly the path ended.

They found themselves standing in front of a high wall, and just to one side Daisy could see a heavy wooden door. 'Where do you suppose that goes?' she asked, and without waiting for an answer she turned and began to hurry back along the path the same way they had come.

'Oh, for cripe sakes,' Will said, hobbling after her,

grabbing her by the arm. 'Come on, Daisy, get real. There's no way we can get in any trouble. Geez us, the house is right there.' He pointed.

Daisy glanced up over the tops of the shrubbery. Will was right. The house was only about thirty feet away from where she stood. But somehow that didn't matter any more. She was frightened. She was going back to the pool to wait there for her mother. 'I'm getting out of here,' she whispered, shaking his hand off her arm.

'Go ahead, then, sissy-face. But you'll have to go alone because I'm going to see what's behind that door.' With that, Will turned round and, still walking gingerly, he went back to the end of the path.

'You don't have the guts!' Daisy yelled, but even as she yelled it, Will reached out a hand, lifted the brass latch, and in the next instant he disappeared.

She stood frozen, not knowing whether to follow, to go back alone, or to stand where she was and scream for her mother to come and get her.

Will made the decision for her. In the next instant he reappeared in the doorway and motioned wildly for her to come, silently mouthing the words Aunt Amanda.

Alternate waves of fear and curiosity swept over her, and in slow motion she made her way to the open door.

'You *have* to look, Daisy,' Will whispered, taking her hand. 'You're the only one of us who's seen Aunt Amanda.'

Trembling, Daisy allowed her brother to lead her through the arched opening and into the garden beyond.

She found herself in a curious kind of place unlike any of the other gardens she had seen. Here, there

195

were no flowers, only great clumps of what looked like grass. Some of it was ten feet tall, some blue, some red, some silver. But it was grass; at least, that's what it looked like to Daisy. 'Where is she?' Daisy whispered.

Will pointed.

Just ahead, where the brick walk disappeared round some tall green shrubs, Daisy could see a woman, the same one who had threatened to bite her only the day before. There was no doubt. It was Aunt Amanda. 'It's her,' Daisy whispered, excitement overcoming fear. Now all they had to do was get close enough to see if she resembled in any way, shape or form the one with the bloody hands.

Keeping as close to the wall as they could, they left the brick walk and inched their way forward, hunching over, making sure they couldn't be seen. Not that Aunt Amanda was looking. She seemed absorbed in her work, frantically digging at what looked like a single rose-bush. And they could hear her muttering, but they couldn't make out what she was saying.

Will dropped to his knees behind a shrub, pulling Daisy with him, and they crouched there, watching. 'Well?' he whispered. 'What d'you think? Are they the same person?'

Daisy shook her head. 'I don't know. I just can't tell.'

'Shit. I can't either. She doesn't really look like the other one, but she could've been wearing a mask.'

'But the other one was much taller.'

'I know. But still, she could've been wearing high heels.' He poked Daisy with one finger. 'Let's get out of here before she sees us.'

But it was too late. In that same instant Amanda jerked round to impale them with a ferocious stare.

196

They had been found out! Thunderstruck by the suddenness of it, Will and Daisy could only stare back.

For a moment Amanda didn't move. Then, with a terrible wrenching movement, she flung her head back and began to wail, a piercing, howling sound like an animal that was being beaten with a whip.

Never in her life had Daisy heard anything so awful, but she couldn't block her ears, couldn't turn away. The sight of this madwoman standing only a few feet away, arms wrapped tightly around herself, swaying back and forth, howling, was almost hypnotic in its effect.

'What's she doing?' Will choked. Like Daisy, he was rooted to the spot.

Daisy could only shake her head. She wanted to run but she was afraid to. Aunt Amanda looked like some kind of wild beast, muscles tensing, getting ready to spring.

'Do you think she's going to attack us?' Will gasped.

At the thought of such a prospect Daisy exploded. 'I'm getting out of here!' she screeched. She scrambled to her feet, but not quickly enough, for in that instant what she saw turned her blood to ice.

Just behind Aunt Amanda, in the very spot she had been digging, something ghastly had risen from the shadows. A vision so horrifying, but so *familiar*, that Daisy sank back to her knees, paralysed with fear.

The mangled hands with their broken, bloody, purple fingers stretched out like tentacles, *reaching for Aunt Amanda*!

But Aunt Amanda did not see her. Just as the hands were about to touch her, she sprang forward with a snarl, eyes blazing, teeth bared, coming straight for Will and Daisy.

The two children came to life simultaneously. Daisy let out one thin, piercing shriek, grabbed Will's hand, and together they ran for their lives, stumbling, scrambling, crashing through the shrubbery, out through the arched door and through the flower-beds, not once looking back, certain of only one horrendous thing.

Aunt Amanda was right behind them!

Chapter Twenty-Two

'Your mother asked me to speak to you, Dickon,' Gillian said, sitting down beside him in the small sitting-area just outside the orangery. 'Do you know why?'

'Sort of.' She heard a trace of nervousness in his voice.

'She wanted me to talk to you about sleepwalking.'

He shifted in his chair, then nodded but said nothing.

'Did you know that I've been a sleepwalker from the time I was old enough to climb out of my bed?'

Again he nodded. 'I guess we have a problem in common. And my mother says that sometimes it's a real help for people to share their problems.'

'Your mother is right.'

'I hope I can help you, Aunt Gillian,' he said seriously.

A little like the blind leading the helpless, she thought, but she didn't say it. 'You've already helped me, Dickon,' she said, smiling. 'Just by letting me talk to you about it. You're the first sleepwalker I've ever met.'

'Me too.' He grinned, clearly relieved. He moved to the edge of his chair and slapped his hands on his knees. 'So. Is there anything else you'd like to discuss?'

'Anything else?' she said, surprised. 'My gosh, I've

only just begun.' She took a deep breath. 'First of all, do you think your night walks are dangerous?'

He sat back, fidgeting with his fingers. 'No, not really. I've woken up in some pretty stupid places though. Like . . . like sitting on the roof outside one of the gabled windows.'

'How d'you get down?'

'After I woke up I climbed back in.'

'What if you'd fallen?'

'I'd probably have killed myself. But don't worry, Aunt Gillian. I'd never fall.' He frowned. She could see he was agitated, as if he were considering something else, but then he shrugged and fell silent.

'That's what I thought too. When I was your age.' Her voice drifted off. It was going to be difficult for her to tell him what she did to her mother but she knew that it was critical. He had to realize how very dangerous his disorder was. To himself and maybe, as Gillian had discovered at age thirteen, to someone else.

She looked him straight in the eye. 'When I was thirteen years old, Dickon, I broke my mother's rules. Just like you do sometimes. I unlocked my door and sneaked out to the grist mill. My mother came after me. She found me up in the loft. But before I tell you what I did' – Gillian paused, reflecting – 'let me ask you a question. Do you ever know what you're doing while you are sleepwalking?'

'No.'

'Do you ever remember it, afterwards?'

He shook his head.

'Doesn't that scare you? That you might do something awful and not be able to stop yourself? And worse, not remember doing it?'

He didn't answer.

Her next words came out quickly. 'Because that's what *I* did. My mother climbed into the loft to help me. Somehow she lost her footing and slipped off the edge, but as she fell she managed to grab on to the beam. She held on until . . . until I stepped on her hands.' She took a quick breath. 'She died.'

Dickon was watching her intently, but he didn't seem at all shocked. It was as if he found her reactions more interesting than his own. 'I bet you suffered a lot,' he said quietly.

'I did. But so did your father and your grandfather and Aunt Amanda. So did a lot of people.'

'It's good for you to talk about it, isn't it?'

She hadn't really thought about that, but it was true. 'Yes, it is. But what about you?'

He seemed puzzled. 'What about me?'

'Do you understand what can happen if you are careless? If you don't pay attention to your mother? If you don't stay put at night?'

'You've convinced me, Aunt Gillian,' he said quickly. 'I'd never do anything like that.'

'Will you mind your mother?'

He nodded.

'Promise?'

'Promise.'

'I hope so.' She felt a sudden rush of gratitude. To Dickon for listening, and to Lenore for having asked her to help. Perhaps, she thought, some good has come from telling him. Perhaps history won't repeat itself.

She stood up and kissed him on the top of his head. 'We'll talk more later. Right now I'd better go find your cousins before they think I've abandoned them.'

* * *

Sometimes, Gillian thought grimly, children tell the most incredible stories. You sit and listen, straight-faced, and you watch their expressions. The wide-eyed excitement, the wild gesturing with the hands, the non-stop flow of words tumbling out, the lurid details calculated to shock the unwary parent.

But not this time. This was different. So different.

Now, Daisy and Will sat across from their mother beside the pool, their faces ashen, eyes downcast, their bodies taut, hands stiff at their sides. They sat as still as stone. Restrained. Controlled. But so, so frightened. They each took turns speaking, but always in whispers, as if they were afraid someone else was listening.

When she first saw them running towards her, trampling through the flowers, she was going to scold them for being so destructive. But when they came closer, she knew there was trouble. Deep, deep trouble. She could see it in their faces. They were terrified. But it wasn't the kind of scary-movie fear that she was used to seeing. Daisy and Will looked the way children do when they've witnessed a ghastly accident. When they've seen blood. When they've seen someone die.

They pulled their chairs close beside her, sat down, and without waiting for Gillian to ask any questions, Daisy began. In a low, deadly serious tone she told Gillian what had happened to her two nights ago in the wine cellar.

Then it was Will's turn. Like his sister, he told his story without any childish embellishments. He too had seen the same grisly apparition up above the tennis courts. He too had been terrified.

And then came the worst revelation, and the most

shocking to Gillian because she had been there herself and hadn't even known about it. Last night her children had seen the same ghostly spectre standing right beside their mother in the meadow.

Gillian listened to that part of the story in utter horror. There was nothing she could say to explain it. But there was no doubt in her mind that they were telling the truth. But why had it happened? Who had been responsible for it? Was it some trickery of Robin's? Or was it Amanda? Was she capable of doing something so fiendish?

Or was it someone, *something* else?

'It wasn't Aunt Amanda,' Daisy said quietly. And then she told Gillian what they had seen only moments ago in the grass garden.

'I don't know which one of them was scarier,' Will said, shivering. 'But Aunt Amanda almost caught us.'

'She was right behind us,' Daisy said. 'I could almost feel her breath on the back of my neck. And then all of a sudden she was gone.'

'Well, thank goodness for that much at least,' Gillian said, still trying to keep her tone light. If she was sure of one thing, it was that she had to stay calm. She was their mother. Their parent. If anyone should be solid and rational it was her. She had to try to offer some explanation. But what? What could she possibly tell them that made any sense? *Max, help, I need you.*

'Do you believe in ghosts, Mom?' Will asked. Both he and Daisy had turned in their chairs and were watching her intently.

She considered carefully before answering. They were in a real mess here, without any answers that made any sense. 'To tell you the truth, Will, I don't know. I don't believe I ever gave ghosts much thought.'

'You believe in God, don't you?' That from Daisy.

'I do.'

'Well, if there's such a thing as God, why can't there be such a thing as a ghost?' Daisy looked nervously away towards the gardens.

'Maybe it's the ghost of our grandmother,' Will said quietly. 'Dickon told us about what happened to her.'

Gillian was aghast. This was something she had never expected. Her children already knew what she had done to her mother. But how could Dickon have told them when she herself had told him only a few minutes ago? She closed her eyes and put her hands to her temples. Dickon had known all along. But who would have told him? Certainly not Lenore. Lenore had asked Gillian to do it, hoping it would help Dickon understand how dangerous it was to be a sleepwalker.

Had Robin been the one?

She felt a sudden surge of anger.

'Mom?' A light touch on her arm. 'Are you okay?'

She opened her eyes to find her children standing close beside her, eyes wide with concern.

'Are you mad at Dickon for telling us?'

'No.' She felt the hot sting of tears but she blinked them back. 'No. I'm just ashamed that I never told you myself. I never wanted you to know what a dreadful mother you have.'

'You aren't dreadful at all,' Daisy said, putting her arm around Gillian, hugging her. 'You are a wonderful mother. What happened to our grandmother, well, it wasn't your fault.'

'Anyway,' Will said, sitting back down on the edge of his chair, 'do you think it could be her? The ghost, I mean?'

'I don't know who is responsible for this,' Gillian said angrily. 'I only know that someone doesn't want us here at Clairemont. Wouldn't you agree?'

Grave-faced, they both nodded.

'So,' Gillian said, exhaling. 'Give me a minute to think about this mess. Decide what's to be done.' There were two unanswered questions. One, who was terrorizing her children? And two, why were they doing it? Not that she herself had escaped unscathed. There *had* been someone in the study this morning. And there *had* been someone beside her in the meadow last night.

She looked at Will and Daisy and, seeing their expressions of absolute trust, she knew she had no choice. No matter what, she was going to have to find the answers to these questions *by herself*. She could not allow her children to be subjected to this terror for one more minute. 'I'm very proud of you,' she said gently. 'You have been brave, you have taken good care of me, you have behaved in the most responsible fashion. But now it's over.' She stood up and held out her hands. 'Come with me. I have to make some phone calls. And then we're off. Away from Clairemont. Tonight you'll both fall asleep in your own beds, safe at home in good old Arlington, Virginia.'

For a moment they stared at her blankly, as if they hadn't understood what she was saying. And then came the dawn. Utter relief flooded their faces and, when she saw it, she knew she had made the best, the only decision she could.

* * *

An hour later, true to their mother's word, they were on their way. Will sat in the back seat of the car, not relaxing a single muscle until he saw the high gabled roofs of Clairemont fade away in the distance. Then he leaned back and let out a long, low whistle. They were safe. They were finally out of there. They were going home.

Even though it had been his turn to sit in front, he had let Daisy sit there with their mother, mainly because he was so happy to be leaving that he couldn't bring himself to argue about anything.

Daisy chattered all the way down the highway, talking about stupid things like the craft fair they were having in July to raise some money for her Girl Scout troop, and about how she bet that Parch would be much happier to see her than to see Will because Will liked to tease. But her blabbing didn't bother him either. Instead of telling her to shut up, he let himself think about things back home. About Scull Pond, for instance.

Scull Pond was one of his favourite places to go in the summertime. Not too far from their house, it was full of minnows and frogs and stuff like that. It was the best spot to be on a hot day when there wasn't anything else to do. A great place just to mess around. He wished he could show it to Dickon. But maybe sometime he would. Maybe sometime Aunt Lenore would let Dickon come to Virginia for a visit.

Will felt a sudden pang of guilt. Neither he nor Daisy had had a chance to tell Dickon about what they had seen in the grass garden. After Mom made the plane reservations she hadn't let them out of her sight even for a minute. In less than an hour he and Daisy had gathered their stuff together (for the second time), had said goodbye to everyone (except

Aunt Amanda), and off they had gone. This time for real.

Oh well, he thought, watching the telephone poles flash by, I'll write him a letter and tell him it wasn't Aunt Amanda. But then on second thought maybe he shouldn't tell Dickon any such thing. Maybe Dickon would be happier if he thought there was still a chance to be rid of her.

Daisy's next question brought him back to the present. 'So, Mom, what did you have to talk to Dickon about?' she asked. 'How come you thought you had to tell him about your mother?'

'I don't suppose it will hurt now to tell you. Dickon is a sleepwalker. Just like me. And Aunt Lenore asked me to talk to him about it. Try to make him be careful. Not to leave his room at night unless he tells her.'

'Wow,' Daisy said. 'I didn't know that. Did you, Will?'

'Nope. But I don't blame him for not telling us. He's probably embarrassed about it.'

'Why would he be embarrassed?' Daisy asked. 'There's nothing embarrassing about it, is there, Mom?'

'Yes, there is, Daisy,' Gillian said. 'It's a terrible worry for the person afflicted and for the people who love him. Especially when you're a child and you don't mind your mother.' She sighed. 'I'm glad neither one of you was ever cursed.'

'I did it once,' Will said. 'Remember when I woke up in the bathroom?'

'You weren't sleepwalking, you cluck,' Daisy said, turning round to glare. 'You were just trying to see how many drops of water it would take to fill the bathtub, and you fell asleep.'

'I was not.'

'Were too.'

'Hush,' Gillian said.

And they did.

The miles rolled by, and the further away they got from Clairemont the more certain Will became that they were out of danger. His fear faded away and, by the time they reached the airport, Will was wondering if maybe he and Daisy had made too big a deal of it.

It wasn't until they were checking their baggage through that his fear came back with a vengeance. Something was wrong. Very wrong. And the reason he knew it was because the only bags checked through were his and Daisy's. 'Where's your stuff, Mom?' he asked, trying to sound normal.

She didn't answer. 'Come along, you two,' she said. 'Gate 6B. It's almost time.'

They sat down in the boarding area, side by side, and no one spoke but, when his mother reached over and took each of them by the hand, Will felt the sick lump of dread coming up in the back of his throat. His fears had been realized. Somehow he knew that their mother wasn't going home with them. 'You . . . you aren't coming to Virginia,' he said.

'No, sweetheart, I'm not. Not right now. You're going home alone. But Dad is going to meet your plane, so everything will be just fine. Not a thing to worry about.'

Hearing it said out loud almost made Will barf. Their mother had kept her promise. He and Daisy were leaving. But their mother was going back to Clairemont! She wasn't safe at all!

'Mom,' Daisy gasped, clutching her mother's hand

tight. 'You can't go back there. You just can't. It's dangerous. I told Will. I told him. You're in trouble, Mom. Not us. *You*.'

Gillian put her arm around Daisy. 'I'm perfectly safe, honey. Even if you don't believe it, I'm a big girl now, and there are things I have to do. Things I have to find out about. Besides,' she said, putting her other arm around Will, 'I have to explain to all of them why I've sent you home. I need to tell them the terrible things that have been happening at Clairemont. Especially your grandfather.' She looked hard from one to the other. 'But don't worry. I'm going to be very, very careful. And tomorrow morning your grandfather will drive me back to the airport and I'll catch the eleven o'clock flight home.' She smiled. 'And tomorrow night Dad is going to take us all out for a big fancy dinner.'

'Does Dad know? Does he know you're going back to Clairemont alone?' Will asked, his mouth bone-dry.

His mother nodded. 'He knows.'

'But does he know about *her*?' Will couldn't help it. His voice shook.

'No, he doesn't, Will,' his mother said firmly. 'Because I don't want him to worry about something he can't fix. There are some things at Clairemont I have to find out for myself. I know you and Daisy are frightened for me. But I don't want you to worry, either. Aunt Lenore will stay with me tonight. I won't walk in my sleep because she won't let me. And tomorrow I'll come home.' She turned her head away, but not quickly enough to hide her tears. 'There's your flight.' She stood up and kissed each of them. 'I know you're tough as nails. So keep being brave and I'll see you tomorrow. '

Sick with dread, Will got in the boarding line behind Daisy.

Their mother moved to one side and waved.

Will was breathing hard. What could he do? How could he help his mother? Desperate, he reached into his pocket. 'Here, Mom,' he said, motioning. 'Take this.'

She came over to him and took the small foil-wrapped package he was holding out to her.

'You keep it close to you all the time. It's my lucky charm. Maybe . . . maybe it will help.'

Daisy turned around, tears running down her cheeks. 'What's that?' she hiccoughed.

'It's the leaf from the Mother of Thousands plant,' Will said, numb.

Daisy gasped. 'You mean you picked one of Aunt Amanda's plants? Oh, Will, that makes things even worse.'

Will ignored her. 'It's a good-luck charm, Mom,' he said, blinking hard to keep his own tears from falling. 'I sure hope you don't need it, but if you do . . .'

'Thank you, Will,' his mother said. 'Now go.'

And with one last fearful glance back, they did.

Chapter Twenty-Three

Amanda's journal. Second entry. 2.30 in the afternoon. 18 June.

> To run over better waters the little vessel of my
> genius now hoists her sails, as she leaves behind her a
> sea so cruel. That is what Dante wrote in the four-
> teenth century but I'm sure he was thinking about me
> at the time. Amanda. A little vessel hoisting her sails.

Amanda leaned back in her chair and chewed
thoughtfully on the end of her pen, reviewing in her
mind the hideous events of the day. This morning
she hadn't stayed hidden behind her armoire for very
long. Reason and intelligence had reclaimed her
within minutes. Had driven away her mindless
terror. After all, if what she had seen at the end of
the hall was truly her dead mother, what of it? There
was nothing to fear from the dead. Amanda knew
from all of her reading that even if ghosts do exist,
they cannot harm the living. They can make every
foolish attempt to frighten, but they cannot cause
physical injury. And if her mother's intent had been
to frighten Amanda, well, she had been very much
off the mark. Amanda was no stranger to adversity.
She was a fighter. A survivor. And she knew from
experience that hiding behind one's armoire was
counter-productive.

With renewed confidence Amanda had crawled

211

out, her mind turned to more important things. Her 'rooms' needed her full attention and, casting all thoughts of her dead mother aside, she had hurried down to assess the condition of her Japanese miscanthus.

And to her shock she had discovered a *single pink tea rose* growing in its midst.

Seventeen years ago Amanda had destroyed every one of her mother's roses. How, she thought, glaring at it, had this one managed to survive? Had her mother's ghoulish spectre replanted it by some trick of sorcery?

At that possibility she had burst into a torrent of outrage, and had attacked the thorny weed with a vengeance, determined to dig every piece of its foul root from the soil. But her trowel had barely touched the earth when she sensed an intruder. *Someone was in her garden.*

She whirled round to see Gillian's grubby offspring crouching behind one of her prized boxwoods. Mortally wounded, her eyes rolled up and she flung her head back, the moan beginning low in her throat, coming out as a shrill, strangled cry. And then she attacked.

The miserable curs turned and ran, but Amanda had no intention of allowing them to escape. They needed to be punished, and she gave chase, growing more infuriated with each step. The vermin were *trampling her flowers*.

As fast as they ran, Amanda ran faster. She was almost upon them when, at the very last moment, like a fish on the end of a line, she was jerked back and spun around.

To face her father.

He stood there, at least ten feet tall, towering over

212

her, a vicious, vengeful look on his face, his hand clamped like an iron vice around her arm. 'Amanda!' he thundered. 'What in hell's name are you doing?'

Breathing hard, she pulled away and looked down at the ground, pretending that she hadn't heard.

'Amanda, you have gone too far.' A severe judgemental tone.

How *dare* he use that tone with me, she thought wildly. She looked up at him, imagining him dead.

'I think it's time I see about getting you some help.'

Help? Help? What for? She had plenty of servants here to do her bidding. Unless . . .

She stared. His eyes looked back at her. Two pieces of sharp, ice-blue glass.

'I don't need any help,' she said crisply.

'Go to your room, Amanda,' he ordered, pointing.

'But I have work to do.'

'Go to your room.'

Amanda pulled herself up to her full height, feeling the anger, feeling the hate. Her tooth began to throb. How *dare* he? How dare he order her? *Damn him.* Amanda never swore, never used profanity, but this was more than she could bear. *Damn him. Damn him to hell.*

Heart pounding, she rolled her slender fingers into mighty fists. She wasn't going to put up with this outrage one minute longer. All her life she had. No more. She took one step towards him, gathering all her strength to strike him across his ugly, hateful, arrogant face but, as her hand came up, another hand came out of nowhere and with surprising force pulled hers back.

Amanda whirled round to stare.

'Mandy,' Lenore said softly. 'How happy I am to have found you. Are we to ride together at three?'

'As usual, Lenore, you have arrived just in time.' The voice of the Father Almighty. 'I was about to take this young woman over my knee.' He glared at Amanda.

Amanda glared back, not flinching, not giving an inch.

'Take charge of her,' he snapped at Lenore. Then he turned to Amanda. 'You have gone too far this time, young lady,' he said coldly. 'Too far. I am going in right now to make some phone calls. Your reign here at Clairemont has come to an end.' With that, he disappeared.

Amanda felt defiled. *What was he suggesting?*

'Have you done something foolish?' Lenore asked quietly, taking Amanda by the hand, leading her back along the path towards the grass garden.

'Of course not,' Amanda shouted. 'I *never* do anything foolish.'

Now, as she sat at her writing-desk, she reaffirmed that sentiment aloud. 'I *never* do anything foolish.'

She put her pen to paper and continued with her entry.

> *To paraphrase T. S. Eliot, the time has come to prepare a face to meet the faces that I meet. The time has come to murder and create. To murder Gillian, to punish Father, and to create a new world order for Amanda Blackmarsh. For the following reasons: first, Gillian is a hateful, deceptive, promiscuous harlot. True, as a result of my courageous attack, she has taken her wretched children to the airport to fly away home. But she is coming back. And that will be her undoing. Tonight she will die. And then Clairemont will be mine. And Father will dance to the tune of its new mistress.*

*Goodbye, Gillian. The little vessel of my genius now
hoists her sails.*

Amanda set her pen back in its holder, closed her
journal, and placed it carefully in its proper spot in
the drawer.

She shivered. In spite of her resolve to see things
through to the end, the task ahead was precarious,
fraught with danger to her should her plot misfire.

She stood up, crossed to the window, and gazed
out over the velvety green lawns and the meticulously tended gardens. You are mine, she thought.
Every bit of you. Every square inch. And in response,
she felt the house fold itself around her and embrace
her. 'I will never let anyone else have you,' she
whispered. 'Once I have disposed of Gillian, no one
will.'

She turned away, crossed to her armoire, and
opened the panelled door. On the floor were four of
her small green enamelled compost pails. She made
certain the lids were on tight, then picked them up
along with her new pigskin gloves and her trans-
planting trowel. She crossed to the door but didn't
open it. She stood waiting for the grandfather clock
in the lower hall to strike three. It was another of
her habits. Never leave on an errand of importance
without waiting for the deep, resonant sound of the
clock. In this instance it served a dual purpose
because she knew that at three o'clock Dickon would
be at the stables, ready to ride off with his mother.

Again, thinking about that, Amanda felt the painful stab of abandonment. Not that Lenore hadn't
asked Amanda to join them. She had. But once
Amanda had regained her composure after her
father's vicious attack, she had replied that it

wouldn't suit. She knew that in order to be perfectly safe from detection she had to go to the wine cellar when Dickon was not around. But even as she had refused Lenore's invitation, Amanda had been surprised by her cousin's reaction. Normally Lenore would have begged her to come riding. But this time Lenore was almost indifferent. And oddly preoccupied. As if she had more important things to think about than Amanda. A *most* painful stab indeed.

Bong. Bong. Bong.

Amanda heard the clock strike the hour and she set off at a brisk pace, down the back stairs, through the kitchens, down another flight to the wine cellars. And beyond.

That evening Amanda did not join the family for dinner. She had an early supper in her room, keeping one eye on her Caesar's salad, the other on the four green pails lined up beside her door. She took her time eating, painstakingly chewing each mouthful of food twenty times. Another of her habits guaranteed to ensure good health.

After she was finished, she went into the bathroom and scrubbed her teeth, flossing meticulously. Another good habit. Then she washed her face and hands. Especially her hands. Even though she had worn garden gloves, one could never be too careful.

At precisely seven o'clock – again she waited for the sound of the grandfather clock – she slipped out into the hall and made her way to the landing. And there she hid in shadow until they all went into the dining-room. She didn't see them, but she heard them. Father with his low, malevolent drone; Gillian, just returned from her journey, speaking in her usual monosyllabic tone; Lenore, trying to seem interested.

216

And Robin. She didn't hear Robin speak but she knew he was there. Robin was always there at the dinner hour. Supervising. Manipulating. Criticizing. She didn't hear Dickon either, but then it was no longer of any concern to her where Dickon was. In a dark hole somewhere, she hoped. Maybe he had fallen from his horse and had broken his scrawny little neck.

When she was sure that they were all settled in their chairs around the dining-table, cramming their faces full of unhealthy food, she returned to her room. Bending over, curving her fingers around the wire handles of her pails, she lifted them gently, careful not to disturb their contents. 'When I finish with this,' she whispered, 'we will all be safe once again.'

The air stirred warmly around her, encouraging her, eager for her to be done with the deed.

Once out in the hall she didn't linger. On cat-like feet she went, full of excitement, full of confidence. From the east wing, where she made her home, she crossed through the gallery and into the west wing. Amanda's prison of old. The place where as a child she had been forced to sleep.

When she came to the door that used to be hers, she paused. For a moment she thought about going inside just to look around. But no. This was not the time. Now she had murder to commit.

She was almost at Gillian's room when to her chagrin she heard footsteps. Someone was coming. But even as she shrank back into the shadow of a doorway the footsteps faded away. 'Come along, my brave Amanda,' she said gently. 'Do what must be done.'

Quickly she took the last few steps to Gillian's

door, set her pails down, reached out and turned the knob. In the next instant she was inside the room, her precious cargo safely hidden behind one of the drapes, she safely hidden behind another.

Now all she had to do was wait. Wait for Gillian to finish dinner, wait for her to say goodnight, wait for her to come to her room, to wash up, to climb into bed, to fall asleep. It would be a long wait, Amanda knew. But it would be well worth it. Because when it was over, Gillian would die. A long and painful death.

She pulled her knees up to her chest and rested her head between them. It was her most effective waiting position. And her remembering position as well.

And she waited.

And she remembered.

When she was eight years old it rained all the time, or so it seemed to her now. And every day that it rained, Amanda's mother would send her here to play in Gillian's room with Gillian's dolls and games. Hideous dolls. Stupid games. Amanda hadn't ever wanted to come into this room. She *never* wanted to play with her sister. And so as soon as their mother left them alone, Amanda would go behind the drapes and stay there, watching Gillian play by herself.

And Amanda would think about Gillian being dead.

Now, almost twenty years later, here she was again. Hiding behind the drapes in Gillian's room. Thinking about Gillian being dead. Only this time it was really going to happen.

In her mind she reviewed again all the things she had read about spiders. She hadn't read about them because she liked the creatures. On the contrary.

218

They repelled her. But she knew that in this instance they might serve a useful purpose. So this morning, immediately after she had seen the spider in the corner of the upper hall, she went down to the library and spent one full hour researching the subject. To determine which of Dickon's species, if any, might be dangerous. And she was elated to find that some were. Dickon's favourites, as a matter of fact. The *Lycosa raptoria* and the *Latrodectus*.

Latrodectus. Such a magnificent name. *Latrodectus*. The black widow. The colour of coal with a red x-shaped marking on its underside.

At first Amanda was intrigued by what she read. What finer way to commit murder than to use the powerful hand of Nature. But as she read further she discovered a disturbing fact. The single bite of the black widow is toxic but rarely fatal. Toxic but rarely fatal. Those words had posed a true dilemma for Amanda. But true to her own genius, she had worked it out. A single bite might not be fatal, but in volume the neurotoxin was deadly. And dear Dickon had eleven of the widows. And what if a number of *Lycosa raptoria*, the wolf spiders, were thrown in for good measure? What would happen then?

Well, we'll see, won't we, she said to herself.

She smiled. She could almost hear them scurrying around in their green prisons, trying desperately to find a way out.

But they wouldn't. Not until that final moment when Amanda lifted the lids and spilled them – eleven black widows and seven wolf spiders – onto Gillian's spread, onto her pillow, onto her *face*.

And patiently, Amanda waited.

Chapter Twenty-Four

It was raining.

Will sat in the back seat of the car right next to Daisy. He could feel her quaking and he knew why. Because he was quaking himself.

'How long do you think it'll take?' she whispered.

'A couple of hours.' Will turned his head to stare out of the window, but through the grey mist there wasn't much he could see. He leaned his head back against the seat and closed his eyes. He was frightened. Had they made a stupid mistake? If this were a movie they were watching would they be saying, 'Those dumb shits. What are they doing? Don't they know they're only getting deeper into trouble?'

But then he thought about his mother, whom he loved more than anyone else in the world, and he knew that he and Daisy had done the right thing.

How weird that only one hour ago they were ready to board a flight that would have taken them safely home to Arlington. And now . . .

'I'm scared,' Daisy whispered.

'Me too.' He went back to his private thoughts, remembering what had happened. After he and Daisy left Mom, they gave their boarding passes to the stewardess and went into the tunnel. They were almost at the end, almost on the aeroplane, when simultaneously they both froze in their tracks, both thinking exactly the same thing.

'She's going to get killed,' Daisy choked, her face like chalk. It was the same look she'd had on her face this morning when they were getting ready to leave, when she'd told him that they were lucky that their mother was still alive. That they were getting away from Clairemont just in time.

Without a word he grabbed Daisy's hand and they turned and ran back into the boarding area.

Mom was nowhere in sight.

'Come on. We have to catch her,' Will said and, running full-steam, they followed the signs to the main terminal.

'Do you remember where she parked?' Daisy panted.

'I think so. By the fire hydrant.'

They flew through the terminal, down the escalator, out through the door.

Lines of cars were waiting in the pick-up area, and they squeezed their way between the bumpers and darted across the service road into the parking lot. And there they came to a screeching halt, trying to catch their breaths, trying to spot their mother, but the rain was pouring down on their heads, driving hard into their faces, making it impossible to see.

'She's gone,' Daisy wailed. 'And even if she's not, it doesn't matter because we'll never find her.'

'Come on, Daisy,' Will said. 'Don't freak out, for Crissake. All we have to do is to go back inside and call Dad. He'll tell us what to do.' Will's stomach was tied in a tight knot, but he managed to keep control. There were people around and the last thing he wanted to do was to burst out crying right in front of them.

Daisy took a big gulp of air, then nodded. 'Okay. We'll call Dad.'

221

Once inside, they found a credit-card phone, and Will punched in the numbers his mother had made him memorize. To his great relief, after only two rings he heard his father's voice.

'You're *what*?' Max said.

'We're at the airport in Windsor Locks but we didn't get on the plane because we didn't want to leave Mom because she shouldn't go back to Clairemont alone and we tried to catch her but we can't so now what do we do?'

'Where's Daisy?'

'Right here.'

'Okay.' There was a pause and some static. 'Will?'

'Yeah?'

'Do you guys have any money?'

'I have six dollars.' He turned to Daisy. 'Got any money?'

She shook her head. 'It's in my duffel bag.'

'Daisy doesn't have any.'

'Well, never mind,' Max said. 'Where are you now? Exactly.'

Will looked around. 'We're across from the USAir ticket counters.'

'Okay. You stay *right there*. Don't move an inch. I'm going to call the cab service at the airport. They'll take you back to Clairemont. Don't worry about the money. I'll take care of it. You just stay right where you are until someone comes for you. Understand?'

Will felt the tight, sick knot in his stomach get tighter. 'Okay, Dad.'

'That was nutty of you two not to get on the plane.'

Silence.

'Your mother didn't tell me, but I think there's trouble at Clairemont.' Now his father's voice was angry. 'There is, isn't there?'

Silence.

'Will, I asked you a question.'

'I think you should come up here, Dad,' Will said.

Another long pause.

'You're right, Will. You are absolutely right. So don't you worry. I'll be there tonight. In the meantime, you do as I say. Wait for the cab driver. Go back to Clairemont. Don't let your mother out of your sight until I get there. Okay?'

'Okay, Dad.'

'Let me talk to Daisy.'

Will didn't hear what he said, but he did see Daisy manage a sickly smile. It wasn't the best smile Will had ever seen, but it was better than nothing.

As they curved along the drive, Daisy stared. She couldn't believe how different everything seemed. So scary now. So ominous. So changed after only three days. She remembered her first impression. The tall, stately trees on both sides, making a shady archway. The vast expanse of new-mown grass which seemed to go on forever, dotted with stone walls and flowering shrubs and winding paths. And the house. Like a castle in a fairy tale. Silvery stone and gabled roofs and high, high chimneys.

Now everything was shrouded in a dusky grey drizzle. But unfortunately it wasn't grey enough to hide the house. An enchanted castle no longer, now it was a sinister granite fortress, looming over them, hiding something terrifying behind its thick walls. And seeing it, Daisy gasped.

Beside her, Will gasped too. 'Geez us,' he breathed.

The cab pulled up and stopped at the foot of the wide stone stairway. 'Here we are,' the driver said. 'Clairemont. It was tough to find but we made it.'

Will opened the door and climbed out.

Daisy followed.

It had stopped raining but it was cold and damp, and she shuddered.

'Thanks,' Will said to the driver.

'No problem. Hope you kids catch up with your Mom.'

'Yeah,' Will mumbled.

The cab rolled away.

Will and Daisy stood at the foot of the stairs, gathering their courage. 'I don't believe this is happening,' Daisy whispered.

'Well, it is. So let's go.'

White-faced, they started up the steps, one at a time, praying that their mother was there, praying that she would rush out to meet them, but there was no sign of her.

They were almost in the front garden when all at once they heard their names being whispered. 'Will. Daisy. Pssst. Over here.'

Through the gloom they saw Dickon standing just inside the walled garden, motioning frantically for them to come.

Daisy didn't feel any safer but, seeing her cousin, she felt a little less hysterical. Somehow she managed to put on a brave face.

'What's going on?' Dickon asked, full of excitement. 'How come you're back?' He didn't wait for an answer. 'Come on. I've got something to show you that you won't believe.'

'Is our mother here?' Daisy asked.

'Yes. They're all in at dinner,' Dickon said impatiently. 'Come on.'

'Shouldn't we tell her we're here?'

'If you do, you'll never get to see what I found,'

Dickon said. 'That's for certain.'

Will and Daisy looked at each other, unsure, then Will said, 'Let's go with Dickon, Daisy. It'll only take a few minutes. Then we'll find Mom. What harm can it do?'

Daisy frowned, but she made no vocal protest, and reluctantly they followed Dickon through a side entrance. 'How d'you know we were coming?' Will asked.

'Your father called. Your mother wasn't back yet so he talked to my mother. And I almost freaked out when I heard what you had done. It took some guts.'

'Yeah,' Will said. 'Guts.'

With an uneasy heart Daisy hurried up the back stairs after the boys. She was sort of curious to see what Dickon had to show them. But underneath . . .

Underneath she was reminded of another time she had felt like this. Scared and curious all at the same time. They had gone to Vermont to visit some friends of Dad's, and had gone ice-skating on a large pond behind the house. It was the first time she had ever been skating and she had been so excited. But at the same time she had been really scared. Because she knew that underneath the silvery frozen layer of ice lay a deep, dark, murky pool of black water. Water that would drown her if she fell in.

Please God, she prayed, don't let the ice break. Please.

Once they were inside Dickon's room, he closed the door quickly and crossed to his bed. He stooped down and pulled something out from under it and held it up so they could see.

Daisy stared. It looked like a mutilated portrait of her own mother!

'It's your grandmother,' Dickon said, laying it

down on the floor. 'And just look at what Aunt Amanda has done to it.'

Daisy and Will knelt beside him. All over the canvas were small cuts, and in most places the paint had been flecked off. The only thing that remained was the face. A sweet, gentle face that looked exactly like their mother's.

'Is this the person you saw last night in the meadow?' Dickon asked. 'Is it?'

Will shook his head. 'I never really saw her face. Only her hands.' He turned to Daisy. 'Do you think it looks like her?'

Daisy frowned. 'I never saw her face either.' Slowly, sadly, she ran her finger over the surface of the painting, feeling the cuts. 'Aunt Amanda must have really hated our grandmother to do this to her picture.'

'Aunt Amanda hates everyone,' Dickon said. 'Except my mother, that is.'

'Where d'you find it?' Will asked.

'In the Play House. It's Aunt Amanda's private place and I'm never allowed to go near it. But today I decided I would anyway. I was sure that if she was hiding something she would hide it there. Like a mask. Or fake hands.'

'The one we saw wasn't Aunt Amanda, Dickon,' Daisy said. And then she told Dickon about what had happened after lunch, in the grass garden.

'That's why Mom sent us home,' Will said. 'But we didn't want to leave her here alone. So we came back.' His voice trailed off.

White-faced, Dickon sat back on his heels. 'What in hell is going on here, I'd like to know? Who's doing this?'

Daisy took a deliberate breath. 'I think a ghost is

haunting us.' She looked from Dickon to Will and back, but she saw no sign of a snicker. No sign of disbelief. Only dread.

'Your grandmother's ghost,' Dickon echoed. 'But why is she after you?'

'She wants us to leave Clairemont, that's for sure,' Will said firmly. 'Our grandfather may have forgiven Mom, but *she* hasn't.'

And as if someone had opened a freezer door, all at once the room grew bitter-cold. A piercing bitter cold. And underneath it there was an odour. Like flowers.

Dickon jumped up and closed the window, but it didn't help.

Daisy looked at Will. He was blowing on his hands to try to warm them. 'What is it?' she whispered, not daring to look behind her.

But before either of the boys could think to answer, the sudden wave of cold had disappeared. The room was warm again.

Daisy felt as if something from a graveyard had just passed through, and she stared at the other two, dazed.

'It must have been the wind,' Dickon said, but he didn't sound at all convinced.

'So . . . so what do we do now?' Will stammered.

'Let's go find Mom!' Daisy exploded, jumping up, heading for the door.

Will and Dickon were right behind her.

Chapter Twenty-Five

Dinner at Clairemont that evening was an awkward affair with little said, each of them lost in thought. As for Gillian, she was a nervous wreck. Driving back from the airport, knowing that her children were safely away, she had expected to feel relieved. Instead she had been haunted by an inescapable feeling of dread. She couldn't stop thinking about the ghoulish creature who had terrorized her children. And the more she thought about it, the more she wondered about Robin. Could it be that he was responsible? Did he want Clairemont that badly? It was true that if she had left Clairemont in despair, if she had never come back again, she would have sold Clairemont to him in an instant. And, with the appearance of the ghoulish spectre, that had almost happened. Had Robin engineered the whole eerie business to suit his own purpose?

Or was someone, *something* else to blame?

And as hard as she tried to deny the existence of a something else, she was deeply afraid.

To add to her anxiety, she had no sooner walked into the house than Lenore came rushing down the stairs. 'Daisy and Will are on their way back,' Lenore said, clearly upset.

'I know.'

'Not on their way back to Virginia, Gillian.' Lenore's face was ashen. 'They're coming back *here*.

228

To Clairemont.' And then she told Gillian about Max's phone call. 'You ought to call him back right away. Poor Max. As if things aren't worrisome enough, he seems to think you need him, and even though you're leaving first thing in the morning he's planning to drive up tonight. So unnecessary.' She flushed. 'I don't know why I should presume to judge. Of course Max should come if you think he should. In any case, he wanted you to phone.'

Gillian was thunderstruck by the news. Daisy and Will had not boarded the plane. Her two frightened children were *coming back to Clairemont*.

She made her way to the phone and called Max.

'They're fine,' Max said, reassuring her. 'I hired a cab and they're on their way. And so am I.'

As stunned as she was, she managed to persuade him not to. Lenore was right. There was absolutely no need, she insisted. She would keep the children under a constant watch until 8.30 in the morning, when they would all leave Clairemont together and be home by noon.

'Gilly, are you sure you're okay?'

'I'm a basket case. But whether you're here or not, I'll still be a basket case, so please, Max, stay home. I intend to take care of things here all by myself. It's important to me. Can you understand?'

'I suppose.'

'So. That's that. You finish up your work. And tomorrow night we'll celebrate.'

Now, as she sat beside her father at the dinner table, stirring her coffee, she tried to collect her thoughts, tried to decide how to begin to ask the questions that had been plaguing her for hours. But before she had a chance, her father asked a question of his own. 'I

229

know you're planning to leave in the morning, Gillian, but must you? Can't I persuade you to stay a little while longer? So we can spend some time together?'

'I wish I could,' Gillian said softly, 'but I can't.'

'Why not?'

'I'm afraid,' she said bluntly.

'Afraid? Of what?'

She managed a weak smile. 'Things that go bump in the night, I suppose. Anyway, even as we speak my children are on their way back to Clairemont and tomorrow morning I have to take them home.'

Her father regarded her with deep concern. 'Gillian, I need to know. Did you send my grandchildren back to Virginia because Amanda chased them out of her garden? Are you afraid of Amanda?'

Gillian was caught off balance. How had her father known about that?

'I saw her,' he said angrily. 'Hounding those poor children like some kind of wild dog.' He turned to Robin. 'I called Dick Wittaker this afternoon. I made an appointment with him for tomorrow.'

'At his office?'

'No. In Hartford. At the Institute. We all know he's tops in his field and maybe he can come up with some suggestions. Something *must* be done. Amanda cannot go on in her usual fashion. At the very least I think she should be hospitalized for a full psychiatric evaluation. And if Wittaker agrees, I'll take steps to have a conservator appointed, should something happen to me.'

'I wish you'd let me talk to her first,' Lenore said quietly. 'We all know how fiercely protective she is of her privacy. I'm sure I can convince her that by frightening Gillian's children she's only making matters worse for herself.'

'You have done enough talking to Amanda to last a lifetime,' William Blackmarsh snapped. 'If it hadn't been for your eternal defending of her, Lenore, had you not continued to shield her every step of the way, she would have been hospitalized years ago.'

Lenore turned pale.

'In my wife's defence,' Robin cut in sharply, 'she's the only one who's ever given a damn what happens to Amanda. And that includes Gillian.'

His father drew back, eyes narrowing. 'Why do you presume to criticize Gillian, Robin, when you know the blame is not hers? The blame is mine.'

Robin did not respond, and after a moment William continued. 'I have one concern right now. After my death, Clairemont will belong to Gillian, and if she is to feel comfortable using the place, even if only as a summer retreat, Amanda must be well established elsewhere. Claire didn't want Amanda and Gillian bound together, nor do I.'

Gillian sat up very straight in her chair. This was not what she wanted to talk about. Clearly her father wasn't aware of the other things that had happened to Daisy and Will. 'I agree that my sister needs help,' she said. 'And I'll do whatever you want me to do to make things right. But Amanda isn't the only one at Clairemont who has terrorized my children.'

Her father stared. 'What are you telling me, Gillian?' he asked, his voice dangerously low. 'Has something else happened here that I don't know about?'

'Yes.' Gillian turned to Robin. 'Do you know what I'm talking about?'

Her brother returned the look without blinking. 'No, I don't.'

'My children have seen a woman here at Clairemont,' she replied as calmly as she could. 'A woman with . . . with crushed, bloody hands.' And she repeated what Will and Daisy had told her, from beginning to end.

A stunned silence followed. And then Robin let out a crow of laughter. 'Good God,' he chortled. 'Is there no end to Amanda's perverted genius?'

'The person they saw wasn't Amanda,' Gillian insisted.

'I'm afraid you don't know your sister,' her father said. 'This would not be the first time we've been witness to one of her fits of lunacy. Her mad exploits in this household are legion.'

'My children saw Amanda in the garden today,' Gillian said. 'But she wasn't alone. The other woman was with her.'

Robin shrugged. 'Our Amanda is quite capable of engineering almost anything,' he said dryly. 'It is well within the realm of possibility to assume that she has an accomplice. Someone she has hired to frighten you all, to drive you away. She hates you, you know.'

Gillian was startled. Not because she didn't know how Amanda felt about her. She had always known. But she had never thought that her sister's dislike was so intense. Was Amanda capable of doing what Robin was suggesting? Was the real tormentor Amanda after all? 'But why?' she said, almost to herself.

'She loves her privacy. She hates intrusion of any kind,' Lenore said quietly. 'Although I cannot imagine that anyone here at Clairemont would be willing to help her.' With a nervous glance at William Black-marsh, she continued. 'But I can ask. Mandy will tell me if I ask.'

There was a long pause.

'In any case,' Robin said, 'I don't think Amanda should be forcibly removed from Clairemont. After all, this is her home. I'm sure Gillian would never want to send her away.'

William Blackmarsh leaned back in his chair. 'Well, well, well,' he said, a frozen smile on his face. 'So Robin has come to his youngest sister's defence. Tell me, Robin, why this sudden solicitude? It wouldn't have anything to do with Claire's will, would it? You wouldn't be thinking that, if Amanda stays here, Gillian will have no choice but to sell Clairemont to you? Would you?'

'If that would suit Gillian,' Robin replied smoothly, 'I wouldn't be averse to such a plan.'

'Well, I'll be damned,' his father said. 'The plot thickens.' His eyes narrowed. 'You haven't discussed this with Amanda, by any chance? I know that nothing would suit her better than if Gillian were to decide she doesn't want to come to Clairemont ever again. But what about you?'

'I love Clairemont,' Robin said in the same level tone. 'I always have. But whatever Gillian decides to do with the place is up to her. And whatever Amanda has been up to has nothing to do with me.'

'I see,' his father said, looking suddenly old, exhausted. 'So it's up to me to find out who's been doing this. And I will. Tomorrow I'll have the answers, I promise you. And then I'll speak to my attorney. Then I'll speak to Amanda. And then I'll take her to see the good doctor.' He turned to Gillian, who was listening intently. 'In the meantime, my

dear,' he said gently, 'I don't think you have anything more to worry about. Whoever has been
responsible for this will be found. There will be no
further trouble.' He gave Robin a dark look, then
turned back to smile pleadingly at Gillian. 'So now
will you consider staying? For a few days at least? I'll
talk to my grandchildren. Make them feel safe. Give
them the moon if they like. What about it?'

'I don't know, Father,' Gillian said miserably.
'Maybe if Lenore can find out . . .' She turned in her
cousin's direction. 'Lenore?'

She saw Lenore open her mouth to answer, but no
words came out, and in the sudden hush Gillian
heard a whisper from somewhere far, far away. So
faint a sound – barely audible – but she heard it
nonetheless.

*Footfalls echo in the memory/Down the passage which
we did not take.*

And the air in the room grew suddenly cold. A
deep, piercing cold which froze Gillian's breath as
she exhaled. She looked around the table and saw
the same stunned, questioning expression on all their
faces.

And then from outside the closed door came the
most anguished sound. A thin, desolate, high-
pitched keening, punctuated by a frenzied pounding
on the walls, as if in the depth of despair someone
were trying to break through into the dining-room.

Out of the corner of her eye Gillian saw her father
start to get up, then stop mid-way, half sitting, half
standing, staring towards the door.

'What the hell . . . ?' Robin said.

And then silence.

Shattered by the sound of footsteps running.

234

The door flew open.

And Will, Daisy and Dickon raced into the room.

There had been no explanation for the sound they had all heard except to blame Amanda. And yet the whole episode had been so terrifying, so other-worldly, that it was hard to imagine how Amanda could have done it.

But what other explanation was there?

Gillian's father had left the dining-room in an icy rage, looking for Amanda, with Lenore and Dickon right behind. Robin had remained where he was, stiff, his face a blank, expressionless. And forcing herself to keep calm, Gillian had taken her children into the kitchen to get them something to eat.

She sat at the kitchen table watching over them, determined not to let them out of her sight. Not for one minute.

'Is Dad on his way?' Daisy asked, picking at her pasta.

'No.'

Will looked up, startled. 'How come?'

'There wasn't any reason, Will,' she said gently. 'I was able to get you tickets on the eleven o'clock flight tomorrow morning, so we will all have to leave Clairemont by 8.30. Honest. All three of us. Cross my heart.'

'So Grandfather hasn't persuaded you to stay?'

'No. I think it's best if we all leave in the morning.'

In spite of her reassurances, Will lost interest in his food, rearranging the pasta on his plate. 'So. Do we sleep in our old rooms tonight?'

Gillian shook her head. 'You will both sleep with me in my room.' She paused. 'And Aunt Lenore will be there too, for extra protection. Just in case.'

Daisy held her breath. 'Did you tell them what happened to us? About the ghost?'

'I did.'

'Everything?'

'Everything.'

'And did they believe you?'

'They did.'

'But do they think she's a ghost?' Will cut in.

'No. Your uncle thinks Aunt Amanda hired someone to frighten us away. And I think your grandfather agrees.'

Daisy and Will exchanged glances. 'We never even thought about that,' Will said.

'If that ghost is a real person,' Daisy said, shivering, 'she's a really good actress.'

She certainly is, Gillian thought. A genius when it comes to special effects.

There was a long pause while they all thought it over.

'So what's going to happen now?' Will asked.

'Aunt Amanda is very sick. Your grandfather is going to take her to get psychiatric help.'

'You mean she's leaving Clairemont?'

Gillian nodded. 'At least for a while.'

'Wow,' Daisy said. 'Dickon's going to be thrilled.'

At precisely nine o'clock – Amanda knew because she heard the clock strike the hour – the door opened and Gillian came into the room, turning on lights as she went. Not that Amanda saw her. She heard her. The sound of footsteps crossing the carpet, the rustle of clothes, the opening and closing of drawers. And then Gillian disappeared into the bathroom, closing the door behind her.

Breathless, Amanda peeped out.

The room was empty, but the door to the hall still stood open.

Amanda heard the splash of running water. Gillian is brushing her teeth, she thought, pulling back into her hiding-place. Any minute now she'll come out of the bathroom and get into bed.

And she'll fall asleep.

And my spiders will find her. And bite her.

And I'll watch while she dies.

Amanda hugged herself tight.

The next thing she heard was the sound of the hall door closing, and for a moment she was confused. Had Gillian come out of the bathroom so quietly that Amanda hadn't heard? And then she heard the scuffing of feet moving across the floor. More than one pair? And then the swish of bed covers. Someone was turning down Gillian's bed. Was it one of the maids?

And from across the room she heard the sound of low, muffled voices.

Amanda moved her head just enough so she could see. And to her supreme shock she saw *Lenore*. Lenore in her night-clothes, sitting on the edge of Gillian's bed!

Without daring to turn her head another inch for fear of discovery, Amanda moved only her eyes. And there, on the other side of the room, she saw *Gillian's children*, spreading their sleeping-bags out on the carpet.

The bathroom door opened and Gillian came out. 'Did you find Amanda, Lenore?' she asked anxiously.

Lenore was looking for her?

'No. She has hidden herself away, I'm afraid. But don't worry. I'll find her. In the meantime, shall I get the children some of Dickon's night-clothes?'

'No,' Gillian said. 'They're fine as they are. They can change tomorrow when we get home.'

And then, with Gillian's next question, the bomb inside Amanda's head exploded. 'Lenore, are you sure you don't mind staying with us tonight?'

'Of course I don't. After what happened with your sleepwalking last night, and after what you told us about Daisy and Will, I don't blame you a bit for wanting company. Not to mention our own ghastly experience at dinner.'

What Gillian said next, Amanda didn't know. *Couldn't know*. Their voices had become disembodied. Sounds among sounds. The only thing she understood was that Gillian's children were back and Lenore was staying in this room with them! Lenore was sleeping here for the night! The one person Amanda loved. The one person Amanda could never imagine hurting.

Gillian had escaped. There would be no death in this room tonight.

And, knowing it, there rose in Amanda's soul a devastation so vast, so complete, that there was nothing left of her. All she could see before her eyes was a dark, wretched, yawning hole of black despair. And she slid towards it, helpless, hopeless, surrendering, wanting only one thing now.

To die herself.

Amanda stayed hidden behind the drapes, curled up in a tight pre-natal ball, stuporous, eyes open wide, seeing nothing, hearing nothing. She stayed that way for a long, long time.

How she managed to carry herself and her deadly cargo out of Gillian's room and back along the dark, silent corridors, she didn't know.

Once inside her own bedroom, she dropped the green enamelled pails on the floor with a thud, stumbling over them, not knowing, *not caring* if the lids were on or off. What possible difference could it make now?

With her last ounce of strength, she crawled into bed. Gripped by the deepest, most suffocating depression, she could barely wheeze out a breath. She was beaten. Destroyed. A broken mind in a broken body.

Stupefied, she sank into the grey mist of oblivion.

Chapter Twenty-Six

In spite of his determination not to close his eyes, not to go to sleep, Will slept. And when he woke up, he woke up so abruptly that he wasn't sure he had been asleep at all. But he could see light streaming in through the window. And then his mother shook him gently. 'Wake up, Will. It's 7.30. Aunt Lenore has gone to see about breakfast and I'm going to take a shower. And in one hour we're off. Grandfather is going to take us to the airport.'

Will watched her disappear into the bathroom. Then he rolled over to see if Daisy was awake.

'What're you looking at?' she said, scowling. She sounded okay but he knew she was nervous.

'You, pea-brain.'

She sat up with a jerk. 'Holy cow, Will. It's morning and we're still alive. And we're leaving!'

'Yep.' He still felt the gnawing lump of fear in his stomach, but he pushed it back. Fully clothed, he climbed out of his sleeping-bag and grabbed his sneakers. 'At least we don't have to get dressed.'

Daisy nodded. 'All I have to do is brush my teeth.'

'I wonder if Aunt Lenore has found Aunt Amanda,' Will said, trying to tie his laces. He was having a tough time because for some reason his fingers were icy-cold, stiff.

'I bet Grandfather is going to give her a whipping for all the trouble she's caused.'

'No way. She's going off to the nut-house.' Finally managing a knot, Will turned his attention to his sleeping-bag, zipping the zipper, rolling it up as tightly as he could.

'I wonder,' Daisy mumbled.

'Wonder what?'

'I wonder if it really was all Aunt Amanda's doing. I mean, did that person behind her in the garden look like her friend?'

Will shook his head. 'I don't think Aunt Amanda even knew she was there.'

'So maybe she's going to take the blame for something she doesn't know anything about.'

Will shrugged. He didn't want to discuss it. Every time they did, it seemed like it brought them bad luck.

'Well?'

'Who cares?' he said sharply. 'I certainly don't. In a little while we'll be out of here. That's all I care about.' He sat down on the edge of the sofa. 'I wish Mom would get out of the bathroom. I have to go.'

'If you're so brave all of a sudden, why don't you just go down the hall to one of the other bathrooms?'

'I will if she doesn't hurry up.'

'Oh, yeah, I bet.' Daisy crawled out of her sleeping-bag, stood up, and went over to the window. 'Holy cow,' she said, pointing. 'That's right where we saw Aunt Amanda yesterday. Trying to dig out that rose-bush. Remember? Come on over here and look.'

Will had no intention of looking at anything. He stayed right where he was.

'Gillian?' A voice outside the door and then a faint knock.

Startled, Daisy jerked around. 'Should we answer it?'

241

'Who is it?' Will said loudly.

'Aunt Lenore.'

'Come on in,' Will said.

She stepped into the room, pale as a ghost. 'Where is your mother?'

'In the shower.'

She began to pace back and forth like a nervous cat.

'Is something wrong?' Daisy asked, throwing an anxious glance in Will's direction.

'I need to speak to your mother,' Aunt Lenore said. She stepped over to the bathroom door and knocked. 'Gillian?'

'I'll be out in a minute.'

Aunt Lenore began to pace again.

Geez us, Will thought. Oh, geez-us-kee-riste. Sometimes you knew when things were going to go bad. Sometimes you just knew. And now, looking at Aunt Lenore, so white-faced, so upset, he just knew.

The bathroom door opened and his mother came out. 'We're all ready,' she said smiling. 'Ready . . .' She stopped mid-sentence. 'Lenore? What is it?'

Aunt Lenore was trembling now. 'It's your father, Gillian. He's . . . he's dreadfully ill. He woke up a half-hour ago with sharp abdominal pains. Awful nausea. And since then he's been drifting in and out of consciousness.' She put her hand on the bed-post to steady herself. 'We've just now called Harris. His doctor. And he's on his way.'

'Oh, sweet God,' Gillian breathed. 'He's not having a heart attack, is he?'

'I don't think so. But you'd better come with me. As soon as he's dressed Dickon will be along to take charge of the children.' She turned to Will, who sat frozen where he was. 'You two stay right here until Dickon comes.'

'I'll be right back,' Gillian said. Then she turned and followed Aunt Lenore out of the room.

Disappointed was not the word for what Will felt. He was panic-stricken. Their grandfather was sick. Now he wouldn't be able to take them to the airport. But surely, Will thought, trying to calm himself, someone else would. One of the servants. Or maybe Aunt Lenore.

'Maybe he's so sick that Mom won't want to leave,' he heard Daisy whisper.

'Oh, shit,' Will groaned. The fear he had managed to hold back came rushing up in his throat, and for a minute he thought he was going to throw up. He sank back on the sofa, shuddering.

Daisy came across the room and sat down next to him as close as she could get. 'We're trapped, Will,' she said in a small, desperate voice. 'Trapped.'

Will didn't answer. He couldn't. He knew his sister was right.

Her father's room was dimly lit, the blinds still drawn. There was a faint odour of disinfectant in the air which couldn't cover the stench of vomit. Her father lay prone, barely breathing, his skin a ghastly bluish-grey.

Barely breathing herself, Gillian stood beside the bed, with Lenore on one side, Robin on the other. 'Christ,' Robin said, 'where the hell is Harris?' And at that moment the door opened and the doctor came in.

They were asked to wait outside.

Don't let him die, Gillian thought, leaning against

243

the wall, dazed. Please God, don't let him die. Not now.

'I think I'd better find Amanda,' Lenore said quietly. 'She needs to know.'

Numb, Gillian nodded.

'And you ought to call Max,' Lenore added, touching Gillian gently on the arm. 'Tell him you won't be on that flight. Maybe you can arrange for something a little later.' She paused. 'Once we know.'

'Go find Amanda,' Robin said sharply. 'We have enough to worry about right now without you adding to it.'

'Of course, you're right,' Lenore said. And she was gone.

Robin took Gillian by the arm and sat her down on the settee across from her father's door, then turned away and began to pace, his face flushed, his fists clenched.

And Gillian sat staring at the closed door.

Waiting.

Amanda is dead, finally at peace in a vast empty sky where no one else exists. She let the spiders loose and now her body lies stiff, lifeless, her breath gone, her eyes sightless. But her spirit is free. She is like a sea creature that has broken away from its shell, leaving it behind empty on the sand. And from somewhere high above her bed, she watches the pathetic soulless corpse as it lies waiting to be discovered.

And soon tears will flow from every eye. And all of them will suffer. Father. Lenore. Robin. Gillian. Knowing in a flash of blinding revelation how much pain they have caused her. How much anguish. And

244

they will weep and lament and beg her to come back. Beg for her forgiveness.

But it is too late.

Too late.

Amanda is dead.

'Amanda?'

She opened her eyes wide. *But how could she?* Her eyes were lifeless. And yet she opened them all the same, to see Lenore standing by her bed.

'Amanda, wake up.' The voice was insistent. The face was . . . angry? Was the face angry?

Amanda stared.

'You must get up at once, Amanda.'

Amanda? She was no longer Mandy?

'Something terrible has happened. Your father is deathly ill.'

'I am the one who is deathly ill,' Amanda rasped. 'No. More than that. I have been careless. I have killed myself. I am dead.'

'You are no such thing. I would never allow it.' Harsh. Impatient. 'Now sit up and listen to me. You must do as I say.'

I must? I must do as you say? Nonsense. But Amanda sat up nevertheless. Something in Lenore's tone alarmed her. But what? And what was this thing she had said about Father?

'Doctor Harris is with him now,' Lenore said. 'I want you to get dressed and come with me at once.'

Amanda couldn't believe her ears. 'Father is ill?'

Lenore nodded.

'Is he dying?' She couldn't help herself. Her voice shook with excitement.

'We don't know, Amanda.' Again, that angry tone.

'I'll get dressed.' Amanda smiled and swung her

245

legs out over the edge of the bed.

'Before you do that, there's something I must say to you. I want you to listen. Don't speak. Don't argue. Just listen. I don't know what you've been up to with Gillian's children. And I don't know what you were doing last night with that dreadful performance. But it *must* stop. Do you understand, Amanda? I cannot save you forever. You must promise me that after you've seen your father you'll come back here to your room and stay here until Gillian has left. No matter how long it may take. *Do you understand?*'

Amanda felt her heart stop. Normally she would never have tolerated such a tongue-lashing. Not even from Lenore. But something Lenore had said frightened Amanda. What had she meant by 'dreadful performance'? Had Lenore seen her last night in Gillian's room? Was that why she was angry? Did she know what Amanda had planned to do? 'I'm sure I don't know what you mean,' was all she could manage to say.

'I'm sure you *do*.' Lenore took one step backward. 'But enough has been said for now. I'm certain you won't disappoint me. I'll be back in a few minutes to take you to see your father.' And so saying, she turned and left the room.

Amanda sat on the edge of her bed, her mind in utter turmoil, tossed around as if caught up in the centre of a monstrous wind-storm. First of all, what had Lenore seen? And second, what about Father? Could it be that he was *dying*? But even if that was true, Amanda had no reason to rejoice. She still wasn't free of Gillian. She had been so close last night to killing her, but instead she had only ended up killing herself.

Hadn't she?

Amanda's eyes widened and she stared down at her hands, her legs, her feet. She raised them up and wiggled her toes. Everything was still in fine working order, still attached to her body, still warm. Still alive. But how? In disbelief her eyes scanned the room.

The spiders were nowhere to be seen.

And where were her four green enamelled compost pails?

Clearly they had all vanished.

But how?

And even more unnerving, *where were they now*?

Chapter Twenty-Seven

It seemed to Daisy that there were two worlds. In one, you were safe and everything was normal and you watched television and read and ate Snickers bars and rode your bicycle and played Capture the Flag. And in the other one, you were afraid to move, to talk, almost to breathe. Clairemont.

She watched Dickon shuffle the deck of cards. They were going to play rummy, not because they really wanted to, but because it was a way of making the time pass. She glanced at the clock beside their mother's bed. 8.15. They had been waiting for a half-hour and still no sign of her.

Daisy picked up her cards and looked at them, but she couldn't concentrate. 'What do you suppose is happening?'

'I don't know,' Dickon said. 'I told you before, all I know is that Grandfather is very sick.'

'We aren't going home,' Will said.

Daisy dropped her cards on the floor. 'I don't want to play any more.'

'Want to go downstairs and have breakfast?' Dickon asked.

Will shook his head. 'Our mother told us to wait here.'

'I know. But she didn't know it was going to take her so long,' Dickon said, nervously. 'And she didn't know that I can't stay here much longer. I have to feed my spiders.'

Daisy shuddered. Could anything be worse than going down into that dark, damp, terrifying cellar? 'Ugh, ugh, ugh, ugh, ugh,' she said.

'What do you feed them?' Will asked, ignoring her.

'Frogs and lizards. But mostly bugs.'

'You mean just regular old bugs?'

'No. I have to special-order them. Want to come with me and watch?'

Will didn't look at Daisy. 'Maybe.'

Daisy had to struggle hard to keep from bursting into tears. Surely Will wouldn't leave her alone again. Not even to watch Dickon feed his spiders.

'I sure wish Mom would hurry,' Will said.

'Me too,' Daisy said, feeling a new wave of panic. Unless her mother was with her, Daisy didn't want to leave this room for anything.

'I'm starved,' Will said for the tenth time. When Will got nervous he always ate like a hog. As for Daisy, right now the mere thought of food made her want to barf.

'Let's go get some breakfast,' Dickon said again. 'First, we'll go down to Grandfather's room and tell your mother what we're doing, and then we'll go eat.'

Will stood up. 'Come on, Daisy,' he said in a positive tone. 'It can't be any worse than sitting here.'

Oh yes it can, Daisy thought, and stuck her hands in her pockets to keep the boys from seeing how badly they were shaking. With a sinking heart she followed them to the door, feeling as if her feet were made of concrete.

Dickon reached out and opened the door.

And to Daisy's profound relief, her mother stepped into the room.

'You go along, Dickon,' Gillian said calmly. 'I want to talk to Will and Daisy for a minute and then we'll all be down for breakfast.'

'Are you going to feed your spiders now?' Will asked.

'I'll wait for you if you like.'

'Okay. See you downstairs.'

Gillian watched as Dickon closed the door. Then she turned to her children. For the past hour Gillian had agonized, not only about her father's condition, but about the two children waiting for her down the hall. And she knew what she had to do.

Now, Daisy and Will sat side by side on the edge of her bed, waiting to hear what she had to say. So grim-faced and, even though they thought they were hiding it, so frightened.

'Is everything all right, Mom?' Daisy asked nervously. 'Are we going home?'

Gillian sat down beside them. 'I can't go home, Daisy,' she said. 'Not yet. Your grandfather is very sick. The doctor is with him now and no one knows yet what's the matter.' She reached out and gently traced the faint purple smudges under Daisy's eyes. 'Didn't get much sleep last night, did you?'

'Nope. But it's okay. I'm fine.'

'I hope so, because I have something very important to discuss with you two. Yesterday, before I took you to the airport, I should've told you I wasn't going home with you. I should've given you credit for being bright, mature young people. I should have told you the truth, and I should have asked you what you wanted to do.' She took a deep breath. 'But I didn't. And for that, I am very, very sorry.'

'You don't have to be sorry, Mom,' Daisy said. 'We know you were worried about us.'

'But you were worried about me too, right?'

They both nodded.

'So now I want you to help me decide what to do. Okay?'

Again, solemnly they nodded.

'First, let me tell you what Aunt Lenore told me just a few minutes ago. She found Aunt Amanda in her bedroom this morning. And she told her that, until we were gone, she was to stay away from us. Not to do one single thing to frighten us ever again. And Aunt Lenore was sure that Amanda would not disappoint her.'

'I guess that means that Aunt Lenore thinks it was all Aunt Amanda's fault.'

'She does,' Gillian nodded.

'Do you?'

'It's the only logical explanation.'

'Oh,' Will said faintly.

'What is it, Will? What's wrong?'

'What if it isn't Aunt Amanda who's responsible?'

Gillian felt totally at a loss. How could she explain what she wasn't sure of herself. 'I don't know, Will,' she said, shaking her head. 'I guess if it isn't Aunt Amanda, then we're all in one terrible mess.'

'Yes, we are,' Daisy said bleakly. 'One huge, terrible mess.'

There was a long pause. Then Gillian brought her hands down firmly on her knees. 'But unfortunately,' she said, 'that's where we are. And knowing that, you must decide what you feel most comfortable doing. Do you want to stay here with me until we find out what's wrong with your grandfather? Or do you want to fly home this morning as planned?' She glanced at the clock. 'There's still plenty of time. Someone will drive you to the airport.' She took each of them by the hand. 'This is not a happy situation. It's a very scary one. But no matter what you decide, you are two of the best, bravest, most wonderful children that any mother could ever hope for.'

'What do you think?' Will asked Daisy. He said it loudly, but Gillian could tell that he was still frightened.

Daisy leaned over and whispered something in his ear.

'For Pete's sake, why don't you ask her yourself? How come I have to?' he said.

Daisy frowned, then turned to Gillian. 'When you find out what's wrong with Grandfather, if it's nothing serious, I mean, will we get to go home right away? Like maybe this afternoon?'

'If it's nothing serious, we will go home this afternoon.'

Daisy took a long breath, and when she spoke her voice was quavering. 'Okay. Here's what I think. We'll stay with you until you find out what's wrong. If it's serious and you have to stay, we'll go home alone. But if it's just the flu or something, we'll all go home together. This afternoon. Right, Will?'

Will nodded. 'It's okay with me, I guess.'

'I know you are both still frightened,' Gillian said. 'I am too. But I think that Aunt Lenore knows what she's talking about. And if we all stick together, I can't believe anything bad can happen.'

252

Daisy buried her face against Gillian's shoulder. 'I love you, Mom. I just hope that everyone is right about Aunt Amanda.'

Will and Dickon went off to feed Dickon's spiders, leaving Gillian and Daisy alone at the breakfast table. But neither one of them ate much. Gillian poured herself a second cup of coffee.

'Where is everyone?' Daisy whispered.

'They're upstairs waiting to hear what the doctor has to say.'

Daisy picked up a bran muffin, took a small nibble, then set it down. 'Do you want to go up?'

'No, sweetheart. I'll stay here with you. Aunt Lenore will tell me as soon as they know anything.'

And so they waited.

But not for long. And for Gillian, as she thought about it later, what happened in the next few minutes marked the beginning of the end of the world as she knew it.

Lenore came in and one look at her grim expression told Gillian that the news was not good. 'Harris has put in a call for an ambulance,' Lenore said in an unsteady voice. 'It should be here any minute.'

'Does he know what's wrong?'

'He's not saying much. Except that your father is in a serious state. He needs to be hospitalized at once.'

'Mother,' Dickon panted, rushing through the door, Will right behind him. 'Something unbelievable has happened!'

Lenore turned.

'My spiders. My black widow spiders and my *lycosa raptoria*,' Dickon said, angrily stamping his foot.

'They're gone. Every single one of them has disappeared.'

At 2.14 that afternoon, in spite of massive efforts to save his life, William Blackmarsh died.

Chapter Twenty-Eight

Gillian didn't cry. Gillian, who always cried for the simplest reasons. She accepted the fact of her father's death and the terrible emptiness it brought with it, but she didn't cry. For the rest of the day she walked the thin line between calm and hysteria. Her father was dead. That was all she was really sure of. The rest was one big question mark. The servants had searched his room and had found Dickon's spiders. But how had they got there? Had they been placed there deliberately? Was that what killed him? Had someone here at Clairemont *murdered* him?

Those questions left her numb. Until there was an autopsy, Robin said, no one would know for certain. There were going to be official inquiries, but again he wasn't sure when.

Gillian called Max and her responses to his questions echoed Robin's. We don't know. We don't know. We don't know.

Max said he would come at once. An eight-hour drive, but if he didn't hit any traffic he'd be there before midnight. And after she hung up the phone she sat motionless, still dry-eyed. Still no tears.

Through it all, Daisy and Will stayed by her side, tense, silent, trying to give comfort by keeping quiet. When Gillian asked if they wanted to leave they shook their heads. They couldn't leave her alone now, they said. Not now.

Emotionally and physically drained, at eight o'clock that evening she and the children went to bed. Lenore had offered to sleep with them again but Gillian had said no. Max would be there in a few hours.

The children unrolled their sleeping-bags and crawled inside.

'I'm awfully sorry he died, Mom,' Daisy whispered huskily.

'Me too,' Will said.

'I know.' Gillian kissed them goodnight.

She climbed into bed and lay stiff, staring up at the ceiling, remembering another time eighteen years ago when there was another death in this house. When she had stayed awake all night, dry-eyed, staring up at the same ceiling.

She still didn't cry, but this time Gillian slept.

In the farthest corner of the east wing, Amanda sat at her open window, staring out across the moonlit gardens. How odd, she thought, that I am still here and he is dead. How wonderfully odd. Like the others, she didn't know why her father had died. She didn't care. All she knew was that he was gone.

She wanted to rush outside and whisper the good news to all of her children. Her begonias, her lobelia, her mignonette, her balsam. But she couldn't. She had been told to stay in her room until Gillian had left Clairemont. And, until she knew what had angered Lenore so profoundly, she would do precisely that.

Somewhere across the hills an old dog howled at the moon, and in the most soul-stirring voice she could muster, Amanda howled back.

* * *

A hundred miles to the south, Max stopped to get gas. Another two hours and he would be there, thank God. He pulled back onto the turnpike and continued north.

Gillian woke up with a start to find her pillow wet with tears, Lenore standing over her. 'Please, Gillian, wake up,' she was whispering. 'I need help.'

Gillian glanced over at the clock on the night-stand. 9.20. She sat up.

'Come out into the hall,' Lenore whispered in a desperate tone. 'I don't want to wake the children.'

Gillian slipped out of bed and as quietly as she could she followed Lenore out into the hall.

'It's Dickon,' Lenore choked. 'He's gone. I've searched everywhere in the house for him.' Tears began to flow. 'Before he went to sleep he was so depressed. Oh, God, Gillian, what if . . . what if he's wandered back to the grist mill?'

Gillian could see fear in her cousin's eyes. Lenore swallowed hard and flushed. 'I'm so sorry, Gillian. I must be mad. I never should have expected anything from you. Not tonight.' She put her hands to her cheeks. 'I'm so sorry. Go back to bed.'

For a moment Gillian hesitated. The last thing she wanted to do was go to the grist mill. But Lenore should never have to go there alone. Not like Gillian's mother had. If Claire had only had someone to help her all those years ago, she would not have died. 'Let me get my robe and slippers,' she said as calmly as she could. 'And we'll go. We'll find Dickon and we'll bring him safely home.'

Tree-tops. And high above, the moon. Still settled in her chair by the window, Amanda watched, caught up in a state of wondrous enchantment. Everything was so still. Nothing stirred. No breeze. No movement of any kind. Just a vast, silent world. Her beloved Clairemont.

Which now belongs to Gillian.

She started. Had she thought the words or had she *heard* them?

She listened.

Silence.

But the damage had been done. Spoken or not, the words were true and Amanda was dashed to earth. Her father was dead, but it was no cause for celebration. Now Clairemont belonged to *Gillian*.

Amanda moaned low in her throat. Goodbye to everything she held most dear. Unable to hold her head up another minute, she leaned forward and let it drop with a dull thud to the windowsill.

Amanda, look!

Through the grey drizzle of despair she heard the words and she responded. She lifted her head and looked out.

Below, following the garden path, she could see two figures, pale and spectral in the moonlight, moving quickly away. But there was no doubt who they were. *Gillian and Lenore*.

But where were they going? What evil was afoot?

Amanda felt a surge of rage. What was Gillian doing? How dare she prowl the grounds in the dead of night? Was she out to harm Lenore?

Amanda jumped to her feet then, remembering Lenore's warning, she sank back into her chair. She had promised her cousin that she wouldn't leave her room.

But that was before. When her father was still in control. Now he was dead, so what possible punishment could be inflicted upon her if she were to disobey Lenore and follow them? She had already lost Clairemont.

Or have you? That voice again.

Were the gods sending her a message?

Was this her last chance? Somehow, tonight, right now, could she be rid of Gillian once and for all? Would Lenore help her?

Go, Amanda! Follow!

Now the words were frenzied, and it didn't matter if they were her own or someone else's. They provided the inspiration she so desperately needed.

On winged feet she flew to the door and slipped out, moving like a shadow among shadows. She would catch Gillian. And once caught, one way or another, Gillian would die.

Will was dreaming. On his way home from school he had walked off the sidewalk into a bed of quicksand. Gasping for breath, flailing his arms wildly above his head, he sank beneath the surface. Only to find that he had ended up in his own back yard! Neat! Now he wouldn't ever have to walk home again. He would just jump off the sidewalk and be home in an instant.

He woke up with a smile on his face, but it vanished when he lifted his head to check the time. His mother's bed was *empty*.

'Daisy,' he gasped, poking her. 'Mom's gone!' He jumped up and ran to the bathroom, switching on the light.

Propped up on the edge of the sink was a piece of notepaper. *If you wake up while I'm gone*, it read, *don't worry. I've gone to find Dickon.*

'Let's go,' he said to Daisy. In spite of the note, something was terribly wrong, he just knew it. And

259

he was filled with the most frantic need to hurry.

'Where?'

'We'll go to Dickon's room. See if he's there. And if he is, and Mom isn't with him, we'll wake the whole house up. We have to find her, Daisy. We have to.'

Farther down the hall, snug in his own bed where he had been since nine o'clock that evening, Dickon Blackmarsh stirred, then rolled over and sank back into a deep, contented sleep.

Chapter Twenty-Nine

Clearly driven by a sense of urgency, Lenore moved quickly, and Gillian followed. Not that Gillian couldn't have found her way by herself. The dark, overgrown path to the grist mill was indelibly stamped in her brain. She would never forget it, and as she went, she shuddered, praying that she would have the courage to see this through. That she would be able to maintain some semblance of control. She had to. Dickon needed her help but, almost as important, so did Lenore. Again she thought about her own mother. If only someone had been there to help her; if only someone had been there to keep her from falling, to keep Gillian from crushing her fingers . . .

They moved on through the forest, the trees starkly white, luminous in the moonlight, but there was no breeze, no sound at all but the crunching of leaves under their feet.

'We're almost there,' Lenore said, looking back.

And then Gillian heard the sound of rushing water as the shimmering trees parted to reveal the dark stone mass that was the grist mill, and her breath left her in a rush.

Lenore put her finger to her lips and opened the door.

For Gillian, stepping inside was a nightmare revisited. Just as she remembered in her most horrible memories, the light from the moon filtered in through the upper windows, casting eerie patches across the threshing-floor. And across the room she could see the ladder that led up to the loft.

'That's where I've found him before. Up there,' Lenore whispered. 'I'll go first. You follow.'

Numb, Gillian waited until Lenore disappeared. Then, one rung at a time, she climbed.

The only person she saw at the top was Lenore.

She looked past her but the loft was empty. Besides herself, Lenore was the only person there. 'He's not here,' Gillian said. 'Oh, Lenore, where could he be?'

Not answering, Lenore pointed towards the edge.

What does she mean, Gillian thought, stunned. *Has Dickon fallen?*

On hands and knees, she crawled across the loft, stopping at the edge, staring down.

Below, no sign of life.

And suddenly, behind her, she heard Lenore move. Horrified beyond belief, she felt hands on her back, *pushing*, and in the same moment, below, she saw Amanda coming through the door.

Lenore saw her too, and jerked back, giving Gillian a chance to roll to one side and lurch around, still on her knees. Her back to the abyss, Gillian stared at her cousin. Lenore had pushed her, and if it hadn't been for Amanda's sudden appearance she would have fallen. But surely it hadn't been intentional. Surely Lenore hadn't intended to *push her over the edge*. Such a fall would have *killed* her. 'I think we should go,' she said stupidly.

Lenore stood where she was, her expression unreadable. And behind her, Gillian saw Amanda appear at the top of the ladder.

'Oh, Lenore,' Amanda said, clapping her hands

together. 'I should have known. How could I not have guessed?' She tipped her head back, filling the air with peals of laughter. 'You *are* going to kill her, aren't you?' she asked, squatting down, an ecstatic smile on her face. 'You can do it, you know. I'll help. Oh, Lenore, dear, dear, Lenore. It's like history repeating itself, isn't it? I followed you tonight just like I did before. When I followed you and Mother.'

'And just as before, I wish you had stayed in your room, Mandy,' Lenore said.

Amanda stiffened. 'Whatever for? You *know* how happy I was that night. Surely you wouldn't deny me the same pleasure now. Would you?' She looked past Lenore to gaze at Gillian, and her voice became melodic, as if she were reciting poetry. 'I saw it all and it thrilled me to death. Mother, scrambling up the ladder to fetch you home, with Lenore right behind. Mother, reaching out to take your hand. Lenore, pushing her. Mother, grabbing the beam. Lenore, stamping on her fingers until they were *broken to bits*. Mother, falling to her death. Thud.'

Gillian's mind went blank with horror. What was Amanda saying?

'Not that Mother didn't deserve it,' Amanda continued. 'She did. She deserved every bit of it. She was going to send Lenore back to Jordan because Lenore wanted to marry Robin. But you are too young to marry anyone, Mother told her. Too innocent. You must go home to your parents. How like Mother,' Amanda scoffed. 'Always intruding. Always passing judgement.' She shook her head sympathetically. 'I felt so sorry for Lenore that I wanted to kill Claire. But Lenore did it for me. And I was fortunate enough to have seen it with my own eyes.'

'Can all this possibly be true, Lenore?' Gillian

whispered in a choked voice.

'Surely you don't think I'm *lying*?' Amanda said, incredulous. 'Tell her, Lenore.'

'As you wish, Mandy,' Lenore replied quietly. 'I don't mind confessing to Gillian.' She picked up the thread of the story, but where Amanda had been bubbling over with excitement, Lenore was dispassionate, as if her only interest in the telling was to appease Amanda. 'That night, when Claire asked me to come here to help bring you home, I came gladly. And when she climbed up into this loft, I killed her.'

A thundering pain filled Gillian's head, and for a split second, although she still knelt upright, she felt as if she had lost consciousness. None of this was happening. Lenore hadn't done any such thing. Gillian had gone mad. This was all a fabrication of her own poor, demented mind.

But that single second passed. And when it was over, Gillian found herself lucid, fully aware of where she was and what had been said, and she was awash in a tide of terror. Her mother's death hadn't been Gillian's doing at all. *Lenore had murdered her*.

Gillian wanted to scream, but all that came out of her mouth was a low whimper and a trickle of blood where her teeth had bitten down hard on her lip. 'But why?' Gillian whispered, still unable to grasp the full implications of what was happening. 'What do I have to do with this?'

Lenore regarded Gillian with renewed interest. 'I am surprised. As a child you were never aware of anything around you, but I thought that you had changed. You were such a spoiled, selfish darling then. Always surrounded by people who loved you. Your mother and your father. But there were others. Those of us who didn't love you at all. Me. Robin.

Amanda. The three of us had one thing in common. We loved Clairemont. And we wanted it to be ours. And when your father banished you, it *was* ours. Since then we have lived here in utter contentment. Your father hated you, never wanted to see you at Clairemont again. Nor did we.'

She made a snorting sound of derision. 'But a few months ago, Robin – blind, stupid Robin – began to worry. What if, after your father died, you decided to come back here to live. We would have to move. And Amanda would be sent away. So Robin took it upon himself to show you how painful it would be for you to live here, to see how much your father still hated you. He was convinced that, faced with the horror of it all, you would give Clairemont to him. Or at least sell it. An absurd notion. I knew better. From the very beginning I knew there would be only one way for us to be sure. Clairemont would be ours only if you were dead.'

'Does Robin know?' Gillian choked. 'Does he know that you mean to kill me?'

'No, he doesn't,' Lenore answered. 'Not that it matters. Robin lives his life and I live mine. As long as we exist together at Clairemont we are happy. But enough about him.' Her face took on an abstract, impersonal look. 'At first I wasn't sure how to kill you. But when Max left, everything came together. After all, I had already enlisted your help with Dickon. What better way to get you alone? And what better place than here at the grist mill?' She looked over at Amanda. 'You almost ruined it, you know, with your silly play-acting. You almost drove Gillian away.'

'And she never would have come back,' Amanda said defensively. 'But then Father interfered. He *forgave* her. And that's when I decided to kill her myself. And *you* are the one who ruined *that*, Lenore. You stayed with her last night.'

'I know what you were hoping, Mandy. I saw you creeping out of Gillian's room last night with Dickon's spiders. But just think. Even if I hadn't been there, she still wasn't alone. Her children were with her and she might not have been the one to die. And then what would have happened? Your father would have found you guilty and had you committed to an insane asylum for the rest of your life.'

Amanda swallowed hard. 'I hadn't thought of that.'

'Well, you should have. But no matter. I always save you. It was I who followed you from Gillian's room last night. It was I who killed the spiders you so carelessly unleashed upon yourself. It was I who carried the others to William Blackmarsh's bedside.'

'Dear God.' A small whimper escaped Gillian's lips. 'You killed my father too.'

'I did. Not that I had considered it a necessity,' she mused. 'I hadn't. But I needed to keep you here for one more night. And what better way than to make him deathly ill. The fact that he actually died came as a surprise bonus, because it meant that he never had a chance to change his will. By the terms of the only existing document, Robin and Amanda will share his estate. And I will remain Amanda's guardian.'

'Oh, Lenore,' Amanda exulted, 'you are the most wonderful human being in the world.' She made a move towards Lenore, but Lenore held up a restraining hand. 'Is there anything else you'd like to know, Gillian?'

Seized by alternate waves of outrage and terror, Gillian could only shake her head. The abundance of horror had rendered her speechless.

'One more thing,' Lenore said, almost as an after-thought. 'You are probably wondering about Dickon. When I told you about his affliction, I was not being truthful. My son is not a sleepwalker, thank heaven. But he is a good-hearted boy, and when I told him I thought it would be great therapy for you if you thought you were helping him, he went along with it. So although you so kindly agreed to talk to him, there really wasn't any need. Rather a nice twist though. In the end you helped me even as I helped your mother.' Her voice grew pensive. 'Sleepwalkers are such a danger to themselves. No one will be the least surprised that you wandered off to the grist mill. Only two nights ago you came here all by yourself. So when they find your body, poor Gillian, they'll all nod their heads and say what an endless curse your affliction has been.'

'But my children know that I came looking for Dickon.' A desperate attempt to save herself.

'*What?*'

'I left them a note.'

Lenore narrowed her eyes, considering. Then she shrugged. 'No matter. Like Caesar's wife, I am above reproach. Besides, Amanda will say that I spent the night with her. Consoling her over the loss of her father. Why you chose to leave your children to go on a futile search for Dickon will remain a mystery. Whether your death is deemed an accident or a suicide is really of no concern to me.'

Gillian heard it all. She absorbed it, knew what was coming, knew she was doomed. Even if Lenore couldn't manage it alone, she had Amanda to help her. The result would be the same. I am going to die, she thought. I am going to be thrown over the edge.

But, God damn it, I'm not going without a fight. Not the way my mother did. I will leave some scars.

Like a cornered animal, she drew back, gathering what was left of her strength, knowing that within the next few seconds it would all be over. She would fight but she would lose. In a few seconds she would no longer be struggling. Or screaming. Or even breathing. She would be nothing more than a broken body on the concrete floor below.

But not yet. Not without a fight.

'She went to *what*?' Dickon asked, sitting up with a start.

'She went to find you,' Will panted. 'That's what she wrote in this note.'

'That's impossible. I'm right here.'

'Oh, shit,' Will groaned. 'So where is she? We'd better get Aunt Lenore.'

The three flew down the corridor. At his parents' door Dickon stopped, then knocked. 'Mother?'

After a moment the door opened. 'What is it?' Robin said, clearly annoyed.

'Where's Mother?'

'She's staying with your Aunt Gillian, I suppose. Why?'

'She isn't there,' Daisy said, tears stinging her eyes. 'And Mom isn't either.'

'Damn.' Robin was exasperated, but he agreed to look. 'Let me get some clothes on and we'll see if we can find them.'

On their way out of the front door, they met Max coming in.

Heart pounding, nauseous with fear, Gillian drew back as far as she could, expecting that at any moment Lenore would strike like a snake, with venomous speed. But Lenore didn't. She came towards Gillian slowly, deliberately, with an almost clinical interest.

Gillian watched, mesmerized. It was as if Lenore had no intention of pushing Gillian over the edge, as if she truly believed that, given enough time, Gillian would throw herself willingly into the void.

Lenore took another step and again Gillian drew back, but only a few inches. She was at the very edge. There was nowhere for her to go but down.

Now, she thought wildly. This is your last chance. But even as she prepared to defend herself, incredibly Lenore stopped moving. Like some kind of mechanical toy that had wound down, she stopped.

Gillian stared in horror.

Lenore hadn't stopped of her own volition. A hand – all white splintered bone and rotting flesh and purple-black blood – had come out of the darkness to rest on Lenore's shoulder. At the same time Amanda let out a shrill, mind-shattering howl.

Lenore whirled round.

Standing in a dim shaft of moonlight, her hideous claw-like hands stretched out as if to embrace Lenore, was a terrifying skeletal figure draped in silver-grey, her long, snarled hair framing what once had been a perfect face but now was a fleshless skull, open-mouthed, screaming a silent scream.

It was all that remained of Claire Blackmarsh.

I tried to save you from this, Gillian. I tried to drive you and the children away. But I failed. And now I have no choice. I must kill Lenore. I can only beg you not to look.

Trembling on the brink of madness, about to go berserk, Gillian heard her mother's desperate plea.

And she obeyed. Unable to turn away, she put her hands up and covered her face.

She didn't see the rest.

But she felt it.

The rush of frigid air as Lenore was *blown* past her.

The terror-filled scream as Lenore hung for one second, teetering on the edge. And then she was gone.

The next thing Gillian heard was the sickening liquid sound of a body, falling from a great height, striking concrete.

And then silence.

The first thing Will saw when his father opened the grist-mill door was Aunt Lenore, asleep on the floor. And sitting beside her, rocking back and forth, humming, was Aunt Amanda.

Will didn't see any more. The three children were told to wait outside while Dad and Uncle Robin went in.

Minutes later, when Dad came out, he had their mother with him. She wasn't hurt, thank goodness, but she looked really sick.

They left Clairemont that afternoon.

It wasn't until late September that Will found out from his father that Aunt Lenore had died. Exactly when or how, Dad didn't say. And if Mom knew, she didn't talk about it.

Will never did see his uncle again. Or Dickon. Or Aunt Amanda.

Sometimes he and Daisy would wonder whatever became of them. And they'd ask.

But Mom would just shrug. Will guessed she didn't know.